APR 0 1 2015

It Had
to Be Him

It Had to Be Him

TAMRA BAUMANN

Montlake
Romance

This is a work of fiction. Names, characters, organizations, places, events, and incidents are either products of the author's imagination or are used fictitiously.

Text copyright © 2015 Tamra Baumann
All rights reserved.

No part of this book may be reproduced, or stored in a retrieval system, or transmitted in any form or by any means, electronic, mechanical, photocopying, recording, or otherwise, without express written permission of the publisher.

Published by Montlake Romance, Seattle

www.apub.com

Amazon, the Amazon logo, and Montlake Romance are trademarks of Amazon.com, Inc., or its affiliates.

ISBN-13: 9781477821282
ISBN-10: 1477821287

Cover design by Laura Klynstra

Library of Congress Control Number: 2014914680

Printed in the United States of America

This book is dedicated to my mother.

Thanks, Mom, for sharing your joy of reading with me.

I hope this story makes you smile, because that's what

I miss the most about you.

CHAPTER ONE

*M*eg Anderson slowed her rust-bucket SUV, cut the engine, then glided quietly down the hill toward the moonlit lake. The lights were all out in her shotgun-packing grandmother's house, but Grandma was a light sleeper.

She'd had buckshot plucked from her ass before and would rather give birth again than repeat that horrendous procedure. Especially because the only doctor in her small hometown had been her oldest brother—doesn't get more embarrassing than that.

She parked behind the equipment shed, then hopped out of the car to perform a little B and E into her grandmother's guesthouse.

When a girl needed somewhere to hide out for the summer, what better place than a teeny-tiny town in Colorado where her middle brother was the sheriff, her father was the mayor, and her sister ran the only hotel. The townspeople lived for gossip when they weren't busy keeping secrets, and that's just what Meg needed. The keeping secrets part. The gossip not so much. Especially because it was usually about her.

And if the stars would all align for the first time in her life, her father would have had a change of heart. Hopefully he would have forgotten that part about how she was never allowed to work for the family business again, because she was out of options. But there was no way anyone was going to take away the one good thing in her life.

Her daughter, Haley.

Meg tested the handle on the guesthouse. It was locked. People didn't lock doors in Anderson Butte as a rule. But Grandma's guesthouse, close to the shore and the hotel, had been used in the past for some naughty times by amorous couples who'd stumbled upon it. Luckily Grandma never figured out some of those fun times had been Meg's.

As she slipped her now-defunct group medical ID card in between the lock and the doorframe, the cricket chirps grew louder, as if tattling on her, the little traitors. Wiggling the card to the left, then sliding some more to the right, she was just about in when a deep voice spoke behind her.

"What are you doing?"

Crap! She'd recognize that voice anywhere. Her brother, Ryan-the-tattletale-sheriff, who lived next door.

Turning around and sending him her most confident smile, she tapped a finger to her lips. "Shhhhh. Haley's asleep in the car. How'd you even know I was here?" Growing up in a small town taught her early on to never lie. Someone always knew the truth and would hold her to it. Instead, she'd become the best conversation diverter west of the Mississippi.

Ryan crossed his arms and cocked a brow. Only two years her senior at thirty, he knew all of her tricks. "You want to answer the question or do I call Dad?"

Damn Ryan. He knew just how to yank her chain.

She lifted her hands in surrender. "Arrest me or go away. It's late and I've had a long day."

There was just enough moonlight reflecting off the lake to see his jaw twitch in annoyance. Of her brothers and sister, she and

Ryan looked the most alike. Except for the suspicious squinty eyes and the five o'clock shadow.

They both had dark hair and Alaskan husky intense blue eyes, but Ryan was full of muscles and attitude while she just had the 'tude. Being a pixie-sized five foot two and surrounded by tall, genetically perfect family members tended to bring out the pit bull in a person.

He tilted his head toward her sad excuse for transportation. "Thought you bought a new car. Why are you still driving this hand-me-down piece of junk?"

She'd rented a car the last time she'd been home. It wasn't her fault they all assumed she was better off than she was. Leave it to annoying Ryan to point it out. "I never sold this, it's handy for moving. What are you doing out here this time of night anyway?"

"Zeke and two of the Three Amigos called and said they saw a car turn down Grandma's drive. Just checking things out."

The Three Amigos, the bane of her existence. A trio of older women who'd always judged her the hardest. "Well, thank you for doing your job, Mr. Perfect. Now go away."

Ryan shook his head as he shouldered her aside and pulled out a key to unlock the door. "What kind of trouble are you in this time, Meggy?"

"Just thought it'd be nice for Haley to spend a summer on the lake." Never mind she needed to hide from Haley's father.

"Right. Need any help here?"

"Nope. Got it. See you tomorrow?"

"Yep." He had the nerve to muss the hair on top of her head like she was still a kid. "Good to see you, Muck."

As was their ritual, she slapped his hand aside and tried to knee him in the crotch, but he was always too quick. "I'd rather you didn't call me that anymore. Especially in front of Haley." Of all the nicknames her family enjoyed torturing her with, Muck, short for "Megan the F-Up," hurt the deepest. Probably because it used to be mostly true. But not since she'd had Haley. "Please, Ry?"

He glanced toward the car where Haley snoozed in her car seat and shrugged. "Yeah, okay. Night."

"Night." She let out the breath she'd been holding and watched him walk away. Ryan and her oldest brother, Ben, were perpetually annoying, but the only truly decent guys she knew. All the others had lied to her, cheated on her, or broken her heart.

Friends told her she had trust issues. But they were wrong. She could trust. She absolutely trusted that any guy she dated was going to hurt her in the end.

Men.

Who needed them?

Anything they could give her, she could take care of herself with the right machinery and a fresh set of batteries.

After cranking the car door open, she lifted her adorable blonde Tasmanian devil onto her shoulder, then kicked the front door to the guesthouse open wider. Moonlight filtering through the windows guided her to the bedroom.

Warmth filled her as she tucked her beautiful baby under the sheets. Technically, Haley wasn't a baby anymore. She was a precocious two-and-a-half-year-old who proudly declared that extra half year to anyone who asked. And she looked just like her father.

As Meg unloaded the few things they would need right away, thoughts of Josh still sent waves of hurt to her heart. He'd wormed his way into her life when she'd been giving a talk about management software at a resort trade show. When his mesmerizing, tiger-like amber eyes had locked onto hers, she'd totally forgotten her next bullet point. During the two drinks they'd shared after her presentation, she had connected with him like she'd never done with any other man.

IT HAD TO BE HIM

But it was his shoes that should have been the giveaway.

Josh stood well over six feet, with thick blond hair worn just a tad too long, working-man broad shoulders, and a naughty you-know-you-want-me grin, all in stark contrast to his slick Armani suits and Italian loafers. Any straight man who paid that much attention to his shoes wasn't going to have time for love.

She'd been an idiot, thinking she'd finally found the *one*. An upstanding guy who, when he made time for her, made her laugh like no one else. After dating a few months, she had moved into his upscale downtown condo that she then shared with him for about four more months. But when she'd accidentally gotten pregnant, the door hadn't had time to hit him on the butt on his way out of their relationship.

Probably because he couldn't stand the thought of baby puke on his shiny Ferragamos.

She'd have to remember to add the shoe thing to her "do not date these kinds of guys ever again" list.

Unfortunately her heart rarely paid attention to her list.

After getting ready for bed, she crawled in beside Haley, pulling her close for a comforting snuggle. Why, after three years without a word, had Josh sent her a text asking where they were and could they please talk? He wouldn't be looking for *her*; he'd made it clear they were through. Maybe he'd grown a conscience and wanted to be a father to Haley? Too late for that. He'd abandoned them, and Haley belonged with Meg.

When she hadn't responded to Josh's text, he'd called the receptionist from her last job and asked about them there too. It was all the incentive Meg needed. She'd been considering coming home anyway. If the residents of Anderson Butte could keep their yaps shut about all the celebrities who returned to the hotel year after year because of the absolute privacy the town provided, then hopefully they'd make sure Josh wouldn't find her and Haley either. No way was she going to let the man who'd charmed her, made her fall in love with him, and then shattered her heart do the same to her daughter.

———————

The next morning, Meg snuggled into her pillow and sighed as the pleasant aroma of coffee filled the air. She cracked an eye open and winced at the bright morning sun streaming through the window, then grabbed the mug her sister, Casey, held out.

Meg whispered so as not to wake Haley beside her. "Ryan has a big mouth. It's probably not even six yet and everyone knows we're here?"

"Hi to you too," Casey said softly as she sank to the edge of the bed. "It's six thirty and yes, everyone knows you're here. Want to talk about it?"

"Can't a girl come home for a visit without getting the third degree?" Taking a deep drink, Meg admired the beautiful sight known as Casey Anderson Bovier. Her sister was tall, willowy, and elegant. The exact opposite of Meg. "Thanks. This is really good."

"You're welcome." Casey's face scrunched into that mom look. The one that told Meg her sister/surrogate mother knew something was up. "What's going on, Meg?"

"Maybe I just wanted to come home for a while?"

Casey sighed. "To the place you can never wait to escape from after you and Dad have another argument? Where people still hold grudges about some of the monumental stunts you've pulled? Sure. That makes perfect sense."

"It's been years since I've tipped cows, egged cars, or thrown rocks through windows at Town Hall in misguided attempts to gain Dad's attention. I'm over begging for his love." Meg reached out and took Casey's hand. "Maybe I miss my brothers and sister. Isn't that enough of a reason?"

"I suppose. And I've missed you too." Casey squeezed Meg's hand. "There's more to this story, though, so I'll just wait you out. You'll give in to my nagging ways eventually."

Meg took another drink, working up the courage to ask her sister what she really wanted to know without exposing the real reason she was there. "You *are* a champion nag. But can I ask you something?"

Casey's right brow cocked in surprise. "This is a first, but sure. Anything."

"How long did it take you to get over Tomas after he ran off with she-who-shall-not-be-mentioned? And how did you get to a civil place where you can share the boys with him?"

"I assume this is about"—Casey glanced at Haley to be sure she was still sleeping—"he-who-you-have-*never*-mentioned? Haley's f-a-t-h-e-r?"

Meg appreciated Casey for not mentioning the F-word in front of Haley. Meg's daughter had never asked about her father, so Meg was waiting until Haley was older to explain things to her.

Meg said, "As bad as your breakup was, you and Tomas seem to get along now."

"He's the boys' father. I'll always care about him to some degree, so I'm civil to him. But I don't *like* him anymore. And I wouldn't mind if he became impotent to pay him back for all the fooling around he did on me." Casey stole the mug from Meg and took a drink. "It's been three years since your breakup. Do you still love him?"

Tears burned Meg's eyes, but she blinked them back. "I used to love him. When we spent time together between his long bouts of work, he was the greatest guy I've ever known. We even talked about getting married. But then one day, out of the blue, he announced he was leaving. I thought we were happy, but he said he feared being a bad father, and we were better off without him. So that was that."

Meg waggled her fingers for the mug. After Casey handed it back, Meg took another drink. "Haley and I are fine without him. I know I've been irresponsible in the past, but now I'm focused on trying to be a good mother."

"You are a good mother, Meg. None of us would have ever believed it if we hadn't seen it for ourselves. So now it's time to get the rest of your act in gear, right? Show Dad he's wrong about you?"

Before Meg could explain she'd been working on that for some time, Haley awoke and said, "Hi, Aunt Ceecee."

Haley still couldn't get Casey's name right. They'd have to work on that too.

Casey's concerned expression morphed into a cheerful one as she turned toward Haley on the other side of the bed. "Good morning, sunshine." Casey scooped Haley up and gave her a tight hug. "Want to come to the hotel with your favorite auntie and find something yummy for breakfast?"

"Yay! Pancakes?"

"Anything you want, darlin'. Say bye to your mom." Casey dangled a laughing Haley upside down over Meg for a kiss.

"Bye, Momma."

"Bye, Bug. See you in a bit." She kissed her daughter's upside-down lips. "Haley needs her asthma medicine after she eats, so bring her right back, okay? And do I get pancakes too?"

Casey stood and flipped Haley right-side up. "Depends. Get settled, then come talk to me. Ryan mentioned you've brought pretty much everything you own with you."

Meg called out to her sister's retreating back. "Hey, you have two of your own kids to boss around now, so how about sticking to them and leaving me out of it for a change?" Why did her brothers and sister think it was their duty to poke into her business like that?

"And give up one of my life's greatest pleasures?" Casey laughed. "The boys are in France with Tomas and the new rich bimbo wife. You're all I've got at the moment."

Lucky me.

Throwing the covers back, Meg aimed to finish her coffee on the dock. Slipping into a pair of flip-flops, she considered putting on some real clothes, but her tank top and gym shorts would do. She was on vacation, after all.

For the day anyway. She needed a job after she'd been fired from another one for missing too much work because of Haley's asthma.

Meg grabbed her phone, then stepped outside and drew in a deep breath of fresh Rocky Mountain air mixed with the familiar scents of pine needles, lake water, hot summers, and cool, dewy morning grass.

She sipped her smooth roasted blend and strolled toward the quiet lake. Mornings were the best, before things got hopping for the day.

The birds flew inches above the water, searching for their breakfast. Little sets of rings slowly grew larger after the insects disturbed the glassy, smooth water. The occasional plop of a fish jumping and the steady crank of a fisherman's reel slowly winding in the bait punctuated the quiet.

Studying the calming view, she drew another deep breath, and the tension slowly eased from her shoulders.

Home. For better or worse.

The half of the town not related to her would sigh and shake their heads when they saw the former bad girl was back again. The other half, her blood relatives, would just pretend they were one big, happy family, even though they knew the truth about Meg's non-relationship with her father. It had taken Meg years to realize that her father, a distant and hands-off parent since her mother's death, either hadn't been willing or was incapable of raising his children. Thankfully her sibs had all banded together and supported one another growing up.

And then there was Amber, her nemesis from high school.

Amber had most everyone in town fooled by her innocent act. But Meg knew the truth. They'd once been best friends, until Amber revealed the black-hearted troublemaker she truly was.

Their friendship was doomed from the start. Amber was a Grant, the family who owned the mine and most of the land surrounding the town. Meg's father owned all the buildings on Main Street, and most of the rest of the town. The power struggle between the Grants and the Andersons went back to Meg's great-grandfather's time.

The only thing that had changed in Anderson Butte in the last decade was Meg. Getting everyone else to believe it was going to be the trick.

Settling on the end of the dock, she dangled her feet over the edge. She was checking her phone, relieved there were no new texts from Josh, when the familiar thump of a cane followed by the shuffle of soft-soled shoes signaled that her tall, cranky, beloved grandmother was approaching from behind.

Meg laid the phone next to her mug, then lifted her hands over her head. "Don't shoot. I'm unarmed."

Grandma grunted. "That joke's getting old, Meggy. You know I didn't mean to shoot you in the patooty." An orthopedic shoe landed between Meg's shoulder blades and she went tumbling over the edge and into the water. "But I meant that!"

Meg found herself at the sandy floor of the icy cold lake. She bounced off the bottom, holding back her laugh until she broke the surface. Flipping her long hair out of her face, she said, "Nice to see you too, Grandma. Just as feisty as ever, I see."

Grandma pointed to her cane. "Next time you want to stay in my guesthouse you can just call and ask like polite folk do. I don't appreciate squatters, so you can get your tiny heinie up here and paint my fence as rent, you hear? And bring Haley with you. I like that girl."

So much for her one-day vacation.

"I was going to call but it got too late. You go to bed before the sun sets these days."

"A woman needs her beauty sleep. The paint's in the shed."

Meg swam to the wooden ladder and pulled herself up. When she got to the top, her grandmother eyed the phone by the mug. Hopefully the text from Josh was low enough on the list she wouldn't see it.

"Paint the fence and you can stay as long as you like. But you should probably know once your daddy found out you were back, he called an emergency family meeting for this afternoon at one. You're not on the guest list because it's about you, but show up anyway. Without Haley. That'd just irritate your father more."

A family meeting? One she wasn't invited to? That couldn't be good.

Her father only called those when something was dire.

CHAPTER Two

*M*eg ripped off her wet clothes and dug through the plastic garbage bags she'd hastily filled with the entire contents of her closet in her rush to leave Denver. Who needed a matching set of Louis Vuittons? There were definite benefits to waterproof, forty-gallon-sized, tear-resistant luggage. Especially if you happened to own an old car with leaky windows and moved as often as she did.

She bypassed the tight tanks and Daisy Dukes she'd been keeping in case her fat-free, pre-Haley body miraculously decided to reappear. Probably her stress-induced chocolate addiction wasn't helping that happen.

Instead, she opted for *acceptable clothing* should her dad pay her an unexpected visit. She plucked out an oversized T-shirt with her college's logo on it and an old pair of jean shorts. An outfit that thoroughly disguised all the parts that made her a girl and wouldn't send her father's blood pressure to stroke levels—and she was caving again, dammit. But she needed a job worse than she wanted to poke at her grumpy bear of a father.

Her dad would most likely start the dreaded family meeting with his usual discourse, pointing out her chronic lack of discipline. Admittedly, being a single mother and now jobless on top of it hadn't been in her mission statement, but it was her life, and she refused to be told how to live it.

Well, right after she painted Grandma's fence.

Grandma and Casey were the only ones she didn't mind bossing her around. Much. They were the ones always there for her. Her father was a different story. It seemed as if he couldn't stand to be in the same room with her. She'd never been sure why.

After Casey had returned Haley, Meg found the pretty pale-yellow paint and brushes, then settled her daughter in a spot where she could watch her. Swatting away the curious dragonflies dive-bombing her, Meg channeled her inner Tom Sawyer and dove in.

Periodically, she glanced over to be sure Haley was still where she was supposed to be. She sat nearby in the shade of a tall pine tree, contently coloring beside Grandma, who'd pulled up a chair to supervise and had promptly fallen fast asleep.

"You doing okay, kiddo?"

Haley held up her masterpiece. "See? Purple cow!" Her shout startled Grandma awake.

And the cow was red. Another thing they'd work on.

Meg was just about to compliment her when Zeke's rusty old voice croaked out. "Never seen me a purple cow before. That's pretty darned special." He smiled at Grandma. "Hiya, Ruth." Zeke, the town handyman who reminded Meg of the scarecrow in *The Wizard of Oz*, wasn't only certified to work on their family's helicopters; he could fix any car, boat, Jet Ski, or beloved toy she'd ever owned as a child. He was more of a father to her than her own.

Grandma scowled at him. "Hello and goodbye. I have somewhere else to be."

Zeke chuckled. "You're about the busiest woman I've ever met, Ruth. When I'm around, anyway." After Grandma left, he leaned down to inspect the picture Haley had colored. "Yep. You got some real talent there, little lady."

Haley beamed with pride, then shoved the picture at him. "For you!"

"Why, thank you." Zeke was nice enough to clutch it to his chest like it was a rare Picasso.

Meg pressed the top back on the paint can, grateful for a break. "Hey, Zeke. Nice to see you."

"Welcome back again, Shorty. Reporting for Haley-sitting duty as requested." He walked over and checked out her handiwork on the fence. "I've been offering to do this for Ruth for over a year, but she wouldn't let me."

"Yeah, well, I'm just special, I guess."

"Or in trouble with her again, I suspect." Zeke cracked a smile. "You know, I could rig you up a compressor, get this done a lot faster."

"That'd be awesome!"

"Why don't you run along to your meeting and me and Haley will go back to my shop and get it all set up? There may be some ice cream involved too, if that's okay?"

She kissed Zeke's wrinkled, stubbly cheek. "My hero."

After making sure Haley was all settled in Zeke's shop—and warned not to touch anything without asking—Meg jogged to the main drag. Hopefully Amber would be busy with her fake do-gooder act somewhere else at the moment because Meg really wasn't in the mood for two confrontations in one day.

Running late, she didn't have time to clean up. Her hands were covered with yellow polka dots and her shirt looked like the canvas for a modern impressionist splatter painting. One more thing that'd irritate her dad. What was one more fail for the day? Her father should probably start a tab.

Finally reaching the stone steps of Town Hall, she took them two at a time, then yanked the heavy door open and slowed her pace as she headed toward her father's office. Her jaw clenched when she spotted the long table set up just inside the door. There sat the Three Amigos, who had always felt *poor, motherless Megan* needed their guidance.

Bless their hearts.

The octogenarian trio headed up the church council and were peddling their newest craft thing that no one wanted but bought to be polite. Luckily, they were busy chatting among themselves, so maybe they wouldn't notice her.

"Megan? Is that you?"

No such luck.

Sucking a deep breath for patience, she changed directions. "Hello, ladies. How are you?"

Mrs. Jenkins, a retired principal, said, "We heard you were back. Pregnant again, dear?"

Wow. Really?

"Nope. Just going to a family meeting. Nice to see you all. Gotta run. You know how my dad hates tardiness."

All three bobbed their gray heads at that, so she was off the proverbial hook. But their pursed lips confirmed they all still thought she was going straight to hell.

Amazing how they couldn't remember where they put their car keys, but they could recite each and every one of Meg's indiscretions since elementary school.

Scurrying down the hall, she forced another smile and greeted her dad's assistant, the dragon lady who loyally guarded the gates to hell, better known as the mayor's office. "Hi, Mrs. Duncan. How are you?"

The assistant looked up from her computer screen and quirked a brow. "So the prodigal child returns home once again, huh? The mayor's in a meeting and since you weren't on the invite list you can just wait over there until they're through."

Before Meg could respond, her oldest brother, Ben, arrived.

"Hey, Muckity Muck." Throwing his big arm around Meg's shoulder, he winked at Mrs. Duncan. "I'm sure Dad didn't know Megan was back when he asked you to send out the details of the meeting. It involves the whole family. You're looking lovely today, by the way."

So much testosterone pumped from Ben that he cast a spell over the entire female race. He was the opposite of her brother Ryan, who spoke only when necessary.

"You're probably right, Doc. Go on in." When the woman's eyelids fluttered seductively, Meg's gag reflex kicked in.

Ben lifted his chin as a farewell, dragging Meg along with him. When they got out of earshot, he whispered, "Welcome back. Bring Haley by the clinic. I want to check her breathing."

"I will. Thanks."

He opened the office door for her to enter first. When her feet refused to move any closer to her raging bull of a father, Ben placed his big hand on her lower back and pushed. "Good luck."

Good luck? That wasn't a good omen.

Her father stopped mid-sentence and his jaw clenched. Before he could yell at her, Ben said, "Sorry we're late. I asked Meg to help me with something." He looked down at her and grinned. "Yellow paint was clearly involved."

Grandma snorted out a laugh. "Come on in, you two. We were just getting started, weren't we, Mitchell?" Her tone dared Dad to disagree with her.

"Why am I not surprised to see you here uninvited, Megan?" The frown lines deepened on her father's weathered face. "Have a seat. Let's get this over with."

The steady thump of a dog's tail signaled at least someone was happy to see her—Dad's dog, Numbskull, who lived up to his name.

She ventured deeper into the room, stunned that even the step-monster was in attendance. Sue Ann never came to these things. Normally the woman was too busy rushing off to Denver and spending Dad's money to worry about the details of how they all made it for her by running the many businesses in their little resort town. She hailed from Texas originally, was only ten years older than Casey, still spoke with a twang, and had perfect makeup, big hair, and even bigger fake boobs. It made Megan wish she'd thought to at least take her ponytail down and brush her hair. "Hi, everyone," she said.

Sue Ann raised a brow, then shook her head as her eyes did the up and down over Meg's outfit. "Lord, you're a mess. As usual."

Nice.

Plastering on a smile as fake as her stepmother's double Ds, Meg said, "Great to see you too, Sue Ann."

Meg found an empty chair next to Ryan, and Ben plopped down next to Casey. Ryan leaned over and gave Meg a shoulder bump in silent greeting.

Sending her brother a weak grin, she braced for the impact.

Wasting no time, Dad asked, "So, Megan, how long are you planning to stay this time?"

No welcome home or how're you doing? As usual. "For the summer season at least. Then we'll see. I want Haley to—"

"And how were you planning to support yourself and Haley this summer? I told you you're not welcome to work for our company after the last time you ran off, leaving us high and dry."

Casey sighed. "She didn't leave us high and—"

"You, Casey." Dad's meaty finger changed direction toward Grandma. "And you, Mother, are the reason Meg's so damned irresponsible. You both baby her and look where that got us." His steely gaze found Meg again. "I'm serious, Megan. You're welcome to see if anyone else in town will have you, but they all know you, and are aware of your stellar track record."

Her father really *was* serious this time. "I'm sorry about before, Dad. But after Haley was born I was just doing the leftovers no one else wanted anyway. I didn't think you'd mind if I left." Her father had lost all respect for her for "getting herself knocked up" and had barely been speaking to her. That was the real reason she'd left, but mentioning it wasn't going to help.

An exaggerated, Texas-sized sigh sounded from the step-monster. "Here we go again."

Ignoring her, Meg pleaded, "I'll sign whatever you need, do whatever job you'd like me to do, and I'll stick to it. No matter what it is. I promise."

"Oh, you'll sign a contract, huh?" Her father laughed and ran a hand through his thick white hair. "Like that's going to change anything. The answer is no, Megan!"

Ben spoke up. "She's apologized, Dad. And she has a point. You did give her the crap jobs after Haley was born. I could really use Megan's computer skills at the clinic."

Thank you, Ben!

Dad replied, "I couldn't give her jobs with any real responsibility because she was breastfeeding every damn time I turned around. She's made her bed and needs to lie in it for a change. We all agreed after she left last time that no one hires her ever again."

What? They'd all gone behind her back and ganged up on her? It wasn't like she was an alcoholic who needed an intervention, for God's sake. And it would have been nice if at least one of her siblings had cared enough to mention it to her. What was she going to do?

While picking at the paint splatter on her hands, Meg searched for the words to get out of the hole she'd dug for herself. She wouldn't get any help from her brothers or sister. Dad held

Ben's massive student loans over his head, forcing him to be the town doctor in exchange for paying them off. Casey, devastated after her ex left her with emptied bank accounts, needed the high-paying hotel job to support her kids—not to mention how much she'd always craved their father's approval. And Ryan? Meg's theory was he wouldn't leave town because the only woman he'd ever loved, Sarah, had married another man. One who, when he drank, turned hot-tempered and mean. Ryan stayed to protect her.

But still. A phone call would have been nice.

Alone in her battle, she had no choice. She was going to have to tell them. "After I lost my last position, I looked for other work in Denver but no one would hire me because I've changed jobs too many times." It killed her to tell them that. But she wouldn't blame it on Haley's asthma. It'd just give her dad another opportunity to tell her how stupid she'd been to get pregnant without a husband. But Haley came first. Always. No matter if it cost her jobs.

Digging deeper and giving up all of the little remaining pride she still possessed, she begged. "Please, Dad? Haley's father has reappeared. I'm afraid he'll want to be part of her life. He's a rich and powerful software developer and I'm unemployed. He'd win a custody battle in a heartbeat if that's his plan. I'm willing to clean rooms if I have to."

Casey gasped. "It was one thing to withhold his name, Meg, but you should've trusted me enough to talk about this. You know how I've battled with Tomas for the boys." The hurt and concern in her sister's eyes cut straight into Meg's heart. "We can't lose Hal—"

"That's enough, Casey. And dammit, Megan!" Numbskull whimpered at her father's raised voice. The veins in Dad's neck puffed and his face turned red as he growled, "You're going to have to figure things out on your own for a change. This is what happens when you sleep around and get yourself knocked up!"

And there it was. It didn't matter that she'd once loved Josh and that Haley had shown her a whole new kind of love between a parent and child she didn't even know existed.

Numbskull sauntered over and laid his big head in her lap, letting out a long, been-there-done-that sigh. Sadly, her only ally in the room was a big goofy mutt.

Appreciating the pooch's loyalty, she rewarded him with a dual ear rub while her brain raced for a solution.

Her sister was the only one remotely capable of changing Dad's mind. "Come on, Casey. You know I can run the hotel as well as you can. You said so yourself when I took over while you were on your honeymoon."

Before Casey could answer, her father said, "No. Maybe the threat of losing the one thing you seem to care about is what it's finally going to take to wake you up. This meeting is over!"

"Not so fast, Mitchell." Grandma raised a hand to silence any protest her son might make. "Megan, you think you can run a hotel as well as Casey? Then it's time you prove it."

"What do you mean?"

"You've owned your other grandparents' house since you were eight years old. They left it to you when they died."

Dad growled through gritted teeth. "Mother, that's enough!"

Grandma ignored him. "Your father never told you because he thought it wasn't fair they left it to you alone and not to all of you kids. The last renters just moved out, so it's sitting there on the other side of the lake falling to pieces. Fix it up into a nice private getaway and show your father you're better than he gives you credit for. Hurt him where it pains him most—in his damn wallet. Steal a few of those richer-than-sin clients away, then you'll be able to keep Haley here where she belongs.

"And you!" Grandma stood and pointed her cane at Dad. "That's your innocent-in-all-of-this granddaughter you just put on the line. I'm ashamed of you, son!" She opened the door, ignoring

Mrs. Duncan, who had obviously had her ear plastered to the other side, and yelled, "Now this meeting is adjourned!"

By the stunned looks of confusion on her older siblings' faces, no one else knew about the house either. Dad's menacing stare silenced the questions they clearly wanted to ask.

She'd always presumed the house had been inherited by her mother, an only child. But because her mom had died when Megan was a baby, it had gone to her father. "I'd gladly share with you guys—"

"Nope." Ryan finally spoke. "If those were their wishes, then we need to honor them. None of us are going to complain, are we?" He slid a stern look Casey's way and then to Ben. When they both shook their heads, Ryan nodded sharply. "Then we're all in agreement. Go for it, Meg."

"Oh, that's rich. How?" Her father leaned back in his chair and crossed his arms over his big barrel chest.

When no one spoke, Dad said, "Megan obviously doesn't have the resources, and I expect you all to keep our bargain. Don't let me catch you loaning her money. She'll never learn if we keep bailing her out. We all agreed on that."

Yeah, and at the end of the day, that's what hurt the worst. None of them had any faith left in her. Well, dammit, she'd show all of them, and herself too, that she could run her new little lodge better than any of them, even if she didn't have any money.

But how?

CHAPTER THREE

Meg fumed as she replayed the family meeting in her mind. She was used to her dad stomping on her heart, but hadn't seen that one coming from her sister and brothers.

She dragged the compressor closer to Grandma's fence, intending to finish the paint job while she decided what she was going to do with her life. It was tempting to just pack up and go, but if she left the fence half-painted, they'd all accuse her of reneging on top of being a screwup.

Too bad she had nowhere else to go. Given a choice it sure wouldn't be Anderson freakin' Butte.

As she leaned down to flip the switch, a familiar voice rang out in greeting.

Meg smiled as Pam, her hairstylist best friend who dressed like a hooker, made her way down the drive. Maybe Meg should point the nozzle at Pam and paint some clothes on her. But then, if Meg had a body like that, she'd probably want to show it off too. "Hey, Pam."

Her friend sashayed closer. Pam put so much bump and grind into her walk she should've carried her own pole. And she looked the part for the job: bleached-blonde hair, curvy body, and a man-eating smile. "Hey, Megs, glad you're back. Heard you were going to open a lodge on the other side of the lake."

It hadn't been five minutes since she'd left her father's office.

The Internet had nothing on the grapevine in Anderson Butte. "Well, uh, I haven't really decided—"

"Because I have a business proposition for you." Pam batted her eyes.

Someone should tell her that only works on men. Meg loved Pam like a sister but she had bigger problems at the moment. "I'm not really sure what I'll do with the place yet. But I'll keep that stellar idea of yours in mind. Now if you'll excuse me, I have to paint this fence."

Pam blinked. "I haven't even told you what it is. Come on, Meg. We've known each other since the first grade."

True. She was mad at her family, not Pam. "Sorry. Bad day. What did you have in mind?"

A sly grin lit Pam's face. "I offered this deal to your father, but we all know how shortsighted he is, right? This could be a way to stick it to him, you know? See, I've been taking an online massage class, and I—" Pam suddenly stopped and her eyes got all gooey. "Oh, hey, Ryan."

As mad at her family as Meg was, she could have kissed Ryan for saving her from Pam's off-kilter idea. Pam giving massages in hotel rooms would surely get someone arrested.

"Pam." Ryan lifted his chin in greeting. "Need to talk to Meg. Excuse us?"

"Sure. Stop by later if you'd like to help me with my massage homework. A body full of muscles like yours is hard to come by in these parts." How Pam raised her chest and made her boobs suddenly swell larger was a mystery Meg didn't want to solve. "We'll talk later, Meg. Bye."

"See you."

Meg and Ryan stood in silence until Pam's swaying hips were at the top of the hill. Meg turned and eyed her brother. "You and Pam?"

"Nope."

Ryan, the man of many words.

"Good. Now, thanks for saving me, but the only thing I have to say to you is—you all suck!"

"Prove us wrong then." He reached into his khaki uniform pants pocket and pulled out a set of keys. "For your new house. Utilities will be on in the morning."

Ryan pressed the keys to their grandparents' house into her hand, then turned to walk back to his place. That he had been the first to say he had no problem with not getting his fair share of the house poked at her heart. "Thanks, Ry."

He didn't bother to turn around, just lifted a hand to say goodbye.

Meg stuffed the keys into her back pocket, flipped the switch on the compressor, and went back to painting the fence. Zeke was right—the paint shot out so fast she'd have the job finished in no time. Then she'd collect Haley from Zeke and go to the diner. She needed Aunt Gloria's comfort food. And some awesome pie. Nothing helped a desperate girl think more clearly than Aunt Gloria's chocolate mousse pie.

When the compressor suddenly stopped working mid-squirt, Meg turned to see what the problem was.

Casey stood with the plug dangling from her long, elegant hand. "We need to talk, Meg."

She dropped the nozzle onto the grass and turned the opposite way. Casey's betrayal had stung the worst. "I have nothing to say to you, Benedict Arnold."

"Good, then you can just listen." In a classic Casey move, she tugged on Meg's ponytail, thwarting her escape. Meg whirled around to give her sister the tongue-lashing she deserved, but before she could start, Casey pulled Meg close, wrapping those mile-long arms around her, trapping her against that tall body. "I'm furious with you for not telling me about Haley's father, but I realized something today." Meg tried to pull away, but Casey's grip only grew tighter. "Apparently you haven't figured out I quit being your mother a long time ago. I've always wished we could just be sisters."

Meg stopped struggling. "Really? Because a sister, as opposed to a *mother* siding with Dad, would have called and warned me about this plan. Not one of you cared enough to make a simple phone call?"

"You expected Ryan to call and tell you? The man hasn't strung ten sentences in a row since he was born."

"Funny. But that doesn't let you and Ben off the hook."

"It's not some big conspiracy. The truth is—Dad's right about this one thing. We do always bail you out. If you'd stop being mad long enough to let your brain kick in, you'll realize it's true. Should I give you examples?"

That was the last thing she needed, to have all her past mistakes thrown in her face. "No! But it's different now that I have Haley. I've changed." She had her work cut out for her to show them all how much she'd changed, but she'd do it.

"The jury's still out on that. But if it's true, then you need a sister more than a mother right now." Casey leaned back and tilted Meg's face up with her soft hands. "A sister is someone you can trust, no matter how big the problem. Sisters can share a glass of wine, bitch about men, and talk about sex."

"I can't talk about sex with . . . you." Meg shuddered. "That'd be like talking to Grandma about it."

"That's my point, Meg. Get over it!" Casey huffed out a breath. "Anyway, the real reason for this chat is that I got a new computer a few weeks ago and my old one is still sitting in the corner of my office. I haven't had time to wipe the hard drive. It has all of our client contact information and the latest version of our management software. Dad said we couldn't help you, but if the computer went missing I wouldn't report it to Ryan." Casey pulled her closer. "As your *sister*, I want nothing more than for you to show Dad what you're capable of. So don't screw this up. Are we good here?"

Megan wrapped her arms around Casey's waist and snuggled close.

A hug felt good after the day she'd had.

But it was still a mom hug. Casey was the closest to a mother she'd ever known. It wouldn't be easy to stop thinking of her in that way, but it might be nice to start over with Casey. Just be sisters for a change. Maybe she'd be able to start over with her dad too. If she could pull off renovating the lodge and make him proud of her for once.

"Yeah, we're good. Thanks for the computer. But could we ease into that whole talking about sex thing? I'm still trying to get over the birds-and-the-bees speech you gave me in the fifth grade."

"Me too. I was only seventeen. I made it up as I went."

No. Knowing Casey, she'd probably read eight books on the subject to be sure she got it just right. "That might explain how I accidently got pregnant."

Casey laughed and gave a quick tug on Meg's ponytail. "See you later, brat. I have work to do."

Her sister had never judged Meg for Haley like their father had. Seems Casey *had* stopped mothering her; she just hadn't noticed.

Meg called out as her sister started up the hill. "Actually, it was equipment failure."

Casey turned around but continued walking backward up the hill. "Careful, Meg. That's dangerously close to having a conversation about sex."

Meg smiled as she leaned down and picked up the paint nozzle. Maybe now everyone in this damn town would leave her alone for a half hour so she could paint the fence—and figure out how to raise enough money to fix up her new lodge.

Drawing in a deep breath of clean, pine-tinted fresh air, Josh Granger walked toward the massive Anderson Butte Hotel, smiling for the first time in years. After being sequestered for three years, breathing fresh air, being able to do whatever he wanted, go wherever he wanted, was fantastic. Just driving his truck on the open road felt like he'd won the lottery. But now he needed to focus.

Interrogating and mining out the truth from life's worst excuses for human beings had left him hollow and empty. The FBI's definition of giving him a break a little over three years ago had been to send him undercover as an employee of a software company the mob ran as a front.

The only good thing to come of the case was that he'd met Meg. A woman as fragile as she was strong. Her external badass attitude couldn't hide from him the sweet woman inside she protected so fiercely. The light in Meg's infectious smile had shown him how far he'd sunk into the darkness and despair of the criminal underworld.

Thoughts of being with Meg again had gotten him through all the lonely days and nights he'd been hidden away. He couldn't wait to see her and finally meet Haley. But Meg wasn't going to feel the same about him.

He closed his eyes and dug deep, conjuring the man Megan thought he was. His training had taught him to act, steal, and mine out the truth, but getting Megan and Haley back wouldn't be easy. He needed to let Meg see enough of the Josh she thought she knew, then he'd feed her the real Josh a little at a time. She thought he was a wealthy software designer who didn't want anything to do with them.

He couldn't tell Meg the truth—yet. While the dangerous criminals were all dead or behind bars, there were still some lingering questions about Meg's father, so the case wasn't closed. He probably should've waited until it was all over before he reappeared in their lives, after they knew her father's fate. Then there'd be no need to lie. But who knew how long that was still going to take? And after three of the longest years of his life, he couldn't wait another day to see Meg's beautiful smile again and to finally meet the daughter he knew nothing about but wanted to know every detail he'd missed. Never having a father, and being orphaned at six, he vowed to be a good parent to Haley.

But how the hell was he going to convince Meg he wasn't the old Josh? Worse, what if she didn't like the man he truly was?

Hitching up his bag, he headed for a set of double doors that slid open as he approached. The lobby was surprisingly sleek compared to the rustic exterior; gleaming wood floors, massive tables with fresh flowers, and oversized leather couches and chairs were all strategically set around flat-screen televisions and a big stone fireplace. There was even a highly polished old-fashioned bar for happy hour that could have come straight from a saloon in the Wild West.

A tall, dark-haired woman behind the reception desk lifted her head and sent him a warm smile. "Hi. May I help you?"

Before he could answer, the elevator doors slid open and a guy who looked familiar exited. Dressed in a T-shirt and board shorts, he lifted a hand to the lady behind the counter and then strolled out the back door toward the lake.

Josh approached the counter and dropped his bag at his feet. "Was that Ashton Kutcher?" He'd watched too much mindless television to pass the time while he'd been hidden away. It was embarrassing he even knew who that was.

"I wish. How can I help you?"

He could have sworn . . . he shook it off and got back to business. "I need a room for a few nights, please."

She shook her head. "I'm sorry, but we don't take walk-ins. Reservations only."

"Would you be willing to make an exception just this once? I tried, but it's impossible to find you on the web to make a reservation."

"We rely on word of mouth only. The closest hotel is about fifteen miles south. Shall I call and see if they have any rooms available?"

What? The parking lot wasn't nearly full, and there weren't throngs of people milling around. What hotel wouldn't have an Internet presence? It didn't make any sense.

Megan didn't talk about her family much, but she'd told him they ran the hotel and owned most of the real estate in the town. And something about the woman's smile seemed familiar. Meg was a petite brunette with stunning blue eyes. This lady's eyes were brown, and she was tall and slender, but her smile and hair color were just like Meg's. "Did Megan put you up to this?"

Her eyebrows spiked. "Who's Megan?"

She was good. But he hadn't been called the human lie detector for nothing. A momentary flash in her eyes revealed she was covering. "I just want to see her and Haley. I'm not here to cause any trouble."

At the mention of Haley, the woman's hand had fisted around the pen she held. "I have no idea what you're talking about. And I'm sorry, but I don't have a room for you, Mr. . . . ?"

"Josh Granger. If you see Megan, tell her I just want to talk. And if she runs, I'll find her again. I'll be at the diner I saw down the road if she wants to make this easier on everyone."

Josh picked up his bag and headed for the sliding glass doors.

Maybe he'd come on a little too strong. This wasn't Denver; it was a small town. Debating a less aggressive tactic, he glanced over his shoulder in time to see her furiously tapping out a message on her cell. Good. Spread the word, because Megan's cell phone indicated she was just north of the hotel. The driveway had a gate and a sign professing to shoot trespassers or he would have gone to the coordinates his tracking software had guided him to first.

He'd sleep in his truck at the end of the driveway if he had to so she wouldn't be able to bolt. Or maybe Megan would make this easy and meet him at the diner.

Two minutes later he pulled open the glass door of Good Eats and Better Treats. The home-cooked scents filling the air reminded him he'd skipped lunch. The diner was packed but for two empty stools at the counter.

The décor, contrary to the rustic Daniel Boone theme he'd expected from a mountain town, was straight out of the fifties. It had alternating black-and-white tile on the floors, red vinyl booths and stools, and lots of stainless steel behind the counter that was either original or a damned good restoration job. It even had little jukeboxes at every Formica-topped table.

The waitress behind the counter was somewhere between fifty and seventy-five. She wore a pink bowling shirt with the name "Gloria" stitched across her chest. Her hair was all piled up on top of her head like Marge Simpson's. Gloria had five—no, make that six—pens sticking out of that bird's nest. But it was the blue eye shadow and the hot-pink lipstick that completed what would be one hell of an impressive Halloween costume.

She held out a plastic-coated menu. "What can I get you? The chocolate mousse pie's to die for."

That was Megan's favorite flavor of pie. She used to eat it in bed after they'd work up an appetite. The sexy moans she made while devouring it made up for the crumbs she'd leave on their sheets.

He slid onto a barstool next to an older man and drew a deep breath.

Patience. Small town. Reel it back.

He returned the menu to Gloria without looking at it and remembered to smile. "Why don't you bring me whatever you like the best and then the pie for dessert? I trust you."

Her eyes squinted as she studied him. "Aren't you the charmer? It's no wonder Me—"

The old guy sitting next to him cleared his throat, cutting her off as he stuck his hand out. "Hi. Name's Zeke. What brings you to Anderson Butte?"

He shook the man's hand. "Josh. Nice to meet you. Have you lived here long?"

"My whole life."

"Then you must know the woman I'm looking for. She grew up here. Megan Anderson?"

The old guy frowned and scratched the stubble on his wrinkled cheek. "Nope. Can't say I recognize the name. But wait. Half the town is here tonight 'cuz of the fish and chips special." He stood and placed two fingers in his mouth, blowing out a shrill whistle an NFL referee would be proud of.

All conversation stopped and everyone turned to stare at them. "So, this here young man says he's looking for a lady named Megan Anderson. Any you all know her?"

*No*s rang out along with head shakes before they all went back to their meals.

Zeke shrugged. "Maybe you got the wrong town?"

Okay, so this was how it was going to be. He'd told the woman at the hotel he was coming here and she'd warned them.

"You mean this town—that's named after her family?"

Zeke laughed. "Probably just a coinkydink? Enjoy your meal."

A plate filled with chicken-fried steak and mashed potatoes slid in front of him, along with a scowl from Gloria. "Figured a slick-talking guy like you would like this better than fish and chips."

It was probably good Meg had people like this to protect her. And as much as he wanted to punch his fist into a wall in frustration with them, Gloria was right. He hated fish and chips. It reminded him of those frozen fish stick meals he ate as a kid. They served them every Tuesday at the orphanage disguised as a boys' ranch where he'd grown up. He'd escaped the ranch on his eighteenth birthday, and hadn't had a fish stick in the twelve years since.

"See, I knew I could trust you, Gloria."

Her frown deepened. "Yeah, but can we trust you?" She sauntered away to top off more coffee cups.

Digging into the best chicken-fried steak he'd ever had, he reevaluated his plan. He hadn't counted on the secret club he'd have to infiltrate.

Just as he finished off the last of his buttery, peppery mashed potatoes, the little bell above the glass door rang and in walked a cop. The man, built like a tank, could probably take down a hyped-up meth addict with ease. After scanning the busy diner, he made a beeline for the empty stool next to Josh's.

Maybe his luck was about to change.

The man sat down and Gloria instantly appeared in front of him. "The usual, Sheriff?"

The guy gave a quick nod, then turned his intense blue-eyed gaze on Josh. "Evenin'."

"Evening." Josh glanced at the man's name tag that read "R. Anderson," and it became clear why his eyes reminded him so much of Megan's. Another Anderson relative and another dead end most likely, but it was worth a try. He held out a hand. "Josh Granger."

The man slowly reached out, then returned a bone-crunching handshake. "Heard you're asking after someone named Megan. What's it to you?"

Gloria returned with his pie and a chicken-fried steak dinner for the cop. After she handed everything out, she stood with her hands on her hips, apparently waiting for his answer too. The old guy next to him laid down his fork and crossed his arms, as the whole diner became Sunday-morning-Mass silent.

How much should he reveal? Probably the lady at the hotel had already told them anyway. "Just want to have a friendly conversation with her."

He slid his fork into the pie and took a bite. The burst of creamy, rich chocolate that filled his mouth almost made him forget he was about to be interrogated.

The cop dug into his meal, taking a few bites then pausing for a gulp of his soda. He thumped the glass down on the counter and finally said, "That's what cell phones are for. Since there's nowhere for you to stay, you'd be smart to move along, Granger."

Yep. Dead end.

He finished off his pie and forced a smile. Throwing two tens onto the counter, he said, "Best meal I've ever had, Gloria. Thank you for the hospitality."

As he headed for the door, the old guy, Zeke, said loudly, "Sheriff, it's legal to shoot a man for trespassing if a sign is clearly posted, right?"

"Yep. And Grandma doesn't miss."

That confirmed the cell phone tracking software on his laptop hadn't steered him wrong. Megan was on the other side of the gate with the "No Trespassing" sign.

He kept on walking as if he hadn't heard them. Talking to Megan was going to be harder than he'd anticipated, but no way in hell was he going to be run out of town like the villain in a low-budget Western.

CHAPTER FOUR

*M*egan caught a fleeing Haley and scooped her up. "I know you don't like the mask, but it'll help you breathe better. If you'll sit really still and take big breaths for Mommy, we'll get pie after dinner, okay?"

Megan carried Haley back to the couch and handed her a stack of her favorite books. "Choose which one and I'll be right back."

"Nooo, Mommy. Pleeeeez?" The books ended up on the floor.

Meg hated the nebulizer too, but Haley had been coughing after being outside all day. Probably the extra pollen in the air around the lake, but Meg wasn't taking any chances. They'd go see Ben to be sure Haley's meds didn't need to be upped.

As if waiting for her cue, as soon as Meg walked back in the room with the machine, Haley flopped onto the couch and kicked, cried, and wailed. A tantrum deserving of an Academy Award.

Crying wouldn't help Haley's breathing, so Meg forced herself to remain calm and got everything set up. Then she sat quietly until Haley realized she wasn't going to win. After a few more last-ditch protests, Haley grew still, so Meg pulled her against her side. She picked up *Goodnight Moon* from her feet, placed it on her lap, and then adjusted the mask across her pouting daughter's face. "Breathe deep until all the medicine is gone. Then we'll go eat." She placed Haley's hands on her stomach so she could feel the air as she drew it into her lungs. "Fill the tummy balloon as big as it can get, then let it all out. Remember?"

Haley's little nod just about broke Megan's heart. Her kid was tough to the core.

They were almost finished when Casey slammed through the front door at a full run. One look at Haley stopped her in her tracks. "What's the matter? Did she have an attack?"

Meg begged with her eyes for Casey to chill out. She didn't want to scare Haley. "No. Everything's great! We're just reading."

She couldn't blame Casey. It had taken Meg a while to get used to seeing that contraption strapped to her baby's face too.

"Oh. Good." Casey slowly nodded and then sat on the other side of Haley. "I need to tell you something as soon as you guys are done, okay?" Casey's gaze tilted to the top of Haley's head and then up to Meg again in a "not in front of the kid" gesture.

They were close enough to done anyway. Freeing Haley from the mask, she said, "You did such a good job, Haley-Bug, you deserve an extra treat." Meg dug her cell from her back pocket and did something she usually avoided, but Casey's intense gaze convinced Meg to make an exception. "You can play any game you'd like for a bit while I talk to Aunt Casey."

Haley's face lit up and she morphed back into her happy little self. "Yay! The birdy one, Momma!"

"You got it." Meg set Haley up with the game and then gathered the nebulizer and all the tubing before heading to the kitchen to clean the parts out. Casey followed right behind. "So what's—"

"He's in town. Josh. He tried to check into the hotel. It was just luck we don't take walk-ins. He's at the diner now."

The air whooshed from Megan's lungs. "Are you sure it's him?"

"Had you ever told me his name I would have known for sure, but how about tall, blond, built, killer smile, Haley looks just like him, Josh Granger?"

Crap!

How had he found them so quickly? Panic rushed through her at the thought of seeing him again. But then determination steeled her spine. She had to protect her daughter. Keep her away from him so Haley would never have to feel the rejection and heartbreak Meg still hadn't fully recovered from. She might not be in the best of circumstances at the moment, but she'd always been sure Haley had everything she needed. They didn't need him.

She rushed toward her bedroom to pack, but Casey grabbed her arm and stopped her. "Let go," Meg said. "We have to leave. I don't want him to—"

"Isn't that what the old Meg would have done?" Casey pulled her back into the kitchen. "You said you've changed. Time to prove it."

Meg's head snapped up at her sister's words. That's what she used to do. Run when things got tough. It seemed easier than confronting the people always so quick to judge her. Like her father and the Three Amigos.

But the problem rarely solved itself and running mostly only made it fester and get worse. Best to make a stand right up front and be sure Josh knew no matter what he planned, she'd shield her daughter from him.

Haley appeared in the doorway. "Pie, please!"

Casey lifted Haley up to her eye level. "After my chef met you this morning he made all sorts of treats just for you, my little pie piggy. Let's go. We'll eat pie while Mommy does some serious thinking."

Her sister didn't know the half of it.

Meg slowly followed behind them down to the sandy shore and toward the hotel. They couldn't take the road and risk running into Josh.

Maybe he wasn't going to ask for custody. Maybe he just wanted to meet Haley. Which could be just as bad. Josh would be so busy working, wrapped up in some big project like before, he'd soon forget he had a daughter, but Haley wouldn't forget him.

Her stomach ached at the thought of seeing him again. She'd finally allowed herself to fall in love for the first time and then Josh had turned around and ripped her heart out. And yet, she didn't hate the man all the way like she should. She needed to remember the pain he'd caused her and stay strong.

Walking beside the serene water, Meg drew a deep breath, desperately digging for some of the lake's calm for herself. She *was* going to stick this time. So what she needed to do was figure out what Josh wanted, and then get rid of him.

Josh stared through his truck's windshield, tapping his fingers on the steering wheel. Meg's phone was still just a few feet away, according to his software. The gate was shut, but that didn't mean he couldn't hop the wall and walk down there. All he wanted was a chance to talk to her. To convince her he wasn't the jerk she thought he was. Unfortunately that would require another lie, but it'd be the last lie he'd ever tell her.

He wished he could tell her the truth about why he'd left. That he'd had to leave for their safety, not because he'd wanted to. Especially because they'd just found out Meg was pregnant. It had been the happiest day of his life. He looked forward to being part of a family, something he'd always longed for after growing up without parents. But then a week later he'd had to make up a new lie and leave Meg. He still hated himself and the FBI for that.

They hadn't found anything to make charges stick in the

online gambling investigation against Meg's father three years ago. Hopefully, for Meg's sake, the FBI wouldn't find any new ones. The truth would come out soon, but not until the agency finished tying up loose ends by reinvestigating some of the smaller players in the scheme.

What would Meg's reaction be when she found out he'd been investigating her and her father when they'd first met? And would it make a difference to her once he explained how he'd opted out of the case as soon as it had become clear she hadn't had any clue about her father's activities, so they could pursue a relationship? Hopefully she'd be able to understand that even though he lied about his identity for his job, he hadn't lied about loving her.

He'd turned in his badge yesterday and now he was ready to do whatever it took to get Meg and Haley back. But when all the facts were finally revealed, would Meg be able to get past the betrayal of being spied on and lied to?

Josh studied the locked gate again, debating if he should wait some more or just jump the damn wall. Meg surely knew he was in town by now. What if she tried to run during the night? Now was the best time to make his move.

He pulled himself up, swung his legs over the stucco wall, and landed softly on the other side. He'd stick to the trees on the side of the gravel drive.

The cop had said his grandmother lived here. Would an older woman really shoot him? They were probably just trying to warn him off.

He hoped.

After a few feet, a break in the pine trees revealed a huge, stunning lake. The lowering sun sent long streaks across the water's smooth surface, producing prisms of color. A few Jet Skis and a speedboat bobbed serenely alongside a long dock.

Why hadn't Meg ever mentioned how great her hometown was? Such a contrast to where he'd spent his childhood after he became an orphan at six. That damned boys' ranch in New Mexico. To think he and Meg had been living only a few hours away from each other all that time when they were kids. It was probably a karma thing that his case had caused their paths to cross . . . if he could shake off the cynic he'd become and convince himself to believe in that kind of stuff.

The FBI had recruited him out of college, promoting the organization as a pseudo-family of men and women all focused on doing good for the world. And it could be at times. It didn't hurt that orphans made the best agents—no one to miss them if they didn't come back from a mission.

To live somewhere like Anderson Butte might have made all the crappy things he'd had to do for his job worth it if he'd been able to come home after an assignment to someplace as beautiful as this. And to someone as beautiful as Meg.

What had made her leave? If he'd grown up here, he'd have put down deep roots. Never joined the FBI to move past his unfortunate childhood.

Hopefully he'd be able to stay.

As he moved closer to the lake, a house with a big wraparound porch and a short, yellow picket fence surrounding a garden came into view, but the glint of sunshine off mostly rusty metal made Josh change course. Megan's car stood beside a shed not too far from a smaller building with its own little front porch.

She was still driving that piece of junk? That would be the first thing he'd do. Buy them a safer car.

Glancing around to be sure the coast was clear, he jogged behind the little house and cupped his hands against a window. There were couches, a couple of stuffed chairs, and a pile of brightly colored books scattered on the floor. A cell phone lay on the coffee table. But no Meg and Haley.

Just as he pulled away to try the front door, a deafening explosion assaulted his eardrums. Hot, searing pain made him clutch the outside of his left arm. He spun around to find a tall, older woman pointing a rifle at him.

"Get off my land. Now!"

He hated getting shot, dammit. That made three times now.

Lifting the hand on his wounded arm to show he didn't have any weapons, he said, "I don't mean you any harm. I was just looking for Megan."

"I'd say now you best be looking for a doctor to take care of that. Get!"

The pain made him grit his teeth. "I just want to have a conversation with her."

"Do you have a learning difficulty of some sort?" The old woman raised the rifle higher. "Because I'd hate to shoot a disabled person. If so, tell me now or start running."

It was like being in the freakin' *Twilight Zone*, but she looked pretty damned serious. He glanced at his wound. Blood trickled steadily down his arm. It was just a flesh wound, but he'd have to find a doctor. He probably couldn't stitch it up himself.

He backed up. "Okay, I'm leaving."

Just as he stepped off the porch, the sheriff's car came barreling down the drive. The older man from the diner got out of the passenger side and called out, "Heard the gunshot and figured Ruthie'd done it again. I tried to warn you, Granger."

The sheriff appeared by his side and took Josh's uninjured arm. Without a word, the cop herded Josh into the back of his police car.

The old lady called out, "Might as well give up. We won't let you take Haley!"

Take Haley? Is that what they all thought he was here to do?

As they drove up the hill, a set of blue eyes met his in the rearview mirror. "You ready to leave town now?"

"No." Josh closed his eyes, fighting against the pain. "And I'm not here to take Haley. I just need to talk to Megan."

"Suit yourself. We're almost there."

Wherever "there" was. For all he knew, the sheriff would throw him in a ditch and let him bleed to death. "Is that woman senile or something? She could have killed me."

"Nope. She holds state shooting records. If she'd wanted you dead, you'd be dead. Under our trespassing laws she had every right to shoot you."

Yeah, he knew that. But he hadn't counted on a sharpshooting granny with a cane. Now he knew why Megan never talked about her wacky family.

When they pulled up in front of a building with "Anderson Butte Clinic" on the glass doors, relief washed through him. He looked for a handle to open his car door, but there wouldn't be one because he was in the backseat like a damned criminal. He was usually the one driving.

When the door flew open, he swung his legs out and stood, hating that he was a little lightheaded. Only a few more feet and he'd be good.

The sheriff took his uninjured arm again.

"I don't need your help."

The sheriff kept tugging. "Can't have you running off before I charge you with stalking and trespassing." He pulled Josh along and then opened the door to the clinic for him.

The cop led him to an examining room and guided him to the table. Just as he got settled, the doctor joined them.

"Hi, I'm Ben Anderson. Hear my grandmother shot you. Any allergies to medications?" The doctor sat on a stool and slid closer.

"No." Another Anderson? If he'd had the strength to run, he would have. He started to unbutton his shirt, but the doctor saved him the trouble and cut it off.

After the doctor poked around a bit he said, "It's just a flesh wound." Then he lifted up a needle.

"That an arsenic injection, Doc?"

"Nah. If I'd wanted to kill you, I'd just leave the air bubbles in the syringe." He nudged Josh onto his back and went to work. "We'll have you fixed right up. Hurts like hell though, right?"

"Yeah." But hell might be better than Anderson Butte. "So how are you related to Megan?"

"I'm her oldest brother. Deputy Dawg over there holding my wall up is her other brother. You've met our sister Casey at the hotel. This may sting a bit."

He hissed as the needle pierced his skin. "Any others of you I should watch out for?"

"Our father," the doctor and the cop said in unison.

While the doctor filled up another syringe, he said, "I'm going to give you something stronger for the pain and to help you sleep. Where are you staying tonight?"

He had to think about that for a minute. Then he remembered. "In my truck. There were no rooms at the hotel, evidently."

"Maybe something has opened up. I'll check for you."

"Not holding my breath." Before long the meds kicked in and his mind went to a very happy place.

While Haley dug into a big piece of pie and ice cream for dessert, Meg stacked dishes into the industrial washer in the hotel's kitchen. "Thanks for dinner, Casey, it was great."

"You're welcome. It's been kind of quiet without the boys, so I enjoyed the company." Casey dug her ringing cell out of her pocket, checking the display before she lifted it to her ear. "Hey, Ben."

Casey listened for a moment, then said, "Hang on. Meg's here, I'll put you on speaker."

As she poked a button and laid the phone down, she said, "Grams shot your ex. Ben wants to ask us something."

"Shot him?" She raced for the counter and yelled into the phone. "Is he going to be all right?"

"Just a nick, he'll be fine."

Meg slumped against the counter in relief. She'd never forgive herself if she'd caused any actual harm to Josh. She just wanted him to go away. "Where is he?"

"Here at the clinic."

"Is he in a lot of pain?"

"Gunshot wounds tend to hurt. I've given him something for the pain. He can't drive. Do you have a room, Casey? Otherwise I have to stay with him here. I have a hot date I'd rather not cancel for a change."

Casey crossed her arms and shook her head. "Then let him sleep in his car! He's trying to steal Ha—"

Megan cut her off. "Who has big ears and is sitting right here? He's hurt. Let him have a room, Casey. Please?"

Casey narrowed her eyes. "Fine. Tell him he can stay but the rate is five grand a night!"

Meg rolled her eyes. "Be reasonable."

"You just got done telling me at dinner he's loaded, so why not?"

"Because it isn't right and you know it."

Casey huffed out a breath. "Okay, he can stay. But the rate is a thousand bucks a night. Take it or leave it!"

Ben laughed. "I'll tell him. Thanks, Casey."

Meg started for the kitchen's swinging doors. "Can you watch Haley for a minute? Ben might need some help getting him here. Be right back."

Before her sister could protest, Meg ran out the front doors and hit Main Street. She hated the thought of Josh being shot—she'd loved him once, after all—but she needed to find out why he was here. It probably wasn't going to help that Grandma shot him if there was going to be a custody battle. She'd better try to smooth things out a little.

She'd just ignore the urge she still had to light all his fancy shoes on fire, and instead make nice, get him settled, and then get Haley out of the hotel and back to the guesthouse.

Then she'd find a way to boot his ass out of town.

Breathing hard from the run, she tugged on the clinic's door. Ben sat behind the reception desk poking at a keyboard. He sent her a questioning eyebrow hitch, which she ignored, so he pointed the way. "I'll help him to my car after I finish this up."

The sight of Josh made her stomach clench. He lay on the exam table wearing just jeans and boots. His chiseled chest slowly rose and fell, his arm sported a big bandage, and his eyes were closed. His color was good and he looked fine. Actually, he looked more than fine. Another reason she should just go. But her traitorous feet moved her closer.

She swiped away a wisp of soft blond hair that had fallen over his eye and studied his handsome face.

It still hurt to look at him. The man had stolen a piece of her heart that hadn't grown back.

When she let out a long sigh, his eyes fluttered open and he smiled. "There you are, Meg. Been lookin' for ya." His words slurred together.

"I heard."

He struggled to sit up, so she helped him.

"Your crazy grandma shot me."

"Don't expect a purple heart. She's shot me too." She threw Josh's heavy arm around her shoulder and helped him stand. "Come on. Let's go find you a bed."

"Where'd she shoot you?" He swayed, nearly knocking her off her feet.

She propped Josh against the exam table while she waited for Ben. "My butt. What did you think all those little scars were from?"

"Oooh, yeah." A slow, silly grin lit his face. "You have a reeeally niiiiccce ass, Meg."

Before she could respond to the nice ass remark, Ben appeared in the doorway, then slid around to Josh's other side and helped him stand. "He'll be a little loopy for a while. Just needs to sleep it off. I'll help you get him to the hotel."

Ben killed the lights and locked up, then they wrestled Josh into her brother's Jeep and strapped him in for the short ride to the hotel.

After they led Josh through the lobby and up to his room, Josh fell flat on his face across the bed. Ben asked, "Can you take it from here? My date's waiting."

"Yeah. Thanks. Have fun."

Megan studied Josh's prone body with all those sexy muscles making their way down to his own very nice ass. Doing her best to ignore the physical desire for him that apparently hadn't gone away, she focused on wrangling off his well-worn pair of boots. She'd never seen anything like them hiding among the slick, expensive shoes in his closet. Or the knife he had strapped to his ankle. Why would a software developer like Josh be carrying a knife?

Carefully she removed it, slid the lethal-looking thing out of the case for a better look, and then laid it on his nightstand. Weird.

Next she needed to get him out of his jeans, so she called out loudly, "Josh. Roll over. We need to unzip your pants."

He lifted his head, winced, and then slowly rolled over and closed his eyes again. His hands went to the top button on his jeans and fumbled for a minute before he fell back asleep.

Pushing his hands aside, she straddled him and then undid the top button. Gingerly she unzipped his fly, careful not to touch anything important, and then nudged him so he'd lift up enough to slide his pants off his legs.

Josh had the physique of a well-trained, professional athlete, not a software desk jockey. And he had a few nasty, painful-looking scars on his chest that hadn't been there before.

Not that she cared.

But she probably needed to leave before her hormones started doing the thinking for her.

When she rolled off him, Josh's strong arm snaked around her middle and he drew her against him. "Don't go. Wanna talk to ya."

She wanted to talk to him too. A little coherence would be nice, though. But then, maybe he'd be more truthful all drugged up.

With Josh spooned against her back just like old times, she ignored her happy hormones and said, "Okay, so talk. Why are you here, Josh?"

He pulled her closer and sighed.

She feared he'd fallen back asleep until he began mumbling something unintelligible. But then she clearly made out "Gotta get her back."

He *was* trying to take Haley away. She pulled out of his grasp and headed for the door. "You'll get Haley over my dead body, Josh."

CHAPTER FIVE

Josh blinked his eyes open. The bed was soft and the sign on the back of a door told him he was in a hotel room. His things were stacked on a dresser next to a flat-screen television. His left side hurt, his head felt like he'd gone on a bender the night before, and he was starving.

When he rolled over, searing pain exploded through his arm and everything came rushing back.

He threw the covers aside with his good arm and sat up. His brain slid around in his skull once before settling enough to notice that the clock on the nightstand showed it was almost noon. His knife lay beside the clock.

How he'd ended up dressed only in his boxers, he didn't recall. But he was pretty sure Megan had something to do with it—which meant he'd better come up with an explanation for carrying a weapon in case she asked about it. And what if she'd found the letter?

He stood and made his way to the dresser. He opened his duffel, shoved the clothes aside, and found the envelope taped to the bottom of the bag where he'd kept it since the day he'd had to break up with her.

For in case things had gone bad.

He couldn't bear for her to never know the truth if he were to die.

The envelope was still facedown and securely taped just the way he'd left it, so it seemed his secret was still safe. He grabbed the first set of clothes his hand landed on and pulled them out to change into after his shower. After that, he'd figure a way around the loonies who lived in Anderson Butte and find Meg.

At least the crazy townspeople hadn't left him naked out by the lake, covered in honey, to be eaten alive by mosquitoes.

Maybe he was starting to grow on them.

After a quick knock sounded, the door swung open and Meg's sister walked in with a brown paper bag and a piece of paper in her hand. "So, you're not dead, huh? Just lazy and sleeping in? I tried calling twice."

"Sorry. It appears I survived my first day in Anderson Butte despite your best efforts. Do you barge in on all your customers?"

"I was hoping for the dead theory." She moved farther inside, stopping a good three feet away like he might bite, and then thrust the bag and the paper toward him. "I'm sure you're eager to get on the road. Here's your bill and some lunch you can take with you."

He dropped the clothes he held and opened the bag. The sandwich, apple, and cookie inside made his stomach growl. Josh grabbed the fat turkey sandwich and took a big bite. "Thanks." As he chewed he studied the bill. It was for a thousand dollars. "I assume you take credit cards?"

"In your case we don't. Cash or debit only. ATM's in the lobby. If it's a debit, we'll transfer it to Megan's account. And put some damn pants on, will you?"

Nope. She was the one busting into his room uninvited. "I'll be happy to transfer any amount of money you want into Megan's account, but not until I've seen her and Haley. Where are they?" He'd collected full pay the last three years he'd been hidden away.

Added to the money he'd never had time to spend, he had plenty that he intended to share with them.

Casey crossed her arms. "Megan's gone for the day. She said to text her with whatever it is you want. And you have a few other bills to settle as well. Stop by the clinic and then the sheriff's office on your way out of town."

He took another bite of his sandwich. "I'll go settle up with the others, but I'm not checking out yet." The games were getting old. "What's it going to take to let me see them, Casey?"

"You'll not see her again unless she wants to see you. Don't make me get the sheriff to evict you, Granger. It's past checkout time." She turned and walked out the door.

Josh finished his lunch, and then attempted to shower without getting the bandage wet. It was after one by the time he ventured out to Main Street. He found his truck at the end of Megan's grandmother's drive where he'd left it, complete with a parking ticket sticking out from under the windshield wiper. It was also for a thousand dollars and was to be paid at the sheriff's department in cash or a debit to Megan. Laughing at the ridiculous amount, he climbed into his truck.

Were they punishing him for not paying child support? He couldn't blame them for that. He'd wanted to send something but couldn't risk a money trail to Megan. He'd make it up to them.

Josh cranked the engine and headed toward the clinic.

He found a parking space in a large lot behind the two-story brick building. After beeping the locks on his truck, he started for the rear entrance. The sound of a helicopter approaching grew increasingly louder. When the wind from the blades became gale force, Josh looked up to see a chopper hovering not twelve feet over his head. Megan's brother Ben was behind the controls with a big smile on his face.

The smartass.

Finally the chopper veered away and landed on the far end of the parking lot. Ben was the man he wanted to see, so he waited until the doctor got out and grabbed his bag.

Ben was still smirking as he got closer. "How's the arm today, Granger?"

"Fine. I'm here to settle my bill."

"Come on in. Haven't gotten around to printing it up yet. Have some patients in the hospital over in Denver."

Josh followed behind as they weaved their way back to Ben's office. Ben held out a hand toward a side chair. "Something to drink? Coffee, water?"

"Water. Thanks." Of all the Anderson siblings, Ben seemed the most reasonable.

Maybe Ben was the key to figuring out how to get to Megan. "A helicopter probably comes in handy for making rounds in Denver, huh?"

"Yep. It saves time. We all learned to fly right after we learned to drive." Ben popped open the door to a mini-fridge and tossed a cold bottle of water Josh's way before he started tapping keys on the computer. "Has Meg ever taken you up? I'll deny it if you tell her I said this, but she's the best pilot of all of us. Except for Zeke, maybe."

Megan could fly a helicopter? How the hell hadn't he known that? "No. We never got the chance, I guess." But he'd spent more hours than he could count behind the stick himself.

"Too busy running out the door and leaving her in a lurch, huh?" Ben slid a bill across the desk. It was for four thousand dollars. "Cash or we can transfer it—"

"Yeah, I know. To Megan's account."

"Shitty thing to do to my sister, Granger. We won't let you take Haley."

He wasn't getting anywhere, so he stood to leave. "I'm not here to take Haley. I'm here to try to make up for my past mistakes. Thanks for patching me up."

Ben called out as Josh headed for the door. "Have your arm checked out tomorrow or the next day for infection. My brother is waiting for you at the sheriff's office in Town Hall. If you see an even bigger old guy with a scowl, that's probably my dad. Run!"

Freakin' crazy town.

Josh shoved the door open and sucked in a deep, calming breath. The woodsy, clean scent was something he'd never get tired of.

Town Hall couldn't be too far away, so he left his truck where it was and made his way out to Main Street.

He turned the corner and nearly tripped over a kid who sat on the raised wooden sidewalk beside a golden retriever twice the little boy's size. His head was bent over one of the dog's big paws.

Josh kneeled down beside them. When the dog whimpered, he reached out and gave it a pat. "Everything okay?"

The kid shook his head. "Wilbur got a splinter from the wood."

"Ah." Josh reached to his belt for the more innocuous Leatherman tool, which he'd decided to carry instead of his throwing knife. Growing up, he'd spent most of his free time with the animals at the ranch and hated to see one in pain. "Mind if I take a look?"

The boy's brow furrowed with confliction. "You're that guy I saw at the diner last night, right?" The boy's grip grew tighter on his dog. "Uncle Zeke said you're trying to take Haley away. We aren't supposed to talk to you."

It was like a broken record.

Josh went to work on the dog's paw. "I was at the diner last night, but I'm not trying to take Haley away. I just want to meet her." He held up the three-inch splinter. "That had to hurt."

"Yeah, ummm, I . . . better go." The boy and his dog scurried off down the street, avoiding the wooden sidewalk this time. The kid looked over his shoulder one last time, as if frightened Josh would follow behind.

Great. His status as a child snatcher had all the little kids in town running scared too? He needed to find a little old lady to help across the street to save his reputation.

With none in sight, he checked out the town that surrounded a large park. In the middle of the grass stood a big whitewashed bandstand, like he'd seen in the movies as a kid. He'd naïvely imagined he'd end up in a town just like this once he got adopted. What an idiot. He soon found out older kids rarely got adopted and, if so, didn't end up in places like this.

Anderson Butte was so Disneyland clean and tidy it seemed fake, like a movie set. He was tempted to go around the back to see if it was all a façade.

Colorful wildflowers everywhere offset the vivid green of the grass and the surrounding gigantic trees. The buildings were a mix of old and new, but somehow they all blended to form a welcoming, peaceful, postcard-worthy sight.

Yeah. He could totally see himself finally living in a town like Anderson Butte.

Families and couples, clearly on vacation, slowly meandered up and down the street perusing the shops. The town had everything a body could want. Besides a few little touristy specialty stores, there was the diner, a place to get your hair cut, a little drugstore, the post office, a T-shirt shop, a water sports shop, a mini-market, and a toy store with matching colorful wooden soldiers as tall as he was, standing guard out front.

He'd never been inside a toy store. He'd never had toys of his own growing up at the ranch. Had he been free to, he would have liked to shop at places like this for Haley's birthdays and the Christmases he'd missed. Hopefully he'd be able to make up for those lost years by spending enough time with her to let her see how much he cared. But right now, he was nothing more than a stranger to his own daughter.

Maybe he should get something for Haley to soften the blow when they finally met. But what? He pulled out his phone and was just about to Google the most popular toys for two-year-olds, but stopped. The shopkeepers probably knew Haley.

He threw his empty water bottle into a green recycling can, pulled the door open, and entered the cluttered little shop. It overflowed with stuffed animals, games, dolls, trucks, and things Josh couldn't identify. A tiny woman, maybe in her late twenties, stood behind the counter and lifted her chin slightly in greeting while she helped a familiar-looking blond man with a couple of kids standing next to him. Josh headed toward the counter as the man tucked his wallet into his back pocket and then spun around.

Another movie star? What were the chances?

The guy smiled at him and hustled his boys out the door.

Josh shook his head, then moved to the counter. "Brad Pitt, huh? And I could have sworn I saw Ashton Kutcher yesterday."

The lady, petite, brunette, and so fragile-looking she reminded Josh of a fairy, blinked her eyes. "You must be mistaken, sir. Why would people like that visit here?" She even had a squeaky little Tinker Bell voice.

He threw his thumb over his shoulder. "That man who was just here with his two kids . . ."

When the shopkeeper blanked her expression in a poor attempt to lie, Josh forged ahead. "I wondered if you knew Megan's daughter, Haley? And if you could suggest something she might like?"

She shook her head. "Meg's an Anderson. Her father owns the whole town and if we want to keep our jobs, we can't help you. You might as well leave."

"I just want to buy Haley a gift." Josh raised his hand to run it through his hair, and the little woman flinched as if he meant to hit her.

What had Zeke and the mayor told these people? That he stole little kids and beat women just for fun?

The timid woman chewed on her lower lip as if debating. "Haley likes to draw and color. That's something a father should know about his daughter. Now please leave."

He read her name tag. "I appreciate the information, Sarah. I'm just looking for a chance to *be* Haley's father. Have a nice day." He swallowed back his rising temper as he headed for the door.

That did it. Time for a much-needed showdown with the local law.

He headed toward the biggest of all the buildings around the town square. As he crossed the grassy park in the middle, he spotted Casey. She was just starting up a set of big stone steps while glancing at her watch.

Increasing his pace, he moved behind her. "Worried I won't be gone when Megan gets back?"

Casey jumped as if startled, then slowly turned around. "Why *are* you still here?"

He surged ahead and held the door open for her. "Need I remind you this is a free country? Or does our great nation's Constitution not apply to Anderson Butte?"

Casey huffed past him and started down a long hall. "Maybe you should go debate that issue with my father." She held out a hand. "The mayor's office is right down there."

"Maybe another time." Like when hell freezes over.

"Or, you can come with me to my brother's office and we'll get you on your way."

"Option B sounds safer." But he wasn't going anywhere. Unless it was in a body bag. Which might be a real possibility with this crowd.

Casey led the way. The sheriff was on the phone when they entered his office. He motioned them inside as he listened to someone who was shouting at him loud enough to hear across the room; Josh couldn't make out many of the words, but "Granger" and "ass" came through loud and clear. After a few moments the sheriff said, "Gotta go, Dad."

He hung up the phone and pulled a piece of paper from a file. "The bill for your trespassing charge."

Josh accepted the paper, although he'd never been arrested or charged with trespassing.

The fine was ten thousand dollars. Before he could protest, the sheriff pushed another slip of paper across the desk. "The trespassing fine along with the hotel, medical, and parking violation adds up to sixteen thousand dollars. You can transfer the funds directly to Megan's account by close of business today, or you can get in your truck and never come back. Your choice."

He picked up the little slip of paper with Megan's bank account number on it and couldn't help his grin. "Not bad. This move may have actually worked if I thought all that money was going to your corrupt little town coffers rather than to Meg." Josh grabbed his cell from his pocket and called up his online banking app. "But instead you've solved a problem for me. Now I know how to give Megan the funds I owe her. And, Casey, let's go ahead and make this an even twenty thousand. I may need to stay at the hotel three or four more days until I find a permanent place to live." He hit the "Transfer" button and then flipped the screen around for them to see. "You can call and verify the funds if you like." He stood, stuffed his phone back into his pocket, then picked up all his receipts. "I'm looking forward to settling in. See you around, *neighbors.*"

The stunned looks on their faces almost made up for being shot.

———————————

Meg stopped scrubbing at the sound of a boat approaching. Zeke, as promised and right on time. After spending most of the day cleaning the old house, she'd hardly made a dent.

She tossed her brush in the sudsy water bucket, then stood and stretched out her weary back. Then she made her way down to the rickety dock. Zeke had offered to help her decide what needed to be done first. There was plenty to choose from. Hopefully that bank loan she'd applied for online from her bank in Denver—a bank not under her father's thumb like the one in town—would come through soon.

After grabbing the rope Zeke threw out, she tied off his boat, hoping the cleats would hold. "Hey there. Careful, the wood is rotting in a few places."

Zeke hopped out with the grace of a man half his age. "You missed all the fun in town today with that man of yours."

"He's not my—is he still there?"

Zeke chuckled. "Yep."

Josh was tenacious when he wanted something. "Haley's still with Grandma though, right?"

"She is. Doubt that boy be dumb enough to step foot on Ruth's land again without permission."

She counted on that. "Okay, so let me give you the grand tour." As they walked toward the big two-story log cabin, she gave him the executive summary. "As you saw, the dock's crap and needs to be replaced, but that's something I can do myself. I need to move some walls and make suites. The roof's questionable, the plumbing moans a bit, I need to add three new baths, and the kitchen needs a total remodel. I'll refinish all the wood floors myself. I'm not sure yet, but if I can clean up the original baths and make them shine, we might just call them vintage."

Zeke chuckled. "Vintage, huh? I suppose that's what you could call me too."

"Maybe. If we could shine you up enough." Meg slid her arm through Zeke's. "You sure you want to be helping me like this? My dad's not going to like it."

"Hell, Meggy, I'm not afraid of your father like everyone else in this town. An old widower with no children doesn't have anyone to help spend all the money I've saved from these celebrities who hand it out like candy. If I never worked another day, I'd be just fine." Zeke pulled a big flashlight from the tool bag he carried. "Now to get under the house and get dirty."

Megan's phone signaled an incoming text, which she ignored. "I'm right behind you."

"You hate spiders, but can't bring yourself to kill them. Never understood that about you. Answer your beep and I'll be right back."

"Thanks." Relieved she'd avoided the creepy crawlspace, she tapped her cell's screen and cringed.

It was from Josh.

You can fly a helicopter? How do I not know this about you, Wonder Woman?

Confused, because she expected him to be angry after his pain meds wore off, not cracking jokes, she typed, What do you want, Josh?

I want you to talk to me while we go for a helicopter ride. I'll pay the full fee. Amusement parks have nothing on the rates Anderson Butte charges.

He'd told everyone he wasn't leaving until he saw her and Haley. The seeing Haley part wasn't happening. Talking to him when he wasn't drugged up was probably inevitable.

She'd have to look into those whiskey-colored eyes again. And if he smiled at her as sweetly as he'd done when he first saw her in the clinic, it was going to hurt. But at least the meeting would be on her terms for a change. In the air. In an environment Josh couldn't control.

Yeah, maybe the perfect venue. And she'd have the added benefit of scaring the crap out of him.

Meet me behind the clinic in a half hour.

CHAPTER Six

*J*osh crossed his arms and leaned against his truck as he waited for Megan, detesting the pit forming in his gut. He hated that he had to keep up the lies, even if for just a while longer. Hopefully the story he'd come up with would convince her to give him a second chance.

He was deep in strategy mode when she slipped quietly next to him, leaning against his truck and crossing her arms too. "Pondering how to make your next million, Josh?"

The sight of her made his heart roll over in his chest. She'd pulled her hair up into a cute ponytail and she had on a little pink T-shirt, jeans, and tennis shoes. Her new, curvier hips were just a bonus. But she wouldn't look him in the eye. Not a good sign. She was obviously still hurt and angry with him.

He couldn't blame her.

He'd just up and left her when she'd been pregnant with their child. He didn't deserve to be taken back, but he hoped to God he'd find a way to make her see how sorry he was for it.

"Nope. Those days are behind me. I was just thinking I was glad that helicopter has doors on it. That way you can't tilt me out and be rid of me."

"Zeke has a smaller helicopter like that. Too bad I didn't think to borrow it. You ready?"

"Yep." Maybe he shouldn't be giving her any ideas.

He stood aside as Megan circled the helicopter, preparing it for flight. "Thank you for meeting with me, Meg. I appreciate it."

She stopped mid-stride and finally met his gaze before glancing at his arm. "Well, if we're being nice to each other, then I'm sorry my grandmother shot you. Let's go."

He climbed inside and buckled in. Mimicking her moves, he slid his sunglasses on and then placed the headset that dangled in front of him over his ears.

Megan's tinny voice sounded through the speakers. "Hang on."

The helicopter rocketed straight up with so much force, all the air whooshed from his lungs. "What the—"

"You want to stop? Okay."

They plummeted toward the hard pavement of the parking lot at breakneck speed.

So this was her game. She was trying to scare him. Fine. He'd play along. He was a seasoned pilot himself, so he knew the maneuver wasn't as dangerous as it might appear. Meg really did have some serious skills, just as Ben had said.

He grunted out a "No!"

"Make up your mind, Josh."

Megan stopped their descent less than six feet from the ground before they headed straight up again.

As they zipped out over the water, he grabbed the handle above the door. "I thought we were being nice."

She huffed out a breath. "What do you want, Josh?"

He loosened his grip on the handle as they flew over the tops of tall pines on the other side of the lake. "I'd like to apologize to you and to meet Haley."

She turned to look at him. "Take off your sunglasses and say that again."

"That's a big-ass mountain just ahead. Don't you think you should—"

"Then you should make it quick!"

He yanked off his glasses so she could see into his eyes. Like it'd do any good. He was trained to cover a lie, but in this case he wouldn't have to. "I'm sorry, Meg. I screwed up. And I want to meet my daughter. Now turn."

She frowned as she tilted them so steeply to the right his head thunked against the door. His body strained against the seatbelt, pulling some impressive Gs.

Megan was quiet for a few moments before she said, "You can't just pop into Haley's life, charm her, make her fall in love with you, and then be so busy working you ignore her and make her feel insignificant—like you did to me."

What was he supposed to say to that?

When in doubt, grovel.

"I'm sorry I made you feel that way. It wasn't intentional. How much have you told Haley and your family about me?"

Megan maneuvered them into a slower, more reasonable turn. "When you refused to come home with me that last Christmas, I realized you weren't committed to our relationship. So I didn't tell my family anything. Haley hasn't asked about you yet."

"We lived together. How is that not committed?" Suddenly they were in a narrow canyon no more than forty feet wide. "You're kind of low, don't you think?"

Ignoring him, she flew deeper into the canyon and over a raging river just a few feet below. "People in committed relationships spend holidays together and meet each other's relatives. You stayed home and worked."

"Growing up with a bunch of kids who tried their best to ignore December twenty-fifth didn't exactly groom me for the 'happy family Christmas' experience you had." But the truth was, by that Christmas his case was going south and he might never have seen her again. He didn't want to make things worse by sharing the holidays with her and then leaving her.

The canyon narrowed by the second and for the first time he was genuinely concerned. Ready to take the controls if he had to, he said, "Meg, seriously. What the hell here?"

"Just a few more seconds."

The canyon walls, along with the river, got closer and closer, but then suddenly the walls disappeared and there was nothing below but a deep valley. Around them were 360 degrees of cliffs and trees, like they were in the middle of a deep, wide hole. Megan swung the copter around to face the way they'd come.

An amazing waterfall plummeted as far as the eye could see below them. Millions of tiny rainbows glinted in the fading sunlight as the water cascaded over the cliff.

Meg slowly maneuvered them over a large, jutting ridge and landed. When she shut down and they hopped out, the roar of the waterfall replaced the engine noise.

Josh dug out his cell and snapped pictures as Megan moved beside him, refusing to look at him again.

He tucked his phone away. "Is this the part where you push me off the ledge and tell everyone I slipped?"

"Don't tempt me, Josh." She crossed her arms and sighed. Then her voice changed to a tone of quiet reverence as she said, "I'll bet fewer than fifty people have ever seen this. You have to know it's here because it's not obvious from above and most pilots won't brave the canyon. Zeke showed me this when I was a little girl. It's my favorite place on earth. So, see? I *was* being nice."

"It's incredible. Thank you for nearly killing me so I could see it too."

Meg smirked as she climbed onto a big rock. "The nearly killing you part was the highlight of my day."

"I don't doubt it." He sat beside her. Just being close to Meg always made it easier to draw a full breath. God, he'd missed her.

But now it was showtime.

"I'm sorry I panicked at the thought of being a father. I want to make things right by you and Haley." He hated that he had to say that to maintain his cover. He'd been overjoyed at the thought of being a father, and being a part of a family.

"We've managed just fine without you." She drew her legs up, wrapped her arms around them, and laid her chin on top of her knees, in full protective mode. "Haley needs consistency and to know she'll always be loved no matter what. *I* give her that. *You* made it clear you didn't want us. You have no right to come back and disrupt our lives."

"Haven't you ever made a mistake you regret so much you can't sleep at night until you make it right?"

"Yes." Pain flashed in her eyes before she closed them. "You're the mistake I regret almost every day. I hate how I got suckered into thinking you were a good man who loved me but just worked too much."

He'd always been that man. "After we broke up, I realized I'd screwed up the best thing I'd ever had. So I quit my job and did some serious soul-searching. I decided to go back to the beginning to get it right. And now I'm hoping you'll give me the chance to do the same with you and Haley. I want to be part of her life . . . and yours."

Meg stared straight ahead, her teeth worrying her lower lip for a few moments before she said, "So I'm just supposed to forgive you? Like my feelings don't matter? Forget it. But what does the going back to the beginning part mean?"

"I wanted something different, a job that would leave time for the people in my life. I'm going to go back to school to get my master's in counseling. I want to work with troubled kids."

Meg finally looked at him. "You gave up the job you loved? *And* all that money?"

"Yep. I'm going to sign up for classes in the fall."

A glimmer of hope sparked in her eyes. "In Denver?"

"Wherever you and Haley are. I can do some of it online. I plan to be a real father to her, Meg."

"You can't just move here and expect me and Haley to forgive and forget, Josh. Go back to Denver with all your shiny shoes and leave us alone." Megan unwrapped her arms and jumped off the rock. "Get in. It's time to go."

Dammit. He'd known it wouldn't be easy to convince her to give him another chance, to regain her trust in him, but that hadn't gone well at all.

He had to find another way.

Meg's heart pounded as they strapped in and took off in silence. She could've flown out the safer way above, but the canyon was faster and she wanted him out of her life as quickly as possible.

It'd just be an added bonus if the flight path scared him again in the process.

She hated the pain she'd heard in his voice when he'd asked if she'd ever made a mistake she'd deeply regretted. She'd made more than her share of mistakes in the past, but she couldn't let Josh threaten her hardened defenses against him. She needed to stay strong for Haley's sake.

When she glanced at him out of the corner of her eye, he sat there so perfectly calm it made her even angrier.

Once they were out of the canyon, he asked, "What would it take to prove to you I've changed, Meg?"

"It's too late. I've seen your true colors. You aren't capable of being the kind of man I need."

"What kind of man is that?"

Years of pent-up anger made her voice rise three decibels. "A man who puts me and Haley before his work. A man who pays attention enough to know what my favorite color is and who wants to be home with me at night, not taking mysterious phone calls and then disappearing, citing some work emergency. And most of all, a man who I can trust to stick around when things get rough. I was sicker than a dog every morning, exhausted after work every night, and after Haley was born, I had no idea how to take care of a baby!"

The last thing her heart could take was having to see him every single day and be reminded of how he'd devastated her. He had to go.

With his thumb, Josh swiped away a tear she hadn't realized had fallen on her cheek. "I'm sorry I let you down. But I paid more attention to you than you realize, Meg. I've done some deep reflecting and I've dealt with what was wrong with me, that I couldn't commit to you."

He didn't deserve any more than a grunt for that lame explanation.

Josh said, "What? Don't you believe people can change?"

She'd changed since becoming a mother, not that anyone believed her. But people only changed if they had a good reason and made the painful effort to follow through. She didn't want to risk giving him a second chance and possibly having Haley's heart broken too.

"So some deep thinking taught you all that, huh? Well, maybe you should go try out those new skills on someone else. Because I'm not interested."

When Josh closed his eyes and ran a hand through his thick blond hair in frustration, just like her father always did, it suddenly occurred to her that she'd ended up loving a man as emotionally remote as her dad.

Way to go, Meg!

"I don't want to go the legal route. I want you to want me around. How about we make a deal?"

Legal route? Her stomach dropped. Maybe she'd have to talk to Casey's divorce lawyer. But how would she pay for that? Josh could afford the best lawyers and keep them in court a lot longer than she could afford to fight. And what if Josh's high-powered attorney found a way for him to share custody with her? Haley might have to spend half of her life with a man not capable of being a committed parent.

That wasn't acceptable.

She slowly turned and met his challenging gaze, daring to hope she had a chance to win whatever bargain he'd propose and be rid of him. "What did you have in mind?"

"Understand that I'm going to be a father to Haley no matter where I end up living. How about I promise to leave town at the end of the summer if you still want me to, but in return, you have to give me a fair chance to make things up to you and Haley?"

"Haley is not going to be part of any negotiation. Ever!"

"Fine. *You* give me a chance and then I get to see Haley when you think she's ready."

Because she'd been stupid enough to hope Josh would change his mind and come back after she'd had Haley, she'd put his name on the birth certificate and sent him a copy. Legally, he probably had every right to see their daughter.

Mucked that one up good.

His proposal might be her only option to get him to leave and keep Haley where she belonged. With Meg, a parent Haley could rely on. Even better, maybe once he figured out it wasn't so easy being a parent, he'd bolt again. It'd just be a few months, then he'd probably leave anyway. He wasn't the sticking kind.

She held her hand out. "Deal."

He sent her that smile that used to make her knees go weak, then curled his big hand around hers. "Thank you. I guarantee you'll see a different man from the one you knew before."

"Doubt it." She yanked her hand from his, ignoring the familiar tingle his touch always sent up her spine as she prepared to make their descent behind the clinic.

After they touched down and she killed the engine, she slowly pulled her headphones off and hung them up, spent.

She'd have to keep her guard up and ignore Josh's soulful eyes.

Just as she reached for the door handle, Josh placed his rough hands along the sides of her face and pulled her close. "I do know what your favorite color is, Meg. It's blue. And your favorite pie is chocolate mousse. Your favorite food group is anything chocolate."

Then he kissed her.

Overwhelming desire that had been hibernating for three long years roared to life.

She'd kissed a few guys goodnight after dates since Josh, but it was as if the beast had been lying in wait and only he could awaken it. No one kissed like he did.

She placed her hands on his hard chest, intending to push him away. Instead, her hands fisted in his soft shirt and pulled him closer. A moan escaped as his tongue moved in a sensual, familiar dance with hers, immersing her completely under the Josh spell. But when the cockpit door swung open and a big hand slipped around Josh's arm, tugging him out and into the parking lot, reality came crashing back.

Her father.

And he was furious.

She jumped from the copter and raced around to the other side. "Dad, stop!"

Dad's fist hovered in front of Josh's face. "Is this the little pissant who doesn't support his own child?"

She maneuvered between Josh and her father. Placing her hands on her hips, she wished for another foot or two of height. "This is Josh Granger, Haley's father. But—"

Dad nudged her aside and then punched Josh in the face. "No one takes advantage of an Anderson without paying the price!"

Of course that's all her dad cared about. That an Anderson was made to look bad. Not that Josh had hurt his daughter and granddaughter.

Josh staggered back a step but remained standing.

Her dad assumed a boxer's pose. "Come on, boy. Let's see what you do with someone closer to your own size."

Josh left his arms at his sides as blood trickled from his nose. "I'm not going to fight with someone your age, sir. I might hurt you."

That had to be about the worst thing anyone could say to her father. Meg moved in front of Josh again and held her palms up. "Stop! No more hitting. Let's discuss this like—"

Because she didn't even come up to Josh's shoulder, she didn't have to duck when her father's fist connected with Josh's eye this time. Josh held his ground. Now blood gushed from his nose, and his eye was going to be sporting a whopper of a bruise in the morning.

Her father, red-faced and breathing hard, spat out, "What are you? Some kind of pansy-ass who doesn't know how to defend himself? Hit me back!"

Meg spotted Ryan approaching. After he joined them, he crossed his arms. "Hit him back, Granger, so we can be done with this."

Josh shook his head. "I'm *not* hitting Megan's father."

Meg whirled on Ryan. "What kind of sheriff are you? You're supposed to be breaking this up. Not egging it on!"

Ryan shrugged and shoved his hands into his pockets.

This wasn't going to end well, so she grabbed the gun from Ryan's holster, flipped the safety, and shot a round into a nearby trash can. The loud explosion stopped the fighting and had all the men staring at her like she'd lost her mind.

She turned to her dad and Ryan. "You both told me I needed to handle my own problems, so back off. I don't need your help!"

Josh sighed, then wiped blood from his chin with the back of his hand. "Let's go, Meg."

She must've said something right, because her father and Ryan stood with crossed arms and scowls on their faces as they let Josh tug her toward his truck.

Ryan called out, "I need the gun, Muck!"

Josh beeped the locks open on his truck, then said, "Flip the safety, Meg."

"It's already on."

He yanked the gun from her, then laid it on the pavement before he handed her up into the front seat of his truck and followed behind. "None of you Anderson Butte crazies should be allowed to own guns." He slammed the door and started the engine. "Did your brother call you Muck?"

Ignoring the question, she found some napkins in the glove box, then scooted over to dab at his bloody face. "I wasn't going to shoot anyone any more than you were going to hit my father, and everyone knew it. It was just the easiest way to cut through all the testosterone back there."

She wouldn't tell him, but she was grateful Josh hadn't stooped to her father's level and hit him back. "Where's your BMW?"

Josh took the napkins from her and pressed them harder against his nose to stop the bleeding. "Traded it in for this. Will you have dinner with me?"

"No! And no more kissing." She moved back to her side and crossed her arms.

"I liked the kissing. So did you."

Yeah, she'd liked the kissing, but that was the last thing she needed. It was so not happening again. "That wasn't part of our deal."

He parked in front of the hotel. They both got out and headed toward the lobby doors. Josh's hand slipped around her shoulder, pulling her close. "Could we make kissing part of our deal?"

Before she could tell him no, Casey looked up from the front desk. When her eyes took in Josh's hand on Meg's shoulder, her right brow arched. "What happened to you, Granger?"

"He finally met Dad." Megan slipped out of Josh's embrace and led the way toward the kitchen to find him an ice pack.

She poked at the swinging door and then pointed at a stool by the granite island for Josh to sit on. Digging through the freezer, she found a bag of peas. "Most guys would have been long gone after being shot. Now we can add being punched in the face too. My dad will make your life here a living hell. You should just leave now, Josh."

He smiled at her as she ran her hand through his soft hair, sweeping it back from his forehead before she placed the bag across his swollen eye and nose.

"Nope. I'm sticking this time. Made the 'running' mistake once before."

As she held the bag against his battered face, his hands moved to her hips and he pulled her so close the peas cooled her cheek as his breath heated her lips. Was he going to kiss her again? Her former bad-girl self hoped so.

Her new sensible self told her to run.

He whispered, "Here's another fun Megan fact: your favorite football team is not the Denver Broncos like it should be, but the Green Bay Packers because you think their quarterback is hot."

"Actually, my favorite team really is the Broncos. And if you want to survive another day here, yours better be too. I just said that back then to see if you were paying attention, *workaholic*."

"I haven't been able to stomach a Packers game since. And no matter what the insane people in this town come up with, I'm not leaving, Meg."

Yeah. That was what she was afraid of. Because Josh was like a vanilla ice cream cone dipped in chocolate on a hot summer's day.

Hard to resist.

CHAPTER SEVEN

After he finished his morning shave, Josh poked at the puffy skin around his eye. The color palette varied in shades from toad green to puke yellow and his nose was still swollen. It might be a good thing he wasn't meeting Haley today. He'd probably scare her.

He'd wanted to tag along with Megan for the day, spend some time with her, but she'd shut that idea down quick enough. But after reminding her of their deal, she'd reluctantly agreed to meet him for a drink to discuss their terms more fully at a place called Brewster's after Haley went to bed.

Maybe he'd even dance with her. Dancing sucked, but it'd give him an excuse to put his hands on her.

He pulled the door closed behind him and headed down to the lobby for breakfast. When the elevator doors opened, he spotted a woman herding a bunch of kids toward the dining room. After reasoning with a cranky child, she looked up at him. When she noticed his battered face her eyes widened.

His probably did too. It was Angelina Jolie.

A sudden sharp pain in his left arm nearly brought him to his knees. Casey squeezed a hand around his bandaged arm as she led him into the kitchen. "I'll serve you breakfast in here today."

"Take it easy, will you?"

Casey released her death grip. "Your face looks so bad, I forgot all about your arm. Have a seat at the island."

Megan's Rottweiler sister had probably chosen his bad arm on purpose.

He pulled out a stool, hoping Casey wouldn't resort to sprinkling rat poison on his food next. "So, why are all these celebrities here? Some special event?"

She crossed her arms. "I have no idea what you're talking about."

"I've seen them all—"

"Our chef will make whatever you like. What'll it be?"

Another brick wall. Must be where Megan got her stubbornness from.

"Anything?" What the heck. "How about a cheese omelet, bacon, hash browns, toast, a side of pancakes, orange juice, and milk?"

"Fine, just stay here in the kitchen, Granger." She frowned at him and leaned closer. "What are your plans for today?"

"Not sure yet. Why am I banished to the kitchen?"

"So I can keep an eye on you."

More like so he wouldn't scare off the celebrities with his face.

Casey scurried to the other side of the room and talked to Dax, their chef. What kind of name that was he didn't know, but the guy was the first sane person in Anderson Butte he'd met. He'd stayed and shared a sandwich and a few beers with Dax last night after the kitchen had closed down.

As Josh waited among the sizzle of bacon and the grinding of fresh coffee beans, he spotted a muted flat-screen on the wall with the words to some fluffy women's show scrolling across the bottom. Just when his brains threatened to leak out of his ears, Dax slid plates of steaming hot food in front of him. "Enjoy, bud."

"Thanks."

He picked up a slice of smoky, crispy bacon, something he hadn't allowed himself in years in his attempt to keep his body mission ready, and dug in. He'd just started on his second piece when Megan busted through the double doors in spitting-mad mode.

She was damned cute when she was all worked up like that.

"There you are! What's with the money in my account, Josh?"

"You'll have to ask your brothers and sister about that."

"I told you I don't want anything from you!"

Casey appeared by Megan's side. "Can you two please bring it down a notch? We have paying guests."

"Meg has just figured out I'm one of your paying customers too, Casey. You deal with it." He started in on his omelet.

Casey dragged Megan to the other side of the big kitchen. After a few minutes of eye rolls, gritted teeth, crossed arms, and huffed breaths, Meg made her way back and sat beside him.

"They thought you'd leave rather than pay their overblown fees. They obviously didn't realize how stubborn you are." She stole his last piece of bacon and popped it into her mouth. "Since when do you eat bacon and eggs?"

"Since I'm on vacation. Isn't that what people are supposed to do?"

"That's what *normal* people do, not health-conscious workaholics. I'll transfer the money back this afternoon."

Not if he could help it.

She took the fork from his hand. "I should probably save you from your bad self." Meg stole a big bite of his hash browns.

Next she started in on his pancakes, deliberately provoking him. She had to remember how much it annoyed him when she used to eat off his plate, but strangely, he kind of missed her little bad habit.

He slid the jam closer. "It's strawberry. Your *favorite*."

She met his gaze for a moment before she picked up his knife and dug into the jam. "That could've been just a really good guess. Strawberry is most everyone's favorite. What's my overall favorite thing for breakfast?"

"Coffee. Best not to talk to you in the morning until you've had at least one cup."

"True." She smiled and stuffed the last of his omelet into her mouth. "You have no idea what you're missing by not drinking coffee."

"Orange juice is better for you."

He gave up all hope of getting any more of the best hash browns he'd ever had and slid his plate in front of her. How someone as small as Megan could eat as much as she did always amazed him.

Megan eyed his juice glass, so he handed that over too. Before she got any more big ideas, he chugged his milk. "Why not keep the money and buy a more reliable car?"

"My car's fine."

"But I owe you years of child support."

"How about you leave right now and keep your money?"

"I'd rather you take the money, Meg."

She wiped the plate clean with his toast and shook her head. "You abandoned us, so as of now, Casey's lawyer thinks it's best not to take anything from you until we work everything out."

"I thought we weren't going to do the lawyer thing."

"Casey called him, not me. But maybe we won't have to get lawyers involved. Maybe you'll see what life in Anderson Butte can be like and decide to leave on your own."

She banged the empty glass down and sent him a cocky grin. "Seriously, after seeing your colorful face in the mirror this morning, you must be having second thoughts about staying here."

"Nope." He'd been beaten and left for dead on some of his worse missions. A few punches from Megan's father were child's play.

She stood to leave, leaning her mouth so close to his ear her warm breath sent a jolt straight to his lap. "We'll see. Thanks for sharing *your* breakfast." She gave his shoulder a pat. "Do we still need to have that drink tonight, or did we just cover it?"

"We still need to talk about Haley."

She let out a long sigh. "Fine."

Meg turned to leave, but he hooked a finger in the back of the waistband of her shorts and pulled her against him. Leaning over her shoulder, trying to ignore how nice her hair smelled, he said, "Maybe two-stepping will even be involved tonight."

She turned her head and cocked a brow. "You stomping on my feet isn't my idea of fun."

"I was hoping you'd lead this time."

She flashed a smile the way she used to for a second before she shut it down. Maybe he was making progress.

"No dancing and no kissing, Josh. Let go. Haley has an appointment to see Ben in a few minutes."

He spun her around to face him. "She's sick?"

"She has asthma. It was getting better, but something about being here at the lake has triggered her symptoms again."

"I had asthma. Grew out of it when I was in middle school."

"Really?" Megan's eyes softened as a slow smile lit her face. "Maybe Haley will grow out of it too, then?"

"Probably."

"God, that's such a relief. Gotta go."

"See you tonight." Guilt stabbed him square in the heart when he'd seen the worry Megan carried about the asthma. Something he could have maybe helped relieve if he'd been around. But how to get her to let him help her now?

While watching Megan's curvy jean-shorts-clad butt disappear through the swinging doors, a plan to get her and Haley that new car took shape in his mind. He scooped up his dishes and took them to the sink. After rinsing them off, he placed the plates and glasses into the big stainless steel washer.

Casey popped up behind him and corrected his placement. "Where'd a guy like you get such good manners?"

By growing up in a group home and then living his adult life alone—except for his time with Meg. "I bought them on the Internet. Speaking of which, can I use your computer? The Wi-Fi isn't working in my room. But that's probably on purpose, right?"

"Yep. What do you need?"

"I want to close that bank account so Megan can't return the money to me. Then I was going to buy her a new car. I wanted to look at some prices before I go in to negotiate. Is there a dealer nearby?"

Casey's brows spiked. "There's a Ford dealer in the next town south. You can use the computer in my office." As she led the way, Casey glanced over her shoulder. "If you really want to help her, stop by the lumber store near the car dealer. She needs materials for a thirty-foot dock. Have them deliver everything to the old Benson place. They'll know where that is. But you can't buy Megan's love, Josh. You have to earn it."

She'd finally used his first name. Maybe he was making progress with Casey too. Something told him he'd have to gain her trust before he won Megan over completely. "I'm not trying to buy anything. I just want them both safe. Why does Meg need a dock?"

"It's not my place to tell. But you'd have a better chance of her taking a dock than the car. She'll only make you take it back."

"Not if she doesn't know it came from me."

After their visit with Ben, Megan fastened Haley's life jacket and tucked her in front of the Jet Ski. "All set?"

"Go fast, Momma!" Haley squeezed Meg's legs in anticipation.

"You got it." Meg pushed off from Grandma's dock and then cranked the gas. Haley's squeals of pleasure put a smile on Meg's face. Haley craved speed as much as she did. The shot Ben had given Haley earlier had perked her right back up to her normal self.

What would it hurt to take a little extra time out on the lake before they got started on the house for the day? Until her loan came through, and please God let that happen, she couldn't afford to buy materials to get started on anything serious anyway.

She spotted a familiar ski boat and headed that way so they could do some wake jumping. The boat belonged to the hotel, and her friend Toby would be at the helm. The first guy she'd ever slept with.

Bleached-blond and gorgeous, Toby had told her right up front he was a man-whore and always would be. He didn't commit, but he'd show her a good time whenever she wanted it.

Strangely, he was the only former lover she was still friends with. Probably because he'd told her the truth. She valued that the most in people.

When they got closer, he lifted a hand in greeting. A kid skiing behind the boat shrieked with pleasure.

Meg circled around and then headed straight into the excellent swells. Haley's little hands dug into Meg's thighs as they went airborne, but as soon as they landed she shouted, "Do it again!"

They jumped a few more waves until the kid skiing hit the water hard. As the towboat slowed and the waves settled, she headed toward the boy to be sure he was okay. As they got closer, the kid's widened eyes and gaping mouth told her he'd probably gotten the wind knocked out of him.

Meg slowed the engine and drifted toward him.

The kid barely squeaked out, "Can't breathe."

She grabbed the back of his life jacket and pulled him up out of the water a bit, sending him a reassuring smile. "Lift your arms over your head and try to relax. You'll be good in just a minute. Does anything hurt?"

The kid shook his head as he lifted his arms.

Haley patted his shoulder. "Fill the tummy balloon as big as you can."

The kid frowned in confusion at Haley, but then after a few attempts he was finally able to draw a deep breath. Megan let out the breath she hadn't realized she'd been holding right along with him. "You okay now?"

The boy smiled. "Yeah. That was scary. Thanks."

Toby maneuvered the boat beside them and Megan helped the kid onboard. She recognized the boy's father. He owned half the real estate in Manhattan and was a regular customer.

Once they determined the boy was fine, Mr. Randall held out his hand for a shake. "Thanks for the rescue, Megan. Toby tells us you're opening up a lodge on the other side of the lake?"

Meg glanced at Toby, who sent her an eyebrow hitch and a cute grin.

She shook Mr. Randall's hand. "Yes, I'm hoping it'll be done in a few months."

"How many will it sleep? My wife wanted to organize a little getaway with her sisters and their families here in September. But someone has already bought the hotel out for the week we wanted."

Yay. Maybe her first customer. "I'm still remodeling, but barring any difficulties, I hope to have four master suites, and a couple of rooms with singles and bunk beds for the kids. It's going to be a little more rustic than the hotel, though."

"Great. Casey knows the dates. Go ahead and bill my account for booking the reservation."

"You got it. Thanks, Mr. Randall. You guys have fun." Megan mouthed a silent "thank you" to Toby and drove off, probably grinning like a lunatic. Because the hotel offered to let their privacy-craving customers buy out the whole place, the customers were used to paying a non-refundable third of the fee. That was just one more good thing about catering to the rich.

"Haley-Bug, we're one step closer to getting the money we need to fix up our new house. A few more reservation deposits like that and we'll be on our way!"

"Yay!" Haley clapped her hands as if she knew what Meg was talking about. How great was it that her daughter was happy just because Meg was? A far cry from the relationship she had with her father. Thank God her sister and Grandma had been there for her growing up. Probably she should remember to thank them for that.

As they pulled up to their rickety dock, Meg spotted a pile of building materials stacked neatly near the shore. After she freed herself and Haley from their life jackets and unloaded their supplies, they went to check out the stack. It was everything she'd need for her new dock. An invoice weighted down by a rock lay on top.

She studied the paid receipt, looking for any clues as to who would have been nice enough to buy her the materials anonymously. Maybe Zeke. He'd seen how bad and a little bit dangerous the dock was. Nothing on the paper gave it away. She'd figure it out and then pay whoever it was back after she got the loan.

Just as she was thinking that moving back home might not be so bad, a voice that had the same effect on her as fingernails trailing down a chalkboard made her cringe.

"Well, there you are, Meg. Funny how you've been back for days and we haven't run into each other."

Not funny. On purpose.

She slowly stood as Haley attached herself to Meg's legs as if Cruella de Vil were approaching. "Hey, Amber. How are you?"

Amber navigated her way down the grassy hill toward them in her ice pick heels. She hadn't changed a bit. Long blonde hair, tall and thin like a model, but with silicone-enhanced curves in all the right places and a fake, stiff smile. Like a Barbie on Botox.

Amber always dressed as if attending a swanky cocktail party. Probably because there weren't any of those in Anderson Butte unless Amber was throwing one. "I wanted to be sure you knew about the fund-raiser for the new children's section at the library we're holding tomorrow. Everyone's coming." Amber leaned down and said to Haley, "There'll be lots of fun games for you, sweetheart. And I'm just dying to meet your daddy."

Haley's head whipped up. "My daddy?"

Frickin' Amber. She'd done that on purpose. "We'll talk about that later. Why don't you go grab a juice box from the backpack while I talk to Mrs. Downey?"

Haley frowned as she slowly headed toward the backpack that lay under a nearby pine tree.

Amber's eyes got fake big and she threw her hand over her mouth. Probably to hide her evil sneer. "Oh, Meg. I'm so sorry. I'd forgotten Haley doesn't know who her father is. But I hear he's a real looker. And he's moving here . . . but doesn't have a job?"

The condescension in Amber's voice raised Meg's hackles. "Yeah, so maybe Haley and I will stop by tomorrow if we have time. Thanks."

"If it'd be embarrassing for you to come and not be able to make a donation, we still need someone to work the ice cream booth from twelve till one."

The old Meg might have "accidentally" poked Amber in the chest and made her totter off her ridiculous heels. But Haley was watching. "The ice cream booth is always fun. Sign me up."

Her evil deed for the day accomplished, Amber beamed a sat-isfied grin. "If your ex is looking for a place to stay, my guesthouse is available. Maybe I can even find a way for a good-looking guy to *work off* his rent. See you tomorrow."

Meg's blood boiled as she watched Amber slither away like the snake she was. Amber's not-so-thinly veiled reference to the time she'd slept with Meg's boyfriend in high school and then later married him had hit its intended target.

That woman, married or not, would probably love to get her hands on Josh just to irritate Meg. A week ago, that wouldn't have bothered her a bit. She would have told Amber they deserved each other and good riddance.

Now she wasn't so sure. It seemed Josh *had* been more invested in their relationship than he'd let on back then. And there'd been other small changes in him too. When he'd mentioned dancing with her, which he hated to do, she'd almost accepted just to see if he'd really do it. Luckily, her brain did its job and reminded her heart not to engage.

He'd only hurt her again.

CHAPTER EIGHT

Josh ran through his to-do list quicker than expected. By noon, he'd scratched off: buy Meg a car, set in place a plan to make it look like Meg won the car, and have materials for a new dock delivered. The last remaining item was the one he had the most trepidation about.

Anderson Butte was only a few hours away from the ranch where he'd grown up after his mother had died. He'd never known who his father was. It had been just him and his mother in their small apartment. Looking back, they were probably poor, but the complex had a pool and a park nearby where they played and had fun.

But then one day, his mother never showed to pick him up from school. The principal had stayed and waited with him until it had become dark, then a stranger came for him and took him to his house. After the apartment manager let them in, the lady who'd picked him up told him to pack a bag of clothes and that he'd never see his mother again because she'd been killed by a man who'd robbed the store where she worked. At six years old he'd become a ward of the state, moving from place to place until he'd ended up at the ranch.

The few memories he still had of his mother were good ones.

He didn't have many fond memories of the ranch, though, and little desire to relive the painful ones, but he needed to close out the circle. Return to that part of his past and do something good for those boys who were like he'd been. Make a positive out of one of the biggest negatives of his life.

And maybe Charlie would still be around.

Mr. Jennings, the only decent counselor he'd ever had, had seemed genuinely happy to hear from him when Josh had called earlier and mentioned he'd like to lend a hand in some way and that he might stop by if he had time.

So, no more stalling.

Josh climbed into his truck and headed south.

With each mile he traveled closer to the ranch, childhood memories of uncertainty and fear about his future kicked around in his gut. Sometimes he'd make himself so sick with worry it'd bring on another asthma attack. If it hadn't been for Charlie, he'd never have survived all the years there. So, he'd embrace his current physical discomfort, file it away, then use it for when it was his turn to help some lost kid in return.

After just under two hours, he approached the tiny town near the ranch, noting the stark contrast between it and Anderson Butte. The neglect, the boarded-up shops, the tumbleweeds, and the pothole-lined streets. There was no nearby lake or hotel for tourism. It was just another of the fast-disappearing small towns in northern New Mexico.

Bumping down the narrow excuse for a road, he finally spotted the familiar sideways double Ds seared into the weathered wood that framed the entrance to the Lazy D's Ranch.

As he pulled up to the main house, a group of boys tending to a broken fence stopped working. Four sets of eyes, all sending him suspicious glares, tracked his progress as he parked and got out of the truck. Newcomers usually brought bad news. Either one of their friends was being shipped somewhere else or heading off to a trial and they'd never see the kid again. Or it might be a new counselor. Someone twice as mean as the last one.

"Hey, guys." Josh lifted a hand in greeting as he approached the tatted-up teens. "Mr. Jennings around?"

The biggest kid in the group crossed his inked-up arms over his puffed chest. "Who wants to know?"

There'd been kids just like this one when he'd lived here too. Mr. Tough Shit.

Just as Josh was about to answer, a familiar voice rang out. "Granger? That you?"

When Josh turned around and spotted the man he'd come to see, he smiled. Mr. Jennings didn't seem so big and imposing anymore; he looked . . . old. Still the same shaggy haircut but with streaks of gray now. What he'd used to think of as arms as big as tree stumps had gone a little flabby with age and his belly had followed along the same path. But the ever-present kindness in his pale-blue eyes hadn't changed.

"Good to see you again, Mr. Jennings." Josh held out his hand for a shake, but Mr. J gave him a bear hug.

"Great to see you, Josh." He released him, then shook his head. "How did a scrawny little kid like you turn out looking like a ripped NFL player?"

Determination to never be the one others picked on ever again. "Just a late bloomer, I guess."

When Jennings leaned back to study Josh more closely, his eyes grew wide. "What happened to your face?"

"Forgot to duck. How are things around here?"

"About the same." Mr. Jennings turned to the kids, who were obviously curious but trying to look too cool to care. "Say hello to Mr. Granger, guys. He grew up here too."

Two of them sneered but the other two lifted their chins in

greeting. After figuring out Josh wasn't a threat, they all went back to fixing the fence. The big guy told the others what to do while he watched.

Mr. Jennings tilted his head and started walking toward the barn. "There's a boy I'd like you to meet. Reminds me an awful lot of you."

Josh wanted to ask about Charlie, but he'd know soon enough if he was still there.

Jennings lowered his voice. "This kid lost his mother in a car accident. Father was a cop killed in the line of duty a few years before his mom died. Eric is older than you were when you first arrived, though. He's ten. His grandmother is his only relative, but had a stroke and is rehabbing, so she can't care for him. We're hoping it's just temporary. He had a little brother and sister who died in the accident too. Talks about his family in his sleep sometimes. The others tease him for it, as you can imagine."

It was always harder on the kids who knew what it was like to come from a nice home. Josh didn't remember the details much, but somehow knew his mom must've cared.

Jennings said, "He's only been here a few months. Hasn't had time to develop the hard shell, you know? Since school got out for summer he spends all his time out here with Buck, my manager, and the horses. I suspect he's getting bullied more than he lets on, but whenever I draw him aside and ask, he says he's fine. I'd appreciate it if you could talk with him. You'd understand better than anyone else."

"I can try." The barn needed a coat of stain, but otherwise was just as Josh remembered. Two long rows of stalls, a hayloft, and tack room. Metal feed buckets stacked in the same corner on the dusty earthen floor. All the stalls were empty, their gates standing open. Dust motes hung in the air above the last stall on the end, and the clang of a shovel against a wheelbarrow meant the mucking out was almost done for the day. He used to hate that part of caring for the horses, but now his hands itched to help.

A skinny, dark-haired kid bobbed his head in time to whatever his earbuds played as he leaned down for the last of the mess. Mr. J said, "These kids. Pump music into their ears so loud they'll be deaf by the time they're twenty. Can't ever get their attention anymore without scaring the crap out of them." He tapped on the kid's shoulder.

The boy's thin frame stiffened before he slowly turned around, his grip tightening on the shovel. The quick flash of recognition in his eyes had the kid quickly lowering the shovel before he tugged his left earbud out.

"Hi, Mr. J."

"Hey, Eric. Like you to meet Josh. He used to live here too. He knows his way around horses."

Eric's right hand instantly extended for a shake. A kid this polite would struggle with the thugs he'd met earlier.

Just like he had.

He returned the shake. "Nice to meet you, Eric. Can I give you a hand with something?"

Eric shrugged his slight shoulders. "I'm done now, but thank you."

Mr. J cleared his throat. "Well, in that case, I'm sure Josh would like a look at the stock. Mind showing him around?"

"Yeah. Okay."

Jennings gave Josh a quick eyebrow hitch before he disappeared. It was now his job to try to get the kid to talk.

Josh followed as Eric led him to the pasture behind the barn. There were a few horses nearby, quietly grazing. They all picked up their heads as Josh approached. They scented a stranger in their midst.

Eric climbed up and stood on the second rung of the fence, his eye level even with Josh's. "So, we have a few boarders. That big brown one there, the black one, and then the spotted white one. The other two are rescues."

The rescues were thin and forlorn. "Never understood how people could let a horse suffer like that. Any others?"

Eric nodded. "Yeah. Some out in the far pasture. I'll go get them a little later."

"Is Charlie still here?" It was probably ridiculous to think he'd still be here after all this time. The ranch made money by boarding and selling horses. Josh had raised Charlie from a colt, but he'd belonged to Mr. J, so maybe?

"Yeah." Eric smiled for the first time. "He's one of my favorites. Mr. J told me he used to come if he was whistled to just right, but I haven't been able to get him to do it."

Josh stuck two fingers in his mouth and blew out the long then short whistle he'd trained Charlie with. It wasn't long before he saw him. A big caramel-colored Arabian thundering toward them at top speed.

Josh's lips stretched into a big smile as all his trepidation about coming back to the ranch instantly faded away. Amazing that Charlie still remembered the whistle.

Eric laughed. "Wow! That's awesome."

Charlie skidded to a halt in front of them. The horse butted Josh's shoulder as if punishing him for being gone so long.

"Hey, buddy." Josh gave Charlie a thorough rub. "He looks great, Eric. You're doing a good job. Ever worked with horses before this?"

Charlie, obviously fond of Eric, moved to the side so the kid could pat him too. "Nope. Buck and Mr. J have been teaching me."

"It's easier out here. Away from the others. Right?"

Eric's response was a shoulder jerk. The pain in the kid's eyes told him things were worse than he let on.

Josh took out his cell and shot a few pictures of Charlie, and then one of Eric with his arm around Charlie's neck. "I'll send you this one." He tucked his phone away. "You can trust Mr. J. I finally did, and things got a whole lot better for me."

"You don't understand. If I say anything, it'll just get worse." Eric hopped down from the fence and walked toward the barn.

Josh gave Charlie one last pat, then followed behind. "Mr. J can help you without the others knowing. Schedule your chores at different times from theirs, things like that. You should tell him."

A fluffy black-and-white puppy scampered in front of Eric, nearly tripping him. Eric quickly scooped the pup up, terror widening his eyes, as two more pups wiggled out from behind the trees.

Pets weren't allowed. It was hard enough to find the funds to feed the kids and the horses.

Josh leaned down and scooped up a pup. "Who are these little guys?"

"Um. They just showed up one day with their mom. I save half my food for them. I don't use any of the ranch's feed." Eric quickly gathered the puppies and put them back in their hiding place. When he reemerged from behind the trees, he asked, "Are you going to tell?"

Eric was too thin as it was. The last thing he needed was to share his food with the dogs. "Nope. What I'm going to do is go into town and buy plenty of dog chow. Then Mr. J won't have any reason to make you get rid of them. But in return, you need to tell him what's going on with the other boys. Deal?"

Eric's eyes searched Josh's for the truth. The kid was in a new world, away from his family, just figuring out that sometimes adults lie—or can't always keep their promises. Eric glanced toward the trees again before he slowly nodded. Eric clearly cared for those puppies. Just as Josh had cared for Charlie.

"Deal."

Josh laid a hand on Eric's shoulder, giving it a light squeeze. "I'll get your e-mail address from Mr. Jennings and send that picture of you and Charlie, along with my cell number. Just in case you ever need anything."

"I'll be fine." Eric worried his bottom lip with his teeth. It looked as though he was going to say something else, but then he turned away and mumbled, "Thank you."

After he disappeared into the trees again, Josh let out a long breath. He couldn't save all of them—he could only do his best to help whomever would take it.

After getting the promised dog chow, Josh had the long drive home, along with a quick stop for dinner, to give himself a pep talk about staying detached. He'd had no problem doing it as an agent. Surely he could do it with the kids.

He tugged the heavy wooden door open and walked into Brewster's for the second time that day. He only had a few minutes to spare before he was supposed to meet Meg.

His arrangement with Brewster to hold a dart-throwing contest giving a car away to the first person who could shoot ten bull's-eyes in a row had its flaws, but if everything went just right, Meg would win a car fair and square and never have to know he was behind it. She was a damned good dart thrower.

He'd whiled away a lot of hours in his solitude working to match her skills. It'd helped pass the time.

When the door closed behind him, he stepped deeper into the packed bar. Loud country music mixed with laughter, and the aroma of fried appetizers filled the air.

As his eyes swept across the dimly lit room, he spotted Meg beside the bar wearing a sexy, soft shirt, tall heels, and tight jeans. She was laughing with Brewster and drinking a beer. He liked that about Meg. That she drank beer, threw darts, and raced Jet Skis, and now he knew she could fly a helicopter too. The perfect woman.

Shouldering his way through the crowd, he moved to the bar. When their eyes met, a little smile started to form on her lips before she caught herself and reined it back. "Hey, Josh. Uncle Brewster has Blue Moon on tap. Want one?"

Uncle Brewster? "Sure. Thanks."

He eyed the big man standing nearby pouring out beers. When Brewster glanced Josh's way, he smirked. "Thanks for sponsoring our contest tonight, Granger. Looks like it's going to be a big hit. But Meg wanted to change the rules a bit."

Megan finally let that smile bloom. "The winters get long here and most everyone can throw a mean game of darts. We're going to put everyone's name in a bucket and draw for the order to shoot. Nice of you to give a car away, Josh."

Crap! Was everyone related to Meg in this damned town?

CHAPTER NINE

Meg moved another inch forward. The press of people in the stuffy bar meant Josh was standing entirely too close to her. The heat pumping from him warmed her back.

With a new car at stake, everyone huddled around the metal Pabst beer bucket as her uncle Brewster dug out the ninth person's name to try their hand at winning it. The good thing was, because most of the Grants frequented a bar just outside of town, there'd be a good chance one of her relatives would win the car.

When her uncle had called earlier and told her what *her man* was up to, she'd quickly amended the rules for the evening. No way was she letting Josh hand her a car. She might not have much, but she still had her pride. And then there was the lawyer part about not taking anything from him.

"It's Toby!" Uncle Brewster called out.

Everyone moved aside to give him room to throw. Toby shot her a cute grin, matching his earlier one on the lake. "If I win, I want the car *and* a kiss from you, Meg." Naughty comments along with loud laughter cheered him on.

Before she could tell him no, Gloria, rocking one of her typical bowling shirts, called out, "Older women have more experience. Sure you don't want to save that kiss for me, Toby?"

"I was saving a kiss for you too, Gloria. After I hit bull's-eye number eleven." That drew an even bigger laugh from the room. Toby was the worst dart shooter in town.

Josh's arm slid around her waist, pulling her against his solid chest. His warm breath on her cheek sent a cool shiver up her spine. "Who's Toby?"

She tilted her head back so she could see his face. "The first guy I ever slept with."

Josh's jaw twitched as he watched Toby throw his first dart. When it barely connected with the bottom of the board and everyone moaned, Josh's eyes locked with hers again. "Are you still sleeping with him?"

She pulled out of his embrace and turned to face him. "Not that it's any of your business, but no. Men aren't a high priority for me right now. And I'm not taking a car from you, Josh."

While everyone else crowded by the bar to see who'd go next, Josh pulled her off to the corner. "I want you both in a car with air bags and antilock brakes, not some—"

Brewster's booming voice called out, "Granger, leave my niece alone so she can get up here and throw some darts!"

Josh narrowed his eyes. "You aren't being reasonable, Megan."

"Probably not." She answered his scowl with her best smirk. Teach him to try to pull tricks on her. If they were going to live in the same town all summer, she had to establish a few rules.

She made her way to the line and picked up the first dart. Just as she drew her arm back, her father called out, "Wait!"

When had he gotten there?

Her dad scanned the crowd, sending them his "don't mess with me" scowl. "Are you asking me to believe nine of you couldn't throw ten bull's-eyes? Or is this a way to help Megan win a car and then sell it for cash to fix up the house? I've warned you all about this! She needs to learn to stand on her own."

She hadn't even thought about taking the car and selling it, but now that she studied people's guilty expressions, maybe they had all been missing on purpose. Well, except for Toby. He was just bad at it.

It made her heart go a little gooey to think they'd all do that for her. And pay fifty bucks apiece on top of it.

"We were just having fun, Dad. I'll skip my turn, we'll return entry fees, and Josh can keep his car."

Her father whirled on her. "Nope. You and I are going to throw until someone misses. The chances of you beating me are slim, but I'll be fair. Winner gets the new car and the entry fees too. They were all going to throw their money away anyway." He turned to the people gawking. "Does anyone have any objections?"

Aunt Gloria said, "I do, but it won't do any good to say so. Good luck, Meggy. I'm outta here."

Gloria had always been her favorite aunt, even though she wasn't married to her uncle Brewster anymore.

When the rest remained silent and looked away, Dad glanced at his brother. "How much is in that pot there, Brew?"

"A grand."

Her father stepped aside and held his hand out. "Ladies first."

Damn him. He always ruined everything. God, she wanted so badly to beat him and embarrass him in front of everybody, but he'd probably just find another way to make her miserable if she did that. Or she could walk out and leave him standing there like a fool. But that would have consequences too. What she wouldn't give to be anything other than an Anderson at the moment.

Josh hated seeing Meg try her best to mask the pain and frustration in her eyes. Most probably wouldn't notice, but he saw it. And it killed him. Meg's father was an ass.

"Hey, Mayor." Josh moved beside Meg and pulled her against his side. Echoing her father's words when they'd first met, Josh said, "Let's see what you can do with someone closer to your own size. You win, you keep the car and fees. If I win, Meg keeps the car and the money."

She whispered, "You won't have a chance. I'll play him, but if I win you'll have to keep the car."

It was time to turn the tables back around in his favor. "Nope." He raised his voice so everyone could hear. "How about I take the mayor on? And let's make it even more interesting. *When* I win, Megan gets the car, the pot, and she has to give me the title to her old car so we can all use it for target practice. I found out the hard way gun ownership is big around here. Any objections?"

Everyone shook their heads again, all careful not to make eye contact with Megan's father.

Meg opened her mouth to protest, but her father cut her off. "I can beat a pansy-ass like you with one hand tied behind my back." Then he turned to play the crowd. "Megan won't be getting any free handouts tonight, people."

Meg's eyes narrowed at her father's remark. Then, probably because she thought Josh had no chance of beating her father, she said, "Let's do it! I wasn't going to take the car anyway."

The stakes had just risen another notch. He had to win the car for Meg's sake. And to show the town how to stand up to Anderson.

Megan's father held his hand out toward the painted line on the floor. "Ladies first, Granger."

Ignoring the mayor, Josh moved into position. He drew his arm back, but stopped and mimicked the way Toby had smiled at Meg earlier. "When I win I want a kiss from Meg too."

While everyone laughed, Meg rolled her eyes. "I'm sure there are plenty of other women here who'd gladly kiss you, Josh."

Meg's friend Pam, the hairdresser, lifted her hand. "Oh, I'd—"

When Meg shot her a "back off" scowl, the woman slowly lowered her arm. "Wouldn't. Nope. Not me."

Maybe Meg still cared after all.

Nice.

He turned and threw his first bull's-eye.

The room grew quiet as a cemetery when Anderson moved into place. Megan's father made a big show out of twisting his left arm way behind his back before he threw a rocket of a bull's-eye of his own. "You won't win, Granger. Might as well give up now and go back to that rock you slithered out from under."

Screw him. Josh ignored the remark and focused on winning Megan the car.

After twelve rounds of bull's-eyes, each with a new insult from Anderson, Josh slowly moved into position. He glanced at Meg, who sent him a tight smile. It'd be a new personal record if he could hit that many in a row.

He rolled his shoulders, took aim, and let the thirteenth dart go.

It landed dead center once again—thank God. He wanted to beat that son of a bitch in the worst way.

As Anderson moved up for his shot, his brother called out, "Number thirteen, bro. Your *unlucky* number. But don't let that get to you. You need that car a whole lot more than Meggy does, so good luck."

Josh glanced at Brewster. The man sent him a slight chin hitch before he threw a little towel over his shoulder and crossed his massive arms. Maybe Megan's uncle wasn't so bad after all.

Anderson wiped sweat from his forehead and growled. "It's the principle of the matter and you all know it." He let the dart fly.

And missed. By a millimeter.

The crowd went silent.

Anderson walked over and drilled a finger into his brother's chest. "You'll pay for that, Brewster." Then he turned and slammed two fingers into Josh's shoulder, just above where he'd been shot.

Stars appeared before Josh's eyes while Anderson yelled in his face. "You're going to be sorry you ever stepped foot into my town, Granger." Then he stomped toward the door.

It took all Josh's control not to react. He'd just let the FBI handle Anderson.

Anderson Butte might be short a mayor soon.

After the door slapped closed behind Anderson, a deafening cheer rang out. Everyone surrounded Josh and Megan and patted them on the back.

Brewster picked Megan up and plopped her on top of the bar. "Here are the keys to your new car and a thousand dollars to help with your remodel. Good luck, kid!"

While everyone congratulated a reluctant Megan, Brewster appeared beside Josh. "You did good tonight, Granger. I don't know what's what with you and my niece, but I swear to God, I'll make you pay if you hurt Meg or Haley again. Got it?"

"Yep."

"Okay, then." After a slap on the back so hard Josh lurched a step forward, Brewster called out, "Drinks are on the house!"

After she'd lost count of how many free drinks she'd downed, Meg thanked everyone again and then slipped off the barstool and onto her four-inch heels that still only made her a normal height. Tucking the keys to her new car into her back pocket, she started for the door.

Then the floor rushed toward her face.

If not for Josh's big hand snaking around her arm to save her, it could have been really embarrassing. And potentially painful.

"I'll walk you home, Meg."

She was still miffed about being tricked into taking the car by that dart shark. The last time she and Josh had played he stunk at darts. She didn't think he'd have a chance to beat her dad when she'd agreed to that bet.

She wanted to yank her arm free, but wasn't sure she'd be able to stay upright without his help. "This is Anderson Butte, not New York City. I'll be fine."

Luckily, he just kept motoring her toward the door, then pushed it open. The cool, clean air slapping her in the face felt good after being in the stuffy bar all night. Her new car sat right out front. She couldn't resist. She lifted the handle on the door, but it was locked, so she grabbed her keys.

Josh plucked them from her hand. "Not happening."

"I wasn't going to drive. Beep the locks." After he did, she opened the door and slid behind the wheel. Tilting her head back against the seat, she drew a deep breath. "Wow, this smells nice. I've never had a new car."

Josh crouched beside her open door. "Then it's about time you had one. Sorry if I caused even more trouble between you and your father tonight. But he's an ass, Meg. No offense."

She rolled her head in his direction. Josh could be so sweet sometimes. "My being born caused even more trouble between me and my father. And yeah. He can be a jerk." She yawned and settled deeper into the comfy seat. Her arms and legs suddenly weighed a ton. "I think maybe I'll just sleep right here." She closed her eyes and pulled more new car smell into her lungs.

"Nope. Time for bed."

She snorted. "My bed, not yours, buddy."

"Your bed it is, then." Josh slipped an arm under her knees and lifted her against his chest. With a bump of his hip, he nudged the door closed, then pushed the button to lock the car. The silly man.

Wait. Did he mean they'd both sleep in her bed? Her neglected-for-far-too-long girl parts liked that idea. A lot. But her almost-pickled brain had just enough working synapses left to shut those urges down. "Separate beds."

"For now."

They'd talk about that later. Mostly because her brain was happily swimming in beer and was in no mood to do its job and think.

As they headed toward Grandma's guesthouse, she turned her face and snuggled into the crook of his warm neck, drawing another deep breath.

Soap, shaving cream, and . . . Josh. Even better than the new car smell. "You don't wear cologne anymore."

He pulled her closer. "Nope."

"And you're damned good at darts now."

"Uh-huh."

"You dress different too." She laid her hand against his chest, which was covered by a simple cotton button-down shirt. His heart beat strong and steady under her palm. "No more slick shoes. I thought you loved fancy shoes."

"They were necessary for the old job. Boots are more comfortable."

"And a good place to hide your scary knife. It's like you're a different person sometimes."

"That's because sometimes people aren't as they appear on the outside."

What? Her foggy mind couldn't quite compute that sentence. She'd just have to think on that some more later. When she wasn't so very . . . tired. Or really drunk.

When she opened her eyes next, she was lying on her back on her nice soft bed. Josh sat beside her, messing with her feet. "What are you doing?"

As his thick fingers fought with the tiny buckle on her heels he said, "Welcome back. Where's Haley?"

"Spending the night with Grandma." She sat up, nudged his hands aside, and undid her shoes. "I can take it from here. Thanks." A loud burp escaped before she could tamp it back.

Charming.

His lips tilted into a cute smile as he moved closer and whispered, "Your shirt looks a little complicated. Maybe I'd better help."

When his finger traced her neckline and then slid lower, the rest of her body woke up too. "Go away, Josh."

His gaze slowly moved from her chest to her eyes. "You still owe me a kiss, remember?"

Had she agreed to that? The beer made that a little unclear. But Josh was a damned good kisser, so what the heck. "Fine. Get it over with."

He slid his big hands on either side of her face and slowly drew her closer. His warm breath on her lips made her part hers in anticipation. She closed her eyes, hating how much she wanted that one last kiss from him.

When his thumb gently caressed her lower lip, she opened her eyes and stared into his darkened ones. "What are you waiting for?"

"I'd rather kiss you when you'll remember it. Night, Meg." His chaste kiss to her forehead was like a bucket of cold water, dousing her smoldering desires.

It was probably for the best. In her current state, she wasn't sure she could have said no if he'd asked for more. That he didn't ask earned him a point.

As Josh walked out the door he said, "I'm looking forward to the fund-raiser tomorrow. And to meeting Haley."

Meeting Haley? "Wait a minute. I didn't . . ."

But Josh was already gone, the sneaky bastard. She was taking that point back.

He'd probably gotten her all worked up on purpose. He had her practically begging him to kiss her, and then he'd dropped his bomb. That much hadn't changed about him. It had always been a challenge to stay a step ahead of him. It was what she secretly liked the most about Josh.

She flopped back onto the bed and sighed. Now that Amber had spilled the beans, Haley was just going to keep asking about Josh until she met him.

How was she going to tell Haley about him? *What* was she going to tell Haley about him? Worse, what if Haley became attached to him before Meg sent him away at the end of the summer?

What a freakin' mess.

CHAPTER TEN

*T*rudging up the stairs to her new home's attic with Haley in tow set off jackhammers in Meg's skull. She and Haley should be in church like all good Andersons were supposed to be on Sunday mornings, but the enthusiastic way the preacher tended to deliver his sermons, at decibels that shook the rafters, would have surely made her head explode.

Her dad and the Three Amigos would give her a hard time about skipping her first week back, but she wanted the time to prepare Haley for meeting Josh.

And that's what she should be doing, but the right words weren't materializing in her aching head. So she'd sort through some boxes and hopefully some kind of epiphany would strike.

The big, light-filled attic held tons of boxes, mostly filled with her grandparents' junk. Her dad must have thrown it all up there after her mom's mother died and locked the door before he rented the place out. She needed to get rid of most of it so she could make the space into a kids' loft for her guests. Children were small enough to fit under the sloping roof on the sides, and they'd love lying in bed and peering out at the lake and at the animals in the trees at eye level from the third-floor perch.

Haley's sudden squeal of delight sent hot daggers into Meg's eyeballs. "What'd you find, Bug?"

Haley ran toward her with a framed photo and plopped onto her lap. Pointing everyone out with her chubby little finger, she said, "Mommy, your daddy, Grandma, a lady, a baby, and a doggy!"

Meg studied the picture. She'd never seen it before. "You're right, that's Grandma, my dad, and my other grandma you never met, but that isn't me, it's my mom. I'm the baby in the picture." Her mom couldn't have been much older in the photo than Meg currently was. She hadn't realized just how much she resembled her mother until now. Her dad had refused to keep any of her mother's pictures in the house after she'd died, so Meg hadn't seen many over the years.

Haley looked up and her forehead scrunched. "Where's *my* daddy?"

It was the second time Haley had asked since Amber had taken it upon herself to let Haley know about Josh. Probably as good a time as any to have the talk. "Actually, your father is staying at the hotel right now. He's very excited to meet you."

"Where's he been?"

Good question. Meg wasn't absolutely sure of the answer. "He's been working. We'll probably see him at the fund-raiser later today."

"Will he live at our house now?"

"No. Not all daddies live with mommies. But he's going to be here visiting for the summer."

"'Kay." Haley pointed at the picture again. "What's the doggy's name?"

Evidently that was all Haley wanted to know about Josh. For now. "Brinkley. He was the best dog ever."

"I want a doggy." The longing in Haley's eyes poked at Meg's "no dogs" policy.

"I know, baby, but we can't have one right now. Why don't you go see if you can find any more pictures of Brinkley for me?"

Maybe since they were staying put this time she'd consider a dog for Haley. After the lodge was open and taking bookings.

Haley huffed out a breath, but then hopped up and started digging through boxes without further fuss. Thank goodness. Stress about Haley meeting Josh made Meg's stomach ache. Luckily, Haley seemed to be taking news of Josh in stride. Hopefully it'd go that smoothly later.

Meg tucked the picture into her backpack thinking Casey might like to see it, and went back to her sorting.

As she dug further she found a box with a faded, barely legible *For Megan* scrawled on it in her grandmother's shaky handwriting. Ripping it open, her heart leapt. Her mother's things. She knew so little about her mom it was like finding buried treasure.

Meg found awards from various school functions, report cards, her mom's high school diploma, the cap from her graduation, and a cute little class ring. She slipped the gold ring with her mom's aquamarine birthstone onto her finger. A perfect fit. Maybe she'd ask the others if they would mind if she kept it.

Digging deeper, she found a couple of legal-sized files lying flat on the bottom. Just as she reached in to investigate, a deep voice called out from downstairs, "Where are the heathens in this damned house?" Her head popped up, thinking it was her father for a nanosecond, but then she remembered Ben said he might stop by with some new meds for Haley. The jerk. Trying to make his voice sound like their father's. Well, turnabout was fair play.

She called out in a high, panicked voice. "Ben. Thank God! We're in the attic."

Footsteps thundered up the stairs. Ben flew into the attic and skidded to a halt. "What's the mat—"

The big grin on her face must've given her away.

The concern on Ben's face turned into a scowl. "You're a brat, Muck."

"I learned from the best. And we're not calling me that any-more. Especially in front of the k-i-d."

Ignoring her, Ben scooped Haley up over his head and made her giggle. "I brought my new super-fast ski boat. Want to ditch your boring mom and go for a ride with your favorite fun uncle?"

"Bye, Momma!"

Wow, she'd never even been dumped by a guy that quickly. "We're having a talk about men and their fast boats when you get older, Haley. And I'll be in the ice cream booth at the park when you're done being fun, Ben."

"Okay." He tossed a little white bag her way. "Don't forget, payback's a bi—" He looked at Haley and, remembering his lan-guage, finished with, "bummer, Megan. You won't know when and you won't know where. Instructions on the bottle. See you."

She sent him her best you-don't-scare-me smirk.

Ben and Ryan were both responsible adults and yet they still lived to tease her like they had when they were little boys. But she could hold her own with those clowns.

After Haley and Ben disappeared down the stairs, Meg closed the lid on the box and put it aside to look through later. She had just enough time to change before she had to go scoop ice cream. And then introduce Haley to Josh.

Josh headed down to the lobby before he set off to the fund-raiser. After Casey finished with a person who had to be Jim Carrey, because no one else had a goofy smile that big, Josh stepped up to the front desk. "Just tell me this. Are his initials J. C.?"

Casey crossed her arms. "Nice try. What's up, Granger?"

"Any tips on how to avoid your father today? I don't want to cause Meg any more trouble."

"Yeah, I heard about the dart game last night." When the phone rang, Casey lifted a finger, cutting him off, then answered it.

While she took her call, he wandered over to the brochure rack. White water rafting looked interesting. He cracked the colorful pages open and studied them. Could be a fun thing to expose the kids on the ranch to.

Casey appeared beside him. "Meg's a fantastic guide. You should ask her to take you sometime."

One more skill Megan had that he didn't know about. "She never said much about growing up here. Did she leave town because of your father?"

Casey sighed. "Again, not my place to tell. But if you want to avoid my dad today, lay low at first. He usually kicks off these fundraisers with a rah-rah speech and then makes a quick round of the booths before his wife, Sue Ann, gets bored and makes him leave."

"Sounds like a plan, thanks."

"You're welcome. But you need one more plan. Finding a new place to stay. It's high season and I may need your room."

So he'd worn out his not-so-welcome welcome. "I'll ask around some today."

"It won't be anywhere in town. My dad sent an e-mail this morning saying no one is to rent you a place. I turned the Internet back on in your room so you can search for someplace nearby."

That son of a bitch. "Thanks. I'll get on it."

He made to leave but Casey called out, "Meg told me you're meeting Haley today. Tread carefully there, Granger."

He'd lain awake all night thinking about meeting his daughter. With few memories of his mother and never knowing his father, he had no idea how to be a parent. But he'd vowed his child would know who he was and that he'd do everything in his power to always be there for her.

As much as Casey could be a pain in his ass, he respected her fierce loyalty to Megan. "I'm not sure what to say to Haley today. Got a plan for that?"

Casey blinked as if taken aback that he'd ask her. He wasn't sure she was going to answer, but finally she said, "Well, I guess just don't try to push it. Let it happen naturally. Meg's done a really good job with Haley. She doesn't need you messing things up."

The not-messing-up part was what weighed on him. "Got it. Thanks. See you later."

Josh headed out the door and toward the town square. He passed by a house with a large workshop on the side. The whine of a power tool piqued his curiosity, so he headed for the big set of open doors. Zeke leaned inside an old tractor's engine. Josh didn't want to scare him and make him hit his head, so maybe he'd poke around the shop until Zeke came up for air.

The guy had some badass tools.

Josh was admiring an air compressor as tall as he was when Zeke called out, "Help ya with something?"

"Just checking out your incredible shop." He moved beside Zeke and stuck his head inside the tractor's engine compartment. Nothing like the simple engines back in the day. A guy could work on one without hooking up to a computer. "What's the trouble?"

Zeke leaned back and slowly wiped his hands on a rag. "Won't start. Slick guy like you know about engines?"

"Worked at a garage all through high school and college."

"That so?" He pointed to a pile of dirty parts on a nearby workbench. "Know anything about rebuilding carburetors?"

"Sure. Need a hand?"

Zeke squinted as he tucked his rag into his back pocket, as if debating. "Not with that. But I could use a young guy like you to help pull a transmission tomorrow. If you've got the time."

Josh missed getting his hands dirty. Anything was better than interrogating lying, scumbag criminals day in and day out. He wasn't missing his old job in the least. "Sure. Eight work?"

"Yep. Going to the doings?"

"Yeah, I thought I'd stop by."

"Let's go."

They started down the drive and then headed toward the town square. Zeke set a brisk pace, surprising Josh. The guy had to be in his seventies.

Josh said, "I met a kid who said you told everyone not to talk to me. Why the change of heart, Zeke?"

"Meggy's mad at you, but she once saw something to like. Curious what that is. And this way I can keep an eye on you."

Casey and now Zeke—Meg's Rottweilers. "Fair enough. So, how are you related to Meg, Zeke?"

"I'm not." The slight hesitation in Zeke's gait and the way his eyes shifted contradicted his answer. "My last name's Grant, not Anderson."

Interesting. Zeke had just told him a big fat lie.

The day was warm and the sun bright, making the ice cream booth a popular place. Ben had dropped Haley off just after noon and, being the typical fun uncle, hadn't thought to ask if she wanted some lunch. So a half hour into Meg's hour-long shift, Haley declared she was starving.

Meg made her a cone.

Skipping church and now feeding her kid an ice cream cone for lunch? Just hand over the bad-mommy blue ribbon now. "Why don't you go sit over in the shade and eat this? I'll just be a little bit longer, then we can go do some of the games."

"'Kay." Haley's mischievous grin told Meg she knew she was getting away with something big.

Reaching for the scoop, Meg looked up and her already shaky gut lurched. The Three Amigos were next in line with determined looks on their wrinkly faces. "Hi, ladies. Chocolate or vanilla?"

Mrs. Thompson said, "We missed you in church this morning, dear."

The only acceptable reason to skip church was if a body was physically unable to attend. They didn't have to know the root of the problem was too much alcohol. "I was puking my guts up this morning. But I feel a little better now. So was it chocolate or vanilla you ladies wanted?"

All three of the grannies' eyes grew wide. When they looked at one another, some Vulcan mind link thing must've happened because they all shook their heads in unison.

Mrs. Ingalls swallowed hard before she said, "We don't care for any ice cream, but we're glad you're feeling better. See you next Sunday?"

"Absolutely. Bye, ladies."

Chuckling, Meg turned back to her line of customers. Pam, the traitor, was next. The speed at which Pam's hand had popped up to volunteer to kiss Josh at Brewster's still irked Meg. Without asking, Meg scooped a half-chocolate, half-vanilla cone for Pam because that was her favorite. "Here you go. You should double your donation for this to make up for last night."

"It was an accident. My hand just sort of jumped before my brain caught up. His hotness must've mesmerized me or something. But I thought you said you were over him. Have your feelings changed?"

Had they? Her stomach had been in knots all day in anticipation of seeing Josh, but that was because of Haley. And on account of drinking way too much the night before. It probably had nothing to do with the kiss she still owed him. "It's just . . . things have gotten a little complicated, that's all."

The way Pam slowly licked her cone had all the guys waiting in line for their ice cream staring. Or maybe it was all the cleavage she was showing.

"Complicated? Sounds like we need a girls' night. That is, if I'm forgiven?" Pam batted her eyes again.

Maybe eye-batting worked on girls after all. She could never stay mad at Pam for long because she loved her. "Oh, all right. Now go away, you're holding up my line."

"'Kay. Call you later."

As Pam sashayed away, a bottle of water appeared on the counter in front of Meg. Josh whispered, "Looks like you need a hand. How's the head today?" He tied on an apron and stood beside her.

She glanced over her shoulder to check on Haley's progress. About half a cone left and a major mess to clean up.

"My head's fine—except for the pounding part. Why don't you take the chocolate and I'll do vanilla?"

"You got it." He reached into the pocket of his nicely fitting cargo shorts and pulled out a little travel pack of aspirin. "Got this for you too."

Hallelujah! Her morning dose of painkiller had worn off. "Thanks."

She ripped open the little packet, tossed the pills back, and chugged the ice-cold water as Josh jumped right in like he'd been serving ice cream his whole life. He scooped both flavors while she took her short break and he introduced himself to everyone like he didn't have a care in the world.

She found it hard to draw a deep breath in anticipation of making the introductions of father and daughter soon. She'd been getting enough curious glances all day to know everyone was hoping for a big show.

She moved beside Josh and grabbed a scooper, ignoring the sexy way his forearms flexed as he doled out ice cream.

They'd just gotten the lines all under control when the number-one pain in Meg's ass, Amber, strolled up.

Josh, having no idea he was dealing with Satan's spawn, smiled like he had at everyone else. "Hi. Chocolate or vanilla?"

Might be good to avoid Amber and go clean the ice cream off Haley, but it'd be cruel to leave Josh alone with the woman. He'd done her a favor by helping her out with the ice cream stand, after all.

Amber's eyes took a long stroll up and then back down Josh's exceptional body. When her lips tilted in a slow, come-hither smile, there was no decision. Meg was staying.

"Welcome to Anderson Butte, Josh." Amber stuck out her claw. "I'm Amber Grant-Downey. It's a real *pleasure* to meet you." She leaned so close her fake boobs almost touched Josh's hand.

He slipped his hand from her clutches, then dove for the scoop. Sending Meg a sideways what-the-hell glance, he said, "Nice to meet you too. Chocolate or vanilla?"

"Oh, no, thank you." Amber ran her hands down her sides and her voice turned all blonde-bombshell whispery. "Maintaining a figure like this doesn't allow for ice cream. I just wanted to welcome you to town. And to offer you a friendly place to stay." She turned to Meg. "You did tell Josh about my guesthouse, didn't you, Megan?" Her knowing smile spiked Meg's blood pressure.

Josh said, "Casey told me earlier the mayor nixed anyone renting me a place in town."

She hadn't heard that. She hated that her father had the power to do that. Why couldn't he just butt out?

Amber waved her hand. "I live just outside of town and couldn't give a flip what the mayor says."

Typical of a Grant.

Haley picked that moment to tap on the back of Megan's shorts and leave a chocolate stain. "All done. More?"

"Nope. We'll go get a sandwich if you're still hungry, sweetheart." She glanced at Josh to gauge his reaction at seeing his daughter for the first time. He completely ignored Amber and smiled at Haley as Amber rattled on about the lovely attributes of her guesthouse.

Luckily Meg's ice cream scooping replacement arrived, so she greeted her, untied her apron, and then passed it over as an idea struck her. "Josh won't be staying in your guesthouse, Amber. He's going to stay at my lodge. We'll find our own ways to work off the rent."

Her replacement worker, and third grade teacher, Mrs. Mitchell, raised a brow.

Yeah. That had come out all wrong, dammit.

She sent a stern glance Josh's way to be sure he knew it was his job to play along, and was met by his naughty grin.

Men. He probably thought he'd get the same sexual favors Amber was clearly offering. "By installing a dock and refinishing floors. That kind of thing. And Haley and I will still be living in Grandma's guesthouse."

Josh's smile never wavered. "Ah." He turned to Amber. "Thanks for the offer, but it looks like I'm all set."

Smart man.

The only reason Amber wanted Josh to live in her guesthouse was to annoy Meg. And probably to sleep with him too. But no way was she letting Josh anywhere near Amber-the-man-stealer. Amber had stolen her boyfriend in high school but wouldn't get away with it again. But that would imply Josh was hers and that wasn't the case. Josh seemed to want to make it the case. But she shouldn't, and didn't, want him back. Did she?

Admittedly, the urge to set all his fancy shoes on fire was finally gone.

She'd have to think on it later. After she dropped the daddy news on her kid. Doing that just right was the most important thing. She didn't want to scar Haley for life. "We're going to hit the bathroom and get cleaned up. Bye, Mrs. Mitchell."

Josh untied his apron and fell in step with Meg as she carried Haley across the square.

Amber called out, "Pity. I was looking forward to getting to know you better, Josh. See you around."

Wench.

"She's a piece of work." Josh opened the door to the blessedly cool hallway to her dad's office. "By the way, I'm partial to being included in my own housing decisions."

She stopped walking and huffed out a breath. "Fine. If you'd rather go live with the Wicked Witch of the West, be my guest. I was trying to do you a favor. We'll be right back and then we'll do the . . . thing!" She slapped the door to the ladies room open and set Haley down. Haley's widened eyes proved Meg had let the pressure of what she was about to do get to her. She'd crossed the line to scary-mommy mode.

She was just about to apologize to Haley when a set of strong hands spun her around and into a tight hug.

Josh whispered in her ear, "We can do the *thing* later. I don't want to cause you more problems with your father by staying at your place."

She hadn't realized how much she'd missed the feel of his arms wrapped around her. Maybe she'd let him hold her for just a minute . . . or two. "Amber knows how to get under my skin. I shouldn't have let her. I'm good now."

He gave her a quick squeeze. "Your call."

Haley looked up at the two of them like they'd both lost their minds. "Only girls can come in here."

Her little rule follower. How a rebel like her ended up with such a sweet kid was a mystery.

Now was probably as good a time as any to break the news. At least they had some privacy. "Josh was checking to be sure we were all right." She wet some paper towels and cleaned Haley's hands. "Josh is your father, Haley. Remember we talked about that a little while ago?" Man, that was lame. Maybe she'd better try that again.

"Uh-huh." Haley grinned around the wet paper towel dabbing at her face. "Do you have a doggy? Mommy won't let me have one."

Really? That's the first thing she says to him? They'd already talked about why they couldn't have a dog. She refused to feel guilty about that much.

Josh said, "Nope." Then he knelt to Haley's level. "But I like dogs. I saw some fun games going on out there. Do you want to try a few with me?"

Haley looked up at her. "Can I, Mommy?"

"Sure."

And that was that? Meg wasn't sure what she'd expected, but it was a pivotal moment in all of their lives. Haley meeting her father for the first time, looking at her mirror image, finally understanding why she didn't look like Meg? Being two and a half and filled with innocent trust must be nice. She hoped Josh wouldn't be the one to make Haley lose that sweet trust by hurting her.

CHAPTER ELEVEN

*J*osh wasn't sure if that had gone well or not. Haley hadn't rejected him outright, so that was good. But she'd seemed more interested in whether he had a dog than in him.

It amazed him how much Haley looked like him. Same blonde hair, and looking into her eyes was like looking into a mirror and seeing his own. He'd always imagined her looking like a mini Meg, not like him.

Suddenly, he had an overwhelming desire to know every little thing about her. What were her favorite things? Did she hate fish sticks too? She had asthma like he'd had—did that mean she hated broccoli like him? He'd missed out on so much that she should feel like a stranger to him, but it was as if he'd known her all his life, even if he didn't know many of the details of hers. He wanted to ask a million questions, but then Casey's words echoed in his head. *"Don't try to push it. Let it happen naturally."*

So maybe he'd just go with the flow and learn as they went along.

He held the bathroom door open as Megan and Haley passed through. Megan's stepmother was closing the door to the mayor's darkened office down the hall. When she noticed them, she pulled up short, tucking the papers she carried under her arm.

"What on earth were y'all doing in there? Lord, you're just always up to no good. You'd think you'd have grown out of that by now, Megan."

"We were just telling Haley that Josh is her father." Megan proclaimed the news like that was a perfectly normal thing to do in a women's bathroom. Then she added, "What were you doing in my dad's office?"

Anger flashed in Sue Ann's eyes before she recovered and raised an indignant brow. "Not that it's any of your concern, but your daddy's down with a headache. He asked me to fetch some papers from his desk he'd forgotten to bring along home with him to work on this evening." She glanced at Haley. "Your shirt's a mess, child. Just like your mother, aren't you?"

Who talked to a little kid that way? His kid, dammit!

When Haley's forehead scrunched, Josh scooped her up. "It's a kid's job to get dirty, right? Let's go see if we can win some prizes. I think I even saw a blue dog you'd like."

"Yay!" Haley rewarded him with a big smile.

Megan rolled her eyes at Sue Ann and then turned and led the way to the door. When they were outside again, her hand curled around his arm and she tugged, so he leaned closer. She whispered in his ear, "Rule number one, Josh. Never make promises you can't definitely keep. Haley's going to expect that blue dog now. If you can't win it, you'll disappoint her."

Disappoint her? Dammit! He'd screwed up in the first five minutes.

He'd just have to win that damn dog for Haley, even if it took all the quarters in town.

———

Stuck holding all the prizes Josh had won with Haley, including the blue dog, Meg stood on the sidelines while the three-legged race participants lined up. Haley, her leg secured to Josh's, sent her a big grin and a wave. They wouldn't have a chance of winning because Haley was so little, but she was loving all the attention from Josh.

Next to them stood Amber's husband, Randy, and their six-year-old, Heather. They both leaned forward in anticipation. Randy was the most competitive guy in town. What she'd seen in the man in high school, other than his good looks, baffled her. He'd surely pick his kid up and make a run for it at the end so they'd win.

Once a cheater, always a cheater. He and Amber deserved each other.

The gun sounded and they all took off.

Zeke appeared at her side. "Looks like Granger's trying. Gotta give him points for that."

"I guess. But it's one thing to play games and have fun and entirely another to deal with the hard stuff and be a parent."

Zeke chuckled. "Never thought I'd see the day words like those came out of the town hellion's mouth. Looks like you've gone and grown up on me, kid."

"Hellion? I prefer rabble-rouser, if it's all the same to you."

He smiled. "Either way, I'm proud of you, Meggy."

Not used to hearing words like that, she shifted the stuff in her hands and wrapped her arm around Zeke's waist for a quick hug. "Thank you, Zeke. That means a lot coming from you."

Clearly embarrassed, he frowned. "Well, I've had enough. See you around, kid."

"Bye."

Zeke walked away as loud cheers rang out. As predicted, Randy and Heather were victorious. Haley and Josh were bringing up the rear and just crossing the finish line, but you'd never know it from the smile on Haley's face.

When Josh held out his fist for a knuckle bump, Haley gave it all she had and then splayed her fingers in a move that matched Josh's perfectly, just the way they'd practiced before the race. Then they both turned and beamed their identical smiles at her.

The concrete wall around her heart cracked a little as she smiled back.

Josh untied them, then lifted Haley onto his shoulders and jogged toward Meg.

Her father had never done anything like that. Made her feel so special. It chipped away another layer of that wall.

Josh flipped a laughing Haley to the ground at Meg's feet and then whispered in her ear, "That guy who won cheated big-time. Who does that in a kid's three-legged race?"

That explained where Haley got her rule following from. She sometimes forgot Haley had two parents. "Randy does. He's married to the piece of work with a guesthouse you met earlier."

"Ah, Amber. Speaking of that, where is my new home, exactly?"

She hoped she hadn't made a mistake by offering up her house in the heat of the moment. "The other side of the lake. Number sixteen. I'll need to get your room ready so maybe you could move your things in tomorrow?"

"If you're sure about your father."

She was done being bullied by her father. "I'm sure." She juggled all the loot and then took Haley's hand. "Well, we'd better get going. Nap time."

Clearly exhausted, Haley lifted her arms to be picked up, but Meg didn't have enough hands.

Josh said, "How about I carry you?"

Haley turned to him without hesitation. After he picked her up, she snuggled her face into the crook of his neck. Just as Meg

---

had when he'd carried her home. With a smile on her face, Haley fluttered her eyes closed, sending another pinch to Meg's heart.

Heading for Gram's guesthouse, she whispered, "Thanks for playing Pluck the Duck with Haley twelve times until she won the dog."

He whispered back, "That's a stupid game. All based on chance. There's no real winning involved unless it takes some skill."

Such a guy thing to say. "She's two and a half, Josh. Standing in line, waiting for her turn, and then getting her to pick just one duck when she has two perfectly good hands is an accomplishment. Believe me."

"If you say so." He shifted Haley to his other arm and leaned closer. "We probably need to talk about my rent." He quirked his eyebrows. "Amber offered some pretty hot terms. What are you offering?"

She swatted his arm. "This is a business deal, pal. Nothing more. Do you know how to hammer nails and strip wood floors? If not, I'll just charge you money and then use it to hire Toby to help me."

That wasn't nice to throw Toby's name out there, but a part of her needed to test Josh some more. She hated how her defenses against him were slipping. Besides, it wasn't easy to rile him, making it that much more fun to try. That she'd slept with Toby clearly bothered him.

He pulled her against his side. "I'll bet I'm a lot better with my hands than Toby." He drove his point home by sliding a big hand down to her rear end and giving it a quick squeeze.

"I don't know. Toby's pretty good." Liar, liar, pants on fire. Literally, because Josh's hand was still on her butt.

He gave her bottom a sharp pat before he opened the door to the guesthouse. "After you."

Smiling because she'd almost forgotten how fun Josh was to flirt with, she dumped the new toys onto a chair and then led the way to the bedroom and pulled the covers back.

Josh laid Haley down and gently tucked the sheet under her chin before he whispered, "She's great, Meg. Thanks for today."

Moved by the tenderness in his eyes as he looked at Haley, she could only nod before she turned to show him out.

They walked side by side in silence. Outside on the porch, he wrapped his arms around her and slowly pulled her against his chest. As he stared into her eyes, Josh maneuvered them until her back pressed against the wooden front door. The desire in his gaze made her heart skip a beat just before he whispered, "I think I'd like my kiss now. And while we're at it, how about I remind you just how skilled my hands are?"

Before she could protest—like she would have anyway—he laid his mouth on hers.

It wasn't a sweet kiss; it was hard, needy, and damned sexy. With his solid body and soft lips pressed against hers, she kissed him back just as urgently. Standing on her tiptoes, she circled her arms around his neck. While his tongue did a primitive dance with hers, his hands wandered all over her body, squeezing, caressing, and driving her even crazier with need.

After she pulled away slightly for some much-needed air, she nipped at his bottom lip. It used to drive him wild.

Josh groaned, pulled her closer, and then dove back in for more.

Very bad-girl thoughts of dragging him inside to the couch and having her way with him were interrupted by the sound of a rifle cocking.

Freezing mid-kiss, they both slowly turned their heads toward the sound.

Grandma narrowed her eyes. "You have to the count of ten to get off my property, boy! One!"

Josh stared deeply into Meg's eyes as he gave her one last long, slow squeeze against his muscle-bound body. "Guess I better go."

"Yeah. Run!"

Grandma was on five by the time he took off at a sprint toward the hotel via the beach.

When he was safely away, she turned and met her grandmother's steely stare. "What? We bet a kiss on the dart game last night. I lost."

"You'd best remember how you moped around for months the last time that boy broke your heart before you end up in his bed again, young lady. And in my day, a kiss for a bet didn't include all that monkey business with his hands."

Grandma saw the getting felt up part?

Lord, just shoot me now.

———————

After a fitful night's sleep thinking of Josh and that kiss, Meg checked her phone for the tenth time as she walked the beach to the hotel. She'd hoped to hear back about her loan from the bank in Denver. No word yet.

She needed to get Josh's room ready for later that evening, but first she wanted to set up her reservation software on the computer in Casey's office. She needed to bill Mr. Randall, her first client, and put that cash to good use on her house.

As much as she would have loved to avoid her grandmother after the kissing episode, Grams and Haley had already made plans to bake cookies. So instead of a quick drop-off and a prom- ise to return in an hour, she had to endure another lecture on the dangers of Josh and his monkey-business hands.

She'd been tempted to remind her grandmother she was twenty-eight years old, not sixteen, but it wouldn't have done any good, so she'd just nodded until Grams ran out of steam.

Her sister, talking on the phone with a client while tapping on her computer's keyboard, lifted her chin in greeting when Meg walked into the office. Casey's usual smile was missing. Either something was wrong with the client she was speaking with, or Meg was in trouble with Casey too.

She'd find out soon enough, so she set out to put Casey's old computer back together.

Casey hung up and started right in. "What's up with you and Granger, Meg? He checked out this morning and said to tell you he's cooking dinner tonight for you guys as a part of his rent."

Josh was going to cook for them? Awesome! "Nothing's up. He's going to be staying, *alone*, at the house, and in lieu of rent, he's going to help with the renovations. He's muscle. That's all."

"So Grandma was exaggerating when she said, and I quote, 'It was like watching a porno movie when I showed up at her door yesterday'?"

Meg laughed. It might have been if Grandma had shown up five minutes later. "Grandma watches porn these days?"

Casey wasn't amused. She crossed her arms and waited for an answer like she'd done when Meg was ten.

"Is this my mother asking or my sister? Because bitching about men and talking about sex was supposed to come with a glass of wine. And it's way too early in the day for that."

"Dammit, Meg. I'm worried about you. Why can't you just talk to me?" Casey closed her eyes and rubbed her temples.

Casey always did that whenever Meg disappointed her. Something that had happened more than she cared to admit.

Feeling guilty, she circled behind Casey's chair and wound her arms around her sister's shoulders. "I'm sorry. You'll always worry about me, and I appreciate it more than you know, Casey." Meg gave her a noisy kiss on the cheek, earning a reluctant grin from her sister.

Meg went back to messing with the computer on the floor. Probably time to go all in on the sister thing. "I haven't slept with anyone since I got pregnant with Haley. I've been on a few dates but wasn't attracted enough to go to the next level. So when Josh kissed me it got a little more heated than I'd planned, that's all."

Casey's jaw dropped. "You haven't had sex in *three years*?"

"Could you shout that a little louder, please? I don't think they heard you on the other side of the lake."

"No one should go without sex for three years. It can't be good for you."

"Wait a minute. You've been divorced for a couple of years now, so who are you having sex with?"

Casey went back to tapping on her computer. "None of your business."

"Oh, no you don't. This isn't a one-way street. Spill!" A memory of a sexy smile across the hotel's kitchen hit her. "It's Dax, right? I've seen the way he looks at you."

"Absolutely not." Casey frowned. "I'd never sleep with an employee. And he doesn't look at me any particular way."

"He does too, but if it's not him, then who?"

Huffing out a breath, she said, "Beau Bailey. But don't you tell anyone or I *will* kill you. Neither of us is looking for another relationship right now so we're keeping it quiet."

"Beau Bailey? He's hot, I'll give you that. And built. But kinda old."

"He's only two years older than me, brat!"

Megan flopped down on the corner of her sister's desk, amazed they'd been able to keep their relationship a secret in their nosy town. "So . . . you guys meet at some seedy motel down the highway, have hot monkey sex, then say see you next Tuesday, same time, same place?"

Casey struggled to keep a straight face. "We have hot monkey sex, but never in seedy motels. Why would we do that when I have perfectly good rooms here?"

"You do it here? Oh my God, Casey. Dad would kill you if he found out!" Meg had a whole new kind of respect for her sister.

Casey beamed a smug smile. "That's why it's handy Beau is a general contractor. If people see him here, they just think he's fixing the plumbing or something."

"Well he's fixing *your* pipes, that's for sure! Wow. This is too much for my traumatized brain to absorb. My sister, Miss Straight As, Miss Perfect, Miss 'why can't you be more like Casey, Megan,' is a ho. And I love it!"

Casey rolled her eyes. "I'm not a ho. I'm a woman with normal needs. The hot monkey sex is just a bonus."

"Stop!" Holding her sides in laughter, Megan said, "As it is I'm not going to be able to look him in the eye the next time I see him."

"The point is, Meg, it's dangerous to scratch your itch with Josh. He's hurt you. Toby has wanted you since the tenth grade. You should put him out of his misery. It'll help you separate sex and co-parenting."

Wiping the tears from her eyes, she said, "News flash. Toby and I have had sex plenty of times and it was just okay. Josh, on the other hand, was stellar. It's made it hard for me to want anyone else."

Casey's eyes narrowed. "It was after your junior prom, wasn't it? When you and Toby came home with those guilty looks on your faces? I knew I shouldn't have let you stay out that long past your curfew."

"Yep. And then we hooked up a lot when I was home in the summers from college. Sometimes we'd go out on the boat and—"

"I don't want to know—he's an employee too. And while Josh has a smokin' hot body—he looks damned good in just his boxers, anyway—you need to figure out if the attraction is just physical or if there are still real feelings involved."

Just his boxers? A hot surge of jealousy stiffened her spine. But Casey would never betray her like that. Would she?

Meg slapped her hands on the desk. "Why have you seen Josh in his underwear?"

"It was an accident. But your reaction told me what I wanted to know. You still have feelings for him, don't you?"

Meg sat beside the computer on the floor again as she pondered her answer. It was her turn to close her eyes and rub her temples, but not because she was disappointed in her sister. "I honestly don't know, Casey. He's changed so much from what he was before, but in some ways he's just the same. He said he realized he needed to switch his priorities and it seems he has. And the way he looked at Haley yesterday was so sweet it melted my heart. Maybe it's because when he smiles I see Haley's smile? I don't know. I'm just so confused."

When Meg opened her eyes again, Casey was sitting right next to her on the floor.

"Sleep with him, then. It's probably the only way you'll know for sure. And if it turns out to be nothing more than fantastic sex, then you deserve some. Just don't hand him your heart until you're sure." Casey pulled her into a hard hug. "But you'd better warn him—if he hurts you again, Grandma told me she's aiming to kill the next time."

CHAPTER
TWELVE

*J*osh crossed the threshold to Zeke's shop the next morning at seven forty-five. Wailing country music pouring out from a boom box from the eighties assaulted his rock and roll-loving ears. He called out for Zeke, but got no response.

He'd been so impressed with the high-tech tools the day before, he hadn't given much thought to the other side of Zeke's shop. A rickety metal desk by the entrance held stacks of papers, one weighted down by a black rotary-dial phone.

He'd never seen a phone like that except on old television shows. He lifted the receiver up and placed it against his ear. A steady dial tone sounded, so he poked his finger in the number seven hole and twirled it around. It made a clicking sound on its slow journey back around the dial. It must've taken forever to dial a number back in the day. Interesting.

The old tube computer screen on the desk and the stacks of handwritten invoices littering the desktop showed Zeke wasn't big on technology. Maybe he'd ask the old guy if he'd like help updating his systems.

Moving deeper into the shop, Josh spotted a pair of jean-clad legs and worn work boots sticking out from under an old rusty truck.

The music was so loud Zeke would never hear him, so he crossed to the boom box, turned it down, and then waited.

And waited.

When Zeke's legs didn't move, Josh kneeled down on the dusty floor and peered under the truck's chassis. Zeke softly snored. His hand clutched a wrench that lay across his slowly rising and falling chest.

Morning nap time, apparently.

Josh stood and, spotting a broom in the corner, figured he'd make himself useful until Zeke woke up.

After the floors were clean, he got the hose out and sprayed down the driveway. While blasting pine needles and dirt along the concrete, he glanced up and spotted Sue Ann walking out the door of a big house down the street and getting into her car. Everyone lived a stone's throw away from one another. Was that a good or bad thing? He'd always wondered what it'd be like to have a big family, but after seeing how screwed-up Megan's was, maybe it wasn't all roses and sunshine.

With the front looking a little more presentable—he'd come out and pull some weeds for Zeke later—he ventured back inside.

Zeke was draining his to-go cup of coffee. "You're late, Granger." Before Josh could respond, Zeke added, "If you're going to work here, we need to go over the rules."

"Okay." So it was a job? He thought he was just helping the guy out for the day.

"Rule one. Don't mess with my music. Got it?"

"Yep."

"Rule two. I like my workspace dirty. Makes me feel like I'm accomplishing something. No more cleaning up."

Not sure what he meant by that, Josh just nodded sharply and said, "Right."

"Rule three is . . . well, I forget what rule three is, but don't do it and we'll get along just fine."

"You got it. So what can I do to help?"

Zeke rubbed his chin. "Well, since you're the new guy, it seems fitting to send you over to the diner for more coffee and some donuts. Then we'll pull us a tranny."

Not bothering to mention he didn't drink coffee or eat donuts, Josh was happy to comply. A year ago, if you'd asked him where he saw himself, it was out of the FBI, but never in a dusty old mechanic's shop in a tiny town. He still wanted to get a counseling degree, but for now, this could work too.

After Meg sent off the paid reservation receipt to Mr. Randall and transferred his third of the weekly fee to her new business checking account, she drafted an e-mail alerting all of their existing clients about the new lodge. Just as she was about to hit "Send," her phone signaled she had a new e-mail. "Cross your fingers for me, Casey. I just got a response from my loan officer."

Casey stopped typing on her computer. "Well?"

Afraid to look, she drew a deep breath and tapped the screen. After she read through the e-mail twice, she let out the breath she held. "It's only half of what I asked for. She said it helped that I had over twenty thousand in my account—thank you, Josh—but that was all the loan committee would approve. She said I could come in this afternoon and sign the papers."

"That's great, Meg, but what about the other half?"

She settled in the guest chair in front of Casey's desk. "I was just getting ready to send an e-mail to all of our clients to drum up some pre-booking money. If I can get enough, I think I can just barely squeak by and have everything ready by September."

"That's risky." Casey's face turned all mama-is-not-happy. "If you spend their money in advance and then have delays and can't open on time, you're screwed. And our clients will be upset with *all* of us."

"I know. But it's the only way I can make this happen on my own. Please don't tell Dad what my plan is. Let's just let him think I got the full loan."

Casey opened her mouth to answer when a knock on her office door interrupted her. Thank goodness. Meg's plan wasn't the best one, but nothing better had come to mind.

Ryan stood in the doorway beside a frowning Ben.

Casey whispered, "We need to talk about this some more, Meg." Then she turned to their brothers. "Hey, guys. What's up?"

"We wanted to talk to Meg about something. Glad you're here too, Casey." Ryan flopped down onto a chair beside Meg as Ben sat on the edge of the desk.

This couldn't be good. She figured the parenting-by-committee thing would stop once she became a mother, but apparently not. "What's going on, Ry?"

"When Granger took my gun from you the other day, he left prints. So I ran them. I've been looking into his background."

"Dammit, Ryan! You promised you'd stop doing that to all my boyfriends." She turned to her sister and Ben. "And you two wonder why I never told anyone Josh's name?"

Casey ignored her and said, "What'd you find on him?"

"I'm sitting right here, you guys. Stop!"

Ryan turned to Casey. "His prints weren't in the database, but his background check is too sterile. It's like it's so clean and perfect, it's fake. Even *my* background report has more information than Granger's."

"Oh, so now it's a crime to have a perfect background check?" Meg stood to leave. "I'm outta here."

"Sit down and talk to us, Megan." The command in Ben's tone made her stop mid-stride. He'd *never* spoken to her like that. He was the one always on her side.

Taking her seat again, she said, "What?"

Ryan asked, "Has he told you where he's been for the last few years? There's virtually no banking activity except for regular deposits I can't trace. And what do you know about his past? How did you two meet?"

She gave them the CliffsNotes version of her and Josh's short relationship.

Ryan took a little pad of paper from his chest pocket. "What was the address of the condo and the name of the business he worked for?"

She told him, then asked, "Why are you guys doing this? Is it a crime to buy me a car? You're the ones who made him give me the money he won't take back."

Ryan flipped his notebook shut. "Yeah, see, that's what's weird. He has a boatload of cash in his bank accounts, but no assets except his truck. He doesn't own any real estate. Doesn't even rent a storage unit for his things that I can find. It just doesn't add up."

"I'm fairly sure accessing his private information without just cause is illegal, Ryan, so either turn yourself in or cut it out!"

Her brother shrugged a big shoulder. "We want to be sure Granger is who he says he is. Did you ever meet any of his friends or people he worked with?"

"Okay, that's it! I'm done. I have to fly to Denver and back this afternoon and then get a room ready for Josh, the apparent serial killer, all by five thirty. See you guys later."

Megan slammed the door closed behind her and replayed Ryan's last question in her mind. She hadn't met a single friend or co-worker of Josh's. If they went out with others, it had always been with her friends. Looking back, that *was* a little weird. She'd ask him about it when she saw him later.

———

Josh put his truck into park just as Megan's new car pulled up beside him. He grabbed the bags of groceries he'd picked up and got out.

When he spotted Meg in a red dress and matching sexy, tall heels freeing Haley from her car seat, he stopped dead in his tracks.

He needed to step up his game and figure out a way to show her that she could trust him again. He wanted to get back to the place they once were. Before he'd hurt her, they'd talked about getting married. But what more could he do?

Haley hopped out and ran toward him with a big smile. That she was happy to see him sent a wave of heat to his chest.

"Hi!" She held up a plastic bag. "Me and Grandma made you cookies."

Doubt rifle-packing Grams knew they were for him. "Thank you, Haley. We'll have them for dessert." He turned to Meg. "It's just spaghetti. You didn't have to get all dressed up for *me*."

She grabbed a duffel and a bottle of wine from the front seat. "It wasn't for you, pal. I had a meeting in Denver." She held up his favorite vintage. "I got my loan today so we're celebrating."

"Congratulations. But I'm still enjoying the dress and the wine, even if they weren't for me."

He couldn't take his eyes off Megan's curvy butt as she led the way to the front door of the large but forlorn cabin that begged for a coat of stain.

She tilted her chin over her shoulder, sending him a cute grin. "Well, look fast, because I'm not done fixing up your room, so I'm losing the dress and heels in about two seconds."

If Haley hadn't been walking beside him, he would have suggested all the fun ways he'd like to help her out of that dress. "Too bad for me. And why wasn't that door locked, Meg?"

"City boy." She rolled her eyes as she tucked the bottle of wine beneath his arm. "Haley will show you where the kitchen is. Be right back."

Haley smiled and led the way. The kitchen was about as vintage as Zeke's shop. Formica counters, avocado-green appliances, and peeling vinyl on the floor, plus an old wooden table in the corner filled with crayons and paper.

Hopefully the appliances still worked.

Haley laid her cookies on the table, then climbed onto a chair. "I'm gonna draw you a picture."

"That'd be great. Thanks."

He dug through the drawers, finally finding a corkscrew to open the wine so it could breathe. Then he started the sauce. It wouldn't be able to simmer as long as he'd like, but it was better than opening a jar and dumping it on top of noodles.

A light tap on his leg made him look down into a set of big brown eyes. "Now we have to put it on the fridge." Haley thrust the paper she'd been working on toward him.

"Wow. This is fantastic." He wasn't entirely sure what he was looking at.

He found a magnet shaped like an ear of corn with "Iowa" scrolled on the bottom, and attached the picture to the green refrigerator at Haley's eye level. Then he knelt beside her. "So, tell me about that." He pointed to the biggest of the three blobs.

Haley slipped her little arm around his neck and snuggled up to his side. "That's you. See? Yellow hair. Like me!" She pointed to the other blobs. "I'm the little one and Mommy is this one. A family."

A family.

Emotion clawed its way up his throat. That she'd accepted him so easily and drew him in the picture sent a pang to his chest.

He whispered, "Thank you, Haley. That's the best picture of a family I've ever seen."

Megan joined them again, wearing jeans, a tight T-shirt, and no shoes, and looking just as hot as she did in the dress. She plopped down beside them and laid a kiss on top of Haley's head. "Good job, sweetheart." Meg smiled at him. "Haley likes that you both have blond hair. All the Andersons are brunettes. She wanted to 'match' someone. She's very big on matching right now."

"Knucks for yellow hair, right, Haley?" He held out his fist for a bump.

Haley fist-bumped him and then ran back to the table. "I'm gonna make you another picture of us!"

"Can't wait to see it." He stood and held out his hand to help Meg up.

She glanced at his hand, but hesitated. Meg hated to appear weak or to need help. She finally relented and placed her hand in his.

She asked, "So, how was your day?"

He pulled her to her feet. "Zeke offered me a job. I didn't realize how much mechanical work there was to be had in such a small town." He poured out two glasses of wine and handed her one. "He even let me take his prized chopper out for a spin after I did some maintenance. I had fun today. It's just a bonus he's paying me."

"So, you're working for Zeke now?" Meg blinked at him. "And you know how to fly a helicopter too? Seriously. How is it that we didn't know that about each other?" She hopped up on the counter next to the stove.

"I didn't know that about you because you never talked about living here or about your family much. I got my license recently so

TAMRA BAUMANN

you wouldn't have known that about me." That was mostly true. He'd gotten a license under his real name right before he'd left the FBI. He'd been dying to take Zeke's chopper up and saw it as an opportunity to stop lying to her about one more thing.

He took a pull from his wineglass and then started on the salad. When he glanced at Meg she was frowning into her glass. "What?"

She laid her glass beside her on the counter without taking a sip. "Speaking of not knowing things about each other, why didn't you ever introduce me to any of your friends or people you worked with?"

Because he was undercover, in the middle of an investigation. They all knew him as Sam Coulter.

He forced his shoulders to remain relaxed and smiled as he worked on the salad. He'd tell her the truth. But not all of it. "Just when I'd make friends as a kid, they'd get adopted, or transferred somewhere else, so I've never been the type to need many. And you know how much I was working back then. I sort of drifted apart from the few friends I had. But the last thing I wanted to do was spend what little free time we had with my co-workers. I spent way too much time with them as it was."

"So it wasn't because you were embarrassed by me . . . or something?"

"No! I just preferred you to myself." He lifted a crouton to her lips. When she opened her mouth, he popped it in. "What brought all this on?"

She waved a hand. "Just something Ryan said. Never mind."

The suspicious sheriff who clearly didn't trust him. The FBI had doctored Sam Coulter's data, but no one except Megan and his handler knew Josh's real name. He'd have to ask Watts about that.

But first he needed to wipe the worried frown off Megan's face.

134

He moved between her legs and leaned close. "Congratulations on your loan. I'm happy for you." He laid his mouth on hers, taking his time, savoring her soft lips, teasing and nibbling until she moaned.

He leaned back and whispered, "That was nice, but I want more. I want what you promised me the other night in the bar."

Her eyes tilted Haley's way before she whispered, "I had too much to drink that night, so no fair holding me to any promises I might have made. And the jury's still out on whether I'm going to sleep with you."

He pulled her into a tight hug so she couldn't belt him. "I'm glad you're considering sleeping with me, but I was talking about your promise to hand over your old car. I need a part from it for another job. Then we'll shoot it up for fun."

"Why didn't you just say that? You are the sneakiest son of a—" He cut her off with another deep kiss.

Her whole body melted into his. If not for Haley, he would have thrown Meg over his shoulder and taken her to bed. Instead, he had to settle for ending their kiss and staring into her pretty blue eyes.

She stared right back. "I hate when you do that. Kiss me stupid, then trick me into saying stuff. But you'd never lie to me, would you, Josh? It's the one thing I can't abide."

He held her steady, searching gaze, hating the FBI, and himself even more, for every single lie he'd ever told her. "I'd rather cut my heart out than lie to you, Meg."

CHAPTER THIRTEEN

After their fantastic dinner—any dinner was fantastic if Meg didn't have to cook it—she turned back the bed-spread and fluffed the pillows on Josh's bed. The mattress was old and sagged a little, but it'd be replaced soon with the same ones they used at the hotel. She'd have to talk to Casey about going in on a larger order so they'd get better pricing.

She turned to go check on Haley and ran into Josh's hard chest. He backed her up until the mattress hit her legs. The next thing she knew she was on her back, pinned to the bed by his big, hard body.

He swiped away a piece of fallen hair from her forehead. "I'm here to convince the jury to vote in favor of forgiving me and giving me another chance."

All his weight should have made it hard to breathe, but it just felt good. Too good. She needed to keep her defenses up. "Where's Haley?"

"She asked if my phone could play movies like yours. We pulled up some Disney thing."

"She's sneaky, like you. Haley would watch movies twenty-four seven if I let her. She's only allowed a few hours a week."

"Okay. Now back to us?"

"It's complicated, Josh."

"I'm honestly sorry, Meg. For everything. Mostly for not being there for you and Haley. You're a great mom, but Haley needs a father too. And I plan to be a good one."

"Kids grow up with one parent all the time and turn out just fine. I did." She stared into his eyes. "Saying you're sorry doesn't make the pain magically disappear and make everything all better. How can I be sure you won't hurt us again?"

He cringed. "I know trust doesn't come easily for you. I didn't help by leaving like that. You and Haley are the best thing that's ever happened to me. I swear I'll never leave you guys again."

She closed her eyes. The sadness in his gaze pierced her heart. She hated how much she missed his touch, missed sharing simple meals, and just . . . being with him. She'd never had such an easy relationship with anyone else. But she couldn't bear it if he left again. Couldn't bear it if he hurt Haley. "So I should just take you at your word, Josh? Just hand over my and Haley's hearts so you can crush them again?"

He sighed. "You need more time for me to prove to you I'm sticking. And that's fine. I can be as patient as necessary. But when I pushed you away, I never stopped loving you, Meg." He tucked his face next to hers and laid a soft kiss on her cheek. "It was nice tonight. Being with you and Haley. Like the family in Haley's picture."

The lonely pain in his words made her eyes sting with tears. How could a man with so few friends and who grew up without parents be so sweet? He should be bitter and cold.

When they'd broken up, he kept telling her it was him, and not her. He wasn't good enough for her. He didn't know how to be a parent or be part of a family. She should find someone who could be a good husband to her because he was afraid he couldn't and she deserved the best. Those all sounded like standard breakup lines to her at the time. Coward's words.

Now, she wanted to believe he'd meant them.

She ached to sleep with him, to feel that connection to him like she'd never felt with any other man, but for the moment she'd be content to lie quietly under him, happy to feel his heart beat slowly against her indecisive one.

She ran her hand through his soft hair and whispered, "You'll be the first to know when the verdict finally comes in."

The front door opened and a deep voice called out, "Anyone home?"

Haley let out a yelp. "Hi, Uncle Ryan!"

"Dammit." Meg poked Josh in the ribs to make him move. "Ryan is being a big . . . brother again."

Josh slowly rolled off the bed and scooped her up with him, plopping her onto her feet. "What does that mean?"

"I'll tell you later. Let's go before he barges in here with his gun drawn."

When they hit the living room, Meg grabbed Ryan's arm and yanked him straight out the front door with her. Hands on hips, she said, "Cut. It. Out! He's Haley's father, for God's sake!"

"What? It's my day off tomorrow. I was just going to offer to help you around here." Ryan tucked his hands into his jeans pockets and at least had the decency to look guilty.

Meg glanced over her shoulder. Josh stood just inside the door, ready to come to her rescue if necessary. She turned back to Ryan and lowered her voice. "Let me guess. You want to help me, then when I'm not looking, go through all of Josh's things for clues, right?"

"Yep." He smiled. "But I'll help with the dock too."

"I'm not letting you search his room. And as much as I could use a hand, Dad said you guys couldn't help me. You don't need him mad at you too."

"Dad said we couldn't loan you money. I'll be here at eight."
His fist landed a light tap to her shoulder. "Just looking out for
you, Meggy."

His quiet show of support made her anger dissipate by the
time he started his truck and backed out of the drive. Sometimes
her brothers and sister could get on her last nerve, but at least she
had family who loved her.

Unlike Josh. Who had no one.

The next morning, hammer in her hand, Meg wiped the sweat
from her brow with her arm as she and Ryan worked on her new
dock. Reaching inside the pouch at her waist, she grabbed another
nail and then pounded it into the decking. The ache in her back
and the growl of her stomach made Meg tug the phone from her
pocket to check the time. Almost noon. They'd made some serious
progress, so she owed her brother a good lunch. She could probably pull something together inside, but it'd be so much easier to
pick something up from Aunt Gloria's diner. "I'll go get us some
subs. Be right back."

Ryan nodded and went back to hammering. She jogged into
the house to get her car keys and spotted the little note Josh had
left for her that morning. "Coffee's on and lots of healthy stuff for
snacks in the fridge. Quit scowling at the healthy part and have a
nice day." Reading it again made her smile. He did know her better than she'd thought.

That he had fresh coffee waiting for her and Ryan when he
didn't even drink it was pretty great too. Maybe she'd pick up a
sandwich for Josh while she was at it and drop it by the shop on
her way back.

After she'd circled to the other side of the lake and checked on Haley and Grandma, who were eating their lunch too, she walked into the blessedly cool diner.

Her father sat at the counter. If she hadn't been starving to death, she might have turned right around to avoid him, but hunger won out. She sat on the stool next to him. "Hey, Dad. How are you feeling? Sue Ann said you had another headache the other night?"

"It was nothin'." Her father took a bite of his sandwich. Probably so he wouldn't have to talk.

Fine by her.

Thankfully Gloria strolled over and sent her a warm smile. "How are you today, sweetheart?" She slid a cold Dr Pepper in front of Meg.

"Starving! Can I get two meatball subs with fries, a turkey-and-avocado sandwich with mustard, no mayo, and a fruit cup all to go?" She took a long drink of her soda and sighed. "Thanks. That hit the spot."

"You're welcome." Gloria tucked a pencil into her beehive. "Funny. A turkey sandwich with a fruit cup on the side is just what Zeke's new employee ordered for lunch yesterday." She winked and walked away to place the order.

Her dad grunted and took another bite of his pot roast sandwich.

When she reached out to take another drink, her father snatched her arm to stop her. "Where did you get that ring?"

She'd forgotten she still had it on. "I found it in the attic. It was Mom's."

"I'm aware of that." He swung around to face her. "I thought all of that had been destroyed. What else did you find?"

His anger made no sense. But then, the man never made any sense to her. "Just stuff. Like her diploma, report cards, things like that. Why?"

His jaw clenched. "Nothing else?"

There were those files at the bottom. Maybe she'd just keep that little fact to herself. "Just the usual. Why would you want to destroy all of Mom's things?"

He shook his head and then turned back to his sandwich. "Heard you signed on a loan yesterday."

Dead end, as always, when it came to discussing her mother. "Yeah. I can get started on the big stuff now."

Dad just nodded as he chewed.

Luckily, Gloria reappeared with three white bags. "Here you go. On the house until you get your lodge done. In return, you and I are going to work out an arrangement for feeding your new guests here sometimes." Gloria sent Dad a smug, in-your-face grin.

Meg snatched up the bags before her dad could protest and leaned over the counter to give her aunt a kiss on the cheek. "Thanks. You're awesome!" Meg dashed for the door, and then hopped into her nice new car.

God, she loved Aunt Gloria.

Next, she pulled up in front of Zeke's shop. What was Amber's Mercedes doing parked out front? Maybe visiting her uncle. But Josh mentioned Zeke was going to be gone most of the day getting parts.

With a sick, familiar feeling from their high school days brewing, Meg hopped out of her car, forgetting all about Josh's lunch.

As she passed through the doors, she pulled up short. Amber had her hand on Josh's chest, smiling up at him.

Haley wasn't with her this time and she'd had about all she was going to take from that man-stealer. Just as she was about to go all crazy woman on Amber, Josh took a step back and raised his palms. "Nothing is going to happen between you and me, Amber. Ever."

Amber smiled slyly. "You're a man. You'll give in eventually. See you around." Then she turned and spotted Meg.

Plastering on a smug grin, she said, "Whoops."

Josh turned and cringed. "This isn't what you're thinking, Meg."

"I was just thinking I kinda liked the way you shut Amber down." With adrenaline still pumping hot through her veins, she closed the distance between her and Josh. She grabbed his face and kissed him. Hard. Amber could just eat her heart out.

When Josh wound his big arms around her and kissed her back with equal intensity, Meg got pulled so deeply under his spell, she almost forgot Amber was there. God, she really missed kissing Josh.

After they finally came up for air, she turned to Amber. "Run along and *maybe* I won't tell Randy about this."

"Nothing to tell. Besides, it'd be my word against yours. And we all know what your word is worth in this town, Meg. Have a nice day, Josh." She added a little extra hip action as she strolled out the door.

After she was gone, Meg said, "Hi. I brought you some lunch."

"Really?" He beamed a big smile that made her knees go a little weak. Well, okay. A lot weak. That he had on a tight T-shirt that highlighted his big muscles, worn but nicely fitting jeans, and work boots didn't help.

Yum.

She took his hand, tugged him to her car, and grabbed a to-go bag.

"Thank you." He frowned as he read the writing on the outside. "Meatball sub and fries? I guess you're still mad at me, then?"

She snatched the bag back and swapped it out for the other. "Those are for me and Ryan. We're doing hard labor today, so we earned them. This boring one is for you and your healthy arteries."

Josh peered into the sack and then slapped a hand over his heart. "You got me a fruit cup on the side? Does this mean you love me again?"

"It means thanks for the coffee this morning. Gotta go."

As she slid behind her steering wheel, he called out, "I don't know. Nothing says love like a fruit cup, Meg."

She sent him an exaggerated eye-roll, but smiled all the way back to the house.

As she and Ryan devoured their subs in silence at the kitchen table, Meg broke it by saying, "I ran into Dad at the diner."

Ryan raised a brow in a "go on" kind of way as he chewed.

"He noticed my ring." She held up her hand. "It was Mom's. When I told him I found it in the attic, he got all bent out of shape. I've been meaning to tell you guys about the box of her things I found."

"What kind of things?"

"You sound just like Dad. Normal high school things. Except for a couple of files I haven't looked at yet."

"Files?" Ryan's sub stopped halfway to his lips. "What kind of files?"

"Legal-size official ones. They're up in the attic. I can go get them after we finish if you'd like."

Ryan dropped his half-eaten sub and started for the attic. Still starving and reluctant to put her sandwich down, she sighed and followed him up the stairs. "What's going on, Ry?"

"Probably nothing. Where are they?"

She pointed out the box. He sat down and tore the lid off, then dug the files out. Slapping the first one open, his face hardened like granite. He scanned the second one and said, "Dammit. He promised me no one would ever find these."

"Who promised you?" She sat beside him and reached for the file, but he held it out of reach.

"Uncle Ray. You don't want to see these, Meg. Nothing good can come of it."

That made her want to see what was in there even more. Especially because Uncle Ray was the former sheriff. Waggling her fingers at Ryan, she said, "Technically, this is my house. Everything in it belongs to me, and you know it, lawman. Hand it over."

Ryan took out his phone and hit a button. After a few seconds, he said, "Mom's missing files were in Meg's attic. You need to be here. Tell Ben too." He hung up and slid the phone back into his pocket.

What the heck? "If you're trying to freak me out, it's working. What's going on, Ryan? How bad can it be?"

"Bad. Can we wait for Casey, please?"

"No! Tell me."

He closed his eyes and pinched the bridge of his nose between his fingers. "Because no one would ever talk about it, as soon as Uncle Ray retired and I became the sheriff, I looked into Mom's car accident."

"And? For once would you please just string a few sentences together and spare me the misery of extracting them from you?"

"Uncle Ray and the others covered up the details of the accident because Mom wasn't alone that day her car slid off the road. You were in the car too, along with another person. You were the only one who survived."

"Oh. So I was in a car wreck with Mom when she died? Why would that be such a big secret?"

"Because . . ." Ryan licked his lips, obviously struggling to say more. "Your father was in the car too."

"What?" That made no sense. But Ryan had said *your* father. They didn't have the same father? How could that be? "So . . . Dad isn't my father? Then who is?"

Her heart pounded as Ryan slowly handed her the files. What the hell was going on? How could this happen? Possibilities buzzed like a hornet's nest in her confused brain.

Ryan said, "The second one has the results from the paternity test. Mom's parents tried to take you away from Dad, but he wouldn't let them. There was a court battle, but Dad had so many inside connections, Grandma and Grandpa finally gave up. I think that's why they left the house to you. Probably because they didn't know if Dad would leave you anything like the rest of us."

So her brothers and sister, the people she loved most in the world, were just half siblings? And her father wasn't her father?

She started to open the file, but stopped. She looked up at Ryan, and her aching heart nearly burst out of her chest. Maybe she didn't want to know? Maybe if she never opened the file, things would just stay the same? "I'm afraid . . ."

Ryan moved closer and threw his arm around her shoulder, drawing her against his side. "It's just DNA. Family is about who cares for you."

Nodding, her eyes burned with tears as she slowly opened the file. She read the paternity results over and over until it finally sank in. How could it be true? She wasn't who she thought she was at all. And how could everyone have lied to her like that?

She wasn't an Anderson.

She looked up at Ryan for confirmation. "I'm a Grant? I'm Buddy Grant's daughter?"

When Ryan nodded, Meg's stomach lurched.

That made her Amber's half sister.

CHAPTER Fourteen

Visibly uncomfortable with Meg's tears, Ryan had snuck out to work on the dock. Ben was in Denver checking on patients. When Casey walked into the kitchen, Meg tried to hold it together but failed. The dam burst.

"I'm sorry, Meg." Casey held Meg in a tight hug.

Torn between betrayal and absolute love for her sister, she held on tight. "How could all of you lie to me like that? Does everyone in town know but me?"

"No, only a few people outside the family know, but others may have suspected. It was a long time ago, no one even thinks about it anymore. Keeping it from you seemed the kindest thing to do."

"To think that Amber is as much a sister to me as you are makes me sick to my stomach."

"Okay, now you're just pissing me off." Casey squeezed tighter and whispered, "It makes no difference. We're family. That's all that counts."

Meg accepted the tissue that magically appeared and blew her nose. After a few more minutes of embarrassing blubbering, Meg pulled it together. "Do you think Amber knows?"

"She found out when you guys were in high school."

"She talked to you about it and not me?"

Casey crossed to the sink to pour a glass of water while she stalled. Meg didn't think her sister was going to answer the question, but as Casey handed over the glass she said, "I'd cornered her to let her know how I felt about her sleeping with Randy and breaking you guys up. We exchanged a few . . . choice words. Eventually she admitted her mother had just told her the truth, so she stole Randy from you out of revenge."

The vision of her sister going after Amber on her behalf would have made her smile any other day. "But that doesn't make any sense. What do I have to do with what our mom did with Amber's father?"

"Amber was hurting and wanted you to hurt too."

"It's weird Amber never brought it up in all of our fights over the years."

"The affair, your father's death, and having to see you around town destroyed Amber's mother. She was never the same person after that. Amber knew it'd embarrass her mother even further if everyone knew."

"But now that I know her kids are my niece and nephew and Haley's cousins, I should probably talk to her about it. God, this sucks!"

Casey leaned against the kitchen counter and crossed her arms. "No one has to know you know. Including Dad."

Her father, who wasn't her father. What was she going to say to him when she saw him next? "Ryan said Dad fought Grandma and Grandpa to keep me. Why would he do that? He doesn't even like me."

Casey shrugged a shoulder. "Who knows with Dad? But he honestly loved Mom. He turned into a different person after she died." Casey shook her head. "Do you have any idea how much you look and sound like Mom? Even some of your mannerisms are similar to hers. I think you remind him too much of her, and it's painful for him to be around you sometimes."

Yeah, well, you'd think he'd have gotten over it by now.

She recalled the picture Haley found in the attic. Even her own daughter had mistaken Meg for her mother. "I wish I'd never found those files. I'm not sure what to do, Casey." She slumped onto a kitchen chair.

"Take some time and think it through. Ryan and Ben won't say anything." Casey crossed the kitchen and laid a kiss on the top of Meg's head. "It's up to you, but it can just be our secret."

People keeping secrets is what got her into the mess she was in now. In a blink of an eye, her whole identity had changed. She had an entire new half family. And Grandma wasn't really her grandmother. Aunt Gloria and Uncle Brewster weren't her family either. She'd been an orphan since the accident and didn't even know it.

But what killed her were the lies. Her whole freakin' life. Being honest was the only thing that felt right.

No. One thing felt right. That Zeke was her great uncle. That, she liked. A lot.

Her sister whispered, "We're still family, Meg. Nothing's changed because you found those files." Casey sat down in a chair across from Meg and took her hand. "Why don't I pick Haley up from Grandma's so you have some time to work through this? I'll keep her all night, if you like."

"Yeah. That might be good. I'll call and check on you guys later."

"Okay, if you're sure you'll be all right? Do you want me to tell Grandma you know?"

"Yeah, you can tell her." Meg sighed. "God, I hate this. It's a little like waking up in an alternate universe. Same players, but you don't really know anyone as well as you thought."

Later that afternoon, after Ryan and Casey left, Meg sat at the end of her new dock. Still numb from the paternity news, she let her feet dangle over the Jet Ski tied below while she processed her new identity. The importance of setting a good example because she was an Anderson had been drilled into her from the moment she could walk. Something she'd often deliberately failed at to get a reaction from her father. To prove he knew she existed. Nothing irritated him more than breaking one of the Anderson family rules.

Andersons didn't skip church. Andersons got good grades, paid their bills on time, volunteered for causes, and raised money for charities all because it was the right thing to do. They went to college and studied what Dad chose, resort management with a minor in computer science, not architecture like Meg had wanted. He'd only pay for a degree that would benefit their town. It was the Andersons' duty to serve the town named after them so it could continue to thrive and be prosperous.

Well, there was evidently one more thing Andersons were damned good at. Keeping huge secrets from her—the one about her being a Grant.

She would never in a million years have seen that one coming. All those times she'd tried so hard to get her father to love her, to at least like her, were a big waste. He had little regard for Grants and it explained his lack of regard for her too.

Josh's voice drifted out from the open kitchen window. "Anyone home?"

Her voice was croaky from crying and her eyes were probably swollen and red. She hated that he'd see her like that. But she wanted to talk to him.

She cleared her throat and called out, "I'm outside."

After a few moments, heavy footsteps from Josh's boots rang

out as he approached from behind. "Hey there." He sat down next to her and drew a deep breath as he gazed out over the lake. "I love the way it smells here. I'll never get tired of it. Where's Haley?"

"Spending the night with my sister."

He tore his eyes from the water and inspected the wood beneath him. "The dock looks great. You and Ryan busted some butt today."

She finally turned and faced him. "Ryan more than me."

"You've been crying. What's wrong?"

"Turns out I've been lied to. For a very long time."

"Lied to?" Josh swallowed hard, suddenly looking as uncomfortable as she felt. "What do you mean?"

The concern in his eyes made her slowly turn her attention back to the lake. She didn't want to start crying again. "Seems my brothers and sister are half siblings. I have a different father."

After she told him about the files, he pulled her onto his lap and held her against his chest. Then he ran a big hand slowly up and down her arm in the familiar way he used to when they'd sit and watch television, or whenever they sat next to each other. "So you're an orphan too, but one with a big family. And there are lots of people in town who think of you as their own. Zeke and Gloria, to name a few. You saw the way everyone at the bar happily missed at darts the other night."

She nodded and laid her head against his shoulder. Josh's embrace used to always make her feel better after a bad day. "Well, they were mostly Andersons. But that *was* really nice of them."

She snuggled closer and closed her eyes. Warm memories flowed through her of the time before he'd left, when she'd felt completely happy and content being with him.

He laid a soft kiss on the top of her head. "Maybe if you talked to your father—"

"I don't know what I'd even say to him right now. I can't

believe everyone I know has lied to me my whole life." She sat up and turned to straddle him so she could lay a kiss on his lips. "Except for you. Thanks for that."

She circled her arms around his waist and tucked her face into the crook of his neck. Mostly, she missed the way he used to hold her after they made love, making her feel like she was the only woman on earth. Like she mattered more than anything else to him.

He tilted her chin with his knuckle so she had to look him in the eye. "Sometimes a lie can be for someone's own good." He laid a gentle, lingering kiss on her lips that made her want to sigh.

When Josh ended his sweet kiss, she leaned back and forced a smile. "I know. But it still hurts."

He nodded and wrapped her up tightly in his arms.

After snuggling with him for a few minutes, her hands wandered under his T-shirt. She ran her palms against the hard ridges on his back while pressing her body closer to his. He had the best physique, all steely muscle covered by soft skin. She wasn't quite ready to trust him again, but God, she wanted to feel that connection they used to have when they made love. What would it hurt?

She nibbled on his neck, then made her way up to his earlobe and gave a gentle bite.

Josh let out a groan that rumbled against her chest, still plastered so tightly against his. Because she was sitting on his lap, she could feel how much he wanted her too. She'd just be clear on the ground rules so there wouldn't be any misunderstandings . . . after.

She whispered, "I want you to take me to bed, Josh. But it doesn't mean I've forgiven you all the way. I just really miss being with you." She had to keep up her defenses until she was sure about him again.

"You don't mean that—"

"Yes, I do." She hoped with all her soul she could do this. Just have casual sex, and not engage her heart any further.

"Meg, the timing's not—"

She stood and pulled off her T-shirt. "Here? Or inside?"

She gave him points for his obvious struggle to keep his focus on her face and not her chest, barely covered by scanty pink scraps of material.

"Meg, don't. You'll hate me afterward for taking advantage of the situation."

She unbuttoned her jean shorts and let them pool around her feet. "It'll be no-strings-attached sex. Isn't that what every man dreams of?" Why wasn't he sweeping her off her feet and hauling her to bed like he used to do at the slightest provocation?

"Not with a woman who's just had her life turned upside down."

She slapped her hands on her hips, feeling rejected by him all over again.

Standing before him in her underwear, humiliated but pretending not to care, she said, "You don't want to have sex with me? Your loss, pal. Maybe Toby will be interested." She turned and retreated as fast as she could toward the house in her matching pink bra and panties, drowning in embarrassment.

"Dammit, Meg." Josh's footsteps followed behind her. When he caught up he said, "I want to make love to you, but not like this. I want it to *mean* something."

She couldn't let it mean anything, couldn't let him in all the way so he could hurt her again. She just wanted to be close to him for a few minutes. Was that too much to ask?

When they reached the bedroom, she turned around and said, "What it'll mean is that it's been a helluva long time since I've had sex, so I'm overdue. That's enough of a reason for me." Wait. That hadn't come out right.

She was just about to correct herself when his jaw clenched, and Meg suddenly realized the seriousness of her mistake.

Moving toe to toe with her, he towered over her and barked, "So I'm little more than a convenience for you? I have sex with you, then instead of leaving money on the nightstand, you just take it off my rent? No thanks!"

Anger flashed in his eyes.

Startled by the intensity of his outburst and feeling like a jerk, she whispered, "I've never seen you this mad, Josh." She reached out to lay a hand on his arm, intending to soothe and apologize, but he jerked it away.

"Damn straight. You want Toby? Go for it!"

He turned and headed for the kitchen, grabbing his keys off the kitchen counter on his way out.

She followed behind. "I'm sorry, Josh. I shouldn't have said that about Toby. I was upset. I didn't mean it."

He spun around and faced her. "You need to figure out what you want from me, Meg, because I won't be THAT GUY you just use for sex!"

She hadn't meant it like that; she had feelings for him. She wasn't the type to just sleep with any convenient guy.

Before she could figure out what to say to make things right, he beeped the locks on his truck, got in, and tore out of her driveway.

And maybe out of her life. But this time it was she who'd pushed him away.

Way to go, Muck.

Not sure where he'd go, Josh started his truck and took off.

He'd been patient, hadn't he? Making it clear he wanted more than just sex from her, but maybe Meg wasn't ever going to wake up and realize how much he loved her. Maybe the woman wasn't capable of forgiveness and trust. Look at the example her father, or whoever he was to her, had set for her.

As he hit the highway, he let out a long, slow breath. No. That wasn't fair. What did he know about parents and setting examples? Hell, what did he know about relationships? Meg was the only woman he'd ever had a real one with, and he'd screwed that up good.

He needed to look at it from her perspective. It was his fault she didn't trust him. He'd just up and left her. Then stayed away for three years, without sending a dime to help raise Haley. He was probably expecting too much, too soon. Maybe when he could tell her the truth they could start over.

But he hoped to God she hadn't been serious about sleeping with frickin' Toby!

After hours of aimless driving, he was so tired all he wanted was to flop face-first into bed. But overwhelming concern made him aim his truck down Meg's grandmother's driveway. He parked next to Meg's car and got out. She'd had a crappy day and their argument couldn't have helped.

He'd probably get shot again if he wasn't careful, but he needed to be sure she was all right.

After softly closing his truck's door, he tested the handle on the guesthouse. It was locked, for a change. He got some tools from his truck, quickly picked the lock, then stepped inside. Walking toward the open door to the bedroom, he pulled up short. A sliver of moonlight shining through the mostly closed curtain showed the bed was made and empty. Haley was spending the night with Casey, so had Megan decided to spend the night with Toby after all?

A whole new wave of anger surged through him. Not caring if Grandma heard him, he slammed the front door, and then his truck's door, before peeling out of the driveway.

He'd been willing to grovel, do whatever it took, but he drew the line at Meg sleeping with other men. If she wanted Toby then she could just damn well have him.

Whatever.

Hope she had a good time.

Not bothering to keep his speed in check, he circled the lake and then pulled into the driveway of the lodge.

He got out, cursed the unlocked front door, then stepped inside the darkened home. Not bothering to turn on the lights, he went into the kitchen and yanked the refrigerator door open. He needed a damn beer. Or three.

He grabbed a bottle, twisted the top off, and drank half of it in one pull before heading for the living room to watch ESPN. Hopefully box scores would remove the image of Meg and Toby going at it that was etched on his brain.

A small lamp in the living room cast its glow on Meg, curled up in a tight ball on the couch. She'd fallen asleep still clutching a candy wrapper in her hand. A pile of tinfoil on the coffee table next to her head indicated she'd been there for a while. When upset, chocolate was her go-to cure.

Her bare legs peeked out from beneath one of his T-shirts. Why her wearing his shirts was sexier to him than any of her fancy underwear was a mystery he'd yet to solve.

She must've been trying to wait up for him like she used to do whenever they needed to talk.

Relieved she hadn't slept with Toby, Josh put his beer bottle on the coffee table, switched off the lamp, and lifted her into his arms. He'd let her have his bed and he'd sleep on one of the twin beds down the hall.

Her eyes slowly blinked open. "Hi. Are you still mad?"

He nodded as he carried her toward the bedroom. That she'd asked him to be nothing more than an end to her sexual drought still pissed the shit out of him.

"I'm sorry, Josh." She laid her hand on his cheek. "I thought you didn't want me so I was embarrassed. I'd never just use you, because I care about you."

"Okay." He pulled the covers back and tucked her in much like he'd done with Haley the other day. "Night, Meg."

He turned to leave, but she grabbed his hand and tugged until he sat on the bed beside her. The last thing he wanted to do was stay and discuss his damn feelings. Telling her that wouldn't do any good. She'd say her piece anyway.

"In the past when I've annoyed you, you'd grumble and maybe even growl at me, but you've never yelled at me. My father has yelled at me my whole life and I hate it. That you never did was one of the things I used to love about being with you."

He'd been trained to hold his temper, especially under duress. It was the one time he'd failed. "I shouldn't have done that."

"I'm glad you did. You're so even-keeled I sometimes forget you can be hurt too."

"You agreed to give me a second chance, Meg. That can't include other men."

"I haven't been with anyone else since you, Josh. So we're good there." She squeezed his hand. "After you left earlier, I realized what I really needed from you was . . ." She stared into his eyes for a moment, then looked away. "Never mind. It's late."

No one else since him?

Slowly tilting her chin so she had no choice but to look into his eyes, he said, "What do you need, Meg?"

She bit her bottom lip, blinking back tears.

Meg wasn't a crier. Her almost-tears destroyed him.

She finally whispered, "Would you hold me? Just until I fall asleep?"

That's what she'd struggled to ask for? He'd thought she was about to ask for his left kidney. His anger with her totally vaporized. "Absolutely."

He stripped to his boxers, then slipped beside her and pulled her against his chest. "Will you do something for me now?"

"Depends. You're sneaky." She snuggled closer. "I'm not agreeing to anything in advance."

"I want a date this weekend. A real one. Just me and you."

"Can't. I already have plans. Friday, Pam's hosting a girls' night. And Saturday is the annual Anderson Butte Founder's Day celebration. All Andersons are required to attend."

He waited to see if she'd connect the dots, but wasn't going to do it for her.

She sighed. "Oh. That's right. I'm not an Anderson, am I?" Meg turned in his arms and faced him. "But I guess I always will be, on paper. I'd like it if you went with me and Haley." She laid a quick kiss on his lips. "I don't usually put out on the first date, but I might make an exception in your case."

"Does that mean you're willing to give me a real chance now?"

"I've been thinking about that all night. Of all the men who have hurt me . . . you wield the sharpest blade, Josh."

He rolled on top of her to drive his point home, and stared into her pretty eyes. "That I yelled at you shows your blade isn't a dull one either. But for me, I know it's because I love you, Meg."

She closed her eyes and huffed out a breath. "Even though I'm probably going to regret this, I'll try. To forgive you and have a relationship. But you should know that my grandmother will shoot you dead if you hurt me again."

No doubt she would. A few others in town might too. "Not going to be a problem." She'd understand why he had to lie to her when the truth came out. He hoped.

"We'll see." She gave him a squeeze. "Night."

"Night." He flipped their positions and tucked her head under his chin. How he was going to keep things G-rated with her hot body so near his all night he didn't know, but he'd finally gotten a real commitment from her.

A big step in the right direction.

———————

Meg blinked her eyes open, spotting a steaming mug of coffee on the nightstand. But the sound of the shower running a few feet away was more tempting than even her beloved first hit of caffeine in the morning. Josh was naked and wet in there.

When she'd woken a few times in the night, Josh's arms had still been wound around her.

Because Josh was pretty much a twenty-minute-cuddle kind of guy, she'd only asked him to stay until she fell asleep, never expecting him to hold her all night long. Her heart glowed warmly at that, but her body ached for him.

She opened the nightstand drawer, hoping Josh had thought ahead and bought condoms. When she spotted a mighty Trojan warrior she smiled and scooped up a package. Reconsidering, she grabbed two.

After throwing the covers back, she drew Josh's big T-shirt over her head and then slipped out of her panties. The shower was a small one, but they'd make it work. Josh had always been inventive in tight spaces.

Just the side of Josh's head was visible above the shower door, but the outline of his big, muscular body through the frosted glass sent heat pooling between her legs. His head swiveled in her direction just as she pulled the door open and slipped between him and the stream of water.

When the arctic spray hit her back, it stole the air from her seizing lungs. "What . . . the . . . ?" She turned around and reached for the hot water handle. It was completely off, so she turned it up all the way, unable to draw a full breath until the water warmed. She tossed the condoms in the soap dish, then faced him again, annoyed by his big smirk. "Jeez, you could've warned me!"

"It was more fun this way." Still chuckling, he drew her against his hard, wet, freezing chest, sending a chill racing up her spine. It was probably how Bella felt when Edward the vampire held her in that movie. Although Edward didn't have all of Josh's big, sexy muscles.

When his cold skin hardened her nipples, Josh groaned. "You being here is defeating the purpose of my cold shower."

"That was the plan." As her mouth found his, she pressed her needy, aching breasts harder against his chest and slipped her arms around him. Her hands moved lower and found his perfect ass, giving it a soft squeeze. God, she'd missed his fantastic body.

Josh's eyes darkened as he pressed her against the cool, lime-green tile at her back. The desire in his gaze as he checked out her body from head to toe set her on fire. He palmed both of her breasts and grinned naughtily.

The steam billowed around them as he lowered his mouth to her chest, sucking and teasing her nipples. When he bit lightly, it sent a jolt straight to her core. Multiple orgasms looked promising. She was already almost there.

Her knees grew weaker with each hot stroke of his tongue. "Josh, I . . ." When his lips moved to her earlobe and nibbled, she forgot what she wanted to say.

His hand slid between her legs and stars appeared before her eyes.

Three years was a long time, dammit. She grabbed his face and kissed him. Hard.

His tongue danced with hers as he pressed her against the

shower wall again. He lifted her legs to his waist as his kisses grew deeper, firmer, and needier.

Any second now he'd put her out of her misery. She wanted to tell him to hurry up about it, but didn't want to stop kissing him long enough to do it. Her whole body was on fire, ready to explode.

At first she thought the buzzing in her ears was caused by the molten blood pounding through her veins, but then it became a voice. Her sister called out from the hallway just outside the master bedroom. "Meg? Where are you? Haley needs you."

The cold water earlier couldn't have squelched her inner fire faster than hearing that.

Seriously? Now?

Dammit!

She called out, "In the shower. Be right there." She pressed her forehead against Josh's and sighed. "I'm sorry."

"Go." He pushed the door open for her, then cranked the hot water off again.

She dried off, wrapped her hair up in the towel, and slipped into her clothes from the day before. While still pulling her T-shirt down, she made her way to the kitchen. When Haley saw her, tears filled her baby's little brown eyes.

Guilt stabbed Meg in the heart for her frustration at being interrupted. Even if it was only for a second. "What's wrong, Bug?"

"It was dark. I got scared." Haley struggled to fill her lungs with air as Casey put her down. "I couldn't find you."

Casey winced. "I left the blackout curtains drawn. She was so sound asleep, I didn't want to wake her. When I went back to check on her a few minutes later she was crying and upset. I'm sorry."

Meg scooped Haley up and forced a smile. It was hard to tell if the crying was making it hard to breathe or if she was having an asthma attack. Stress could trigger them. "Everything's fine now, baby. Did you take your medicine?"

When Haley shook her head, Casey said, "She wanted you to give it to her. I brought it along."

Haley had to eat before she took her meds, so Meg yanked the refrigerator door open and dug through all the food Josh had thankfully added. While she looked, Josh, who'd arrived a few seconds earlier but hadn't said anything, came up behind her and took Haley from her arms. "There's oatmeal in the cupboard, Meg."

After he nodded a greeting at Casey, who couldn't have possibly missed that they'd both come from the master bedroom with wet hair, he set Haley on the countertop. "I had asthma when I was your age too. Know what I used to do when I'd get scared and had a hard time breathing?"

Haley shook her head as she panted for air.

"I used to take care of lots of animals on the ranch where I grew up, but I had a favorite one named Charlie. All I had to do was close my eyes and think of him. It helped me breathe better."

"Was Charlie your doggy?"

"Nope. He's a horse, and he still lives on the ranch. He was just a colt, a baby, when he came to stay with us."

Haley's eyes grew wide. "You had a baby horse?"

Josh fished his phone from his jeans pocket. "He isn't mine, he belongs to someone at the ranch. But he was my best friend while I lived there. Want to see some pictures?"

When a smile lit Haley's face as she leaned closer to see Josh's phone, Meg's shoulders relaxed. It was just the crying making it hard for Haley to breathe. She was fine now.

Casey found a little plastic jar of honey shaped like a bear to sweeten the oatmeal and handed it to Meg as they waited for Haley's breakfast to heat in the ancient microwave. Casey whispered, "Granger carries pictures of a horse in his phone? Never would've guessed that one."

It was sweet that Josh carried pictures of Charlie in his phone, and at the same time sad that Josh's best friend had been a horse. Meg whispered back, "Me either. Now I'm curious to see what other pictures are in there."

"While you're at it, you should delete the one he probably took a few minutes ago of you, naked, in the shower. Wouldn't want it to end up on the Internet one day . . . ho!"

Meg laughed as she shot an elbow into Casey's ribs. Keeping her voice to a whisper, she said, "You're still the bigger ho. We didn't get to finish."

Casey pulled Meg close. "Maybe that's a good thing. Ryan is worried. You need to be careful."

She was worried too. Not that Josh was anything but what he said, but that she'd handed her heart over to a man she still feared would hurt her again.

When the microwave beeped, Meg got Haley's breakfast ready. Josh sat her in front of it at the table.

Haley happily dug in, and then with her mouth full said, "I'm gonna ask Santa for a horse, or a doggy. Then I can breathe better like you, Daddy."

Josh's mouth tilted into a big grin. Probably because it was the first time she'd ever called him Daddy. "Good idea, Haley."

What? No!

As her traitorous sister chuckled, Meg opened her mouth to do damage control, but Josh was quicker. He laid his mouth on hers and kissed her.

When she didn't have enough working brain cells to tell him he was in trouble, he leaned back and shot her a cute smile. "Gotta go. Have a nice day, ladies." Then he strolled out the door.

She'd have to set him straight later on the dog thing. Preferably when he and his sexy mouth were far across the room.

CHAPTER FIFTEEN

*J*osh and Zeke, working side by side to classic rock because it was Josh's day to pick the music, stripped the salvageable parts from Meg's old car. There weren't many to choose from.

A chime sounded from his back pocket. Josh wiped his hands on a rag before pulling out his cell. The text was from his former handler, Watts. Heads up. Someone's coming to look into that matter. Suggestions on times?

The cryptic message referred to the reason Josh couldn't tell Meg about his past as an agent yet. While the mobsters behind the online gambling ring had either killed one another or were behind bars due to Josh's testimony, there were still loose ends to tie up. Meg's father being one of them.

His thumbs tapped. Saturday. Picnic in the afternoon/evening. Should keep him occupied.

Watts wrote, Got it. Done with your little vacation? You can have your job back anytime.

Vacation? It would have been just a matter of time until every bit of his soul had been sucked away if he hadn't quit. Nope. How soon before it's over?

Going for the source. Soon.

That probably meant they were going to place tracking software on the mayor's computers to see if he was bouncing his signal to hide activity. Could be that Meg's father just gambled online sometimes, unknowingly involving himself in their case. But where there's smoke . . . Let me know when.

Will do. Still can't believe you gave up a stellar career for a woman.

That didn't even deserve a response.

Meg was what he'd been missing his whole life. He'd tried once to mix those lives and lost Meg. This time would be different.

Just as Josh was about to put his phone away, it beeped again with an e-mail from Eric.

thx for the pix and the dog food. mr. j says I can only keep 1 pup. can u help me find homes? A picture of all three black-and-white balls of fur appeared under the text.

Haley would happily take one of them off Eric's hands. Maybe he'd just have to adopt one himself. Meg couldn't complain because the dog would technically belong to him.

I'll ask around. Everything else going okay? Josh poked the button to send the e-mail and then put his phone away.

Zeke cocked his head. "Now that you're done with your fancy phone there, want to get back to work? This whole shooting the car up was your big idea, after all. Should be a good show."

"Yep." Josh leaned down to start on the trigger device. He'd run into the fire chief, Abe, at the diner earlier. Abe had been at the bar for the dart competition the other night and asked if he could use Meg's old car for a fire drill once they were done shooting it up. Two birds. One stone.

Besides, blowing up stuff was fun.

———

Meg squared her shoulders and then yanked on Town Hall's main door. She didn't have an appointment, which Dragon Breath would hate. But it wasn't anyone else's damned business if she wanted to have a private discussion with her own . . . father. Or whatever he was to her.

She'd considered doing it at the house, but then the stepmonster would surely invite herself, just as she always did. It needed to be between her and Dad. And she wasn't leaving until she got the truth.

But first, she had a dragon to slay.

Meg stood quietly in front of Mrs. Duncan, waiting for her to finish her phone call. The woman's eyes locked with Meg's. "Hang on a sec, Barb, trouble just walked in." She slid a hand over the mouthpiece. "What do you want, Megan?"

A little respect would be nice. "Just need to talk to my dad for a few minutes . . . please." The *please* killed her.

Mrs. Duncan raised a brow. "Your father mentioned you might stop by. He said to tell you he'd speak to you later—after working hours." She made a shooing motion with her hand and then went back to gossiping with her friend.

He knew. Why else would he anticipate her visit? It wasn't like she ever dropped in unless summoned.

Grandma must've told Dad about the files. Good. It'd save time.

Meg slipped around the desk and headed for the coward's door. Ignoring Mrs. Duncan's protests, Meg stepped inside, dismayed to see Sue Ann sitting on the corner of the desk. She was smiling sweetly at her father. "Thanks, sugar. I'll be better about the spendin' next month. I promise." She batted her eyes just like Pam always did.

Ick.

Meg considered leaving before they noticed her when Mrs. Duncan barreled into the room. "I told her not to bother you, Mayor. But she disregarded me just like she ignores anything else resembling a rule!"

Sue Ann chuckled at Dragon Breath's joke. "So true."

Dad lifted a hand for silence. "Meg, have a seat. If you ladies will excuse us, please?"

Mrs. Duncan frowned on her way out, but Sue Ann just sat there blinking. Finally, she said, "Surely you don't mean me too, Mitch?"

Dad nodded. "You were on your way to Denver, so don't let us hold you up."

Sue Ann's eyes narrowed as she stood to leave. On her way out she glared at Meg. "Don't be doing anything to upset your daddy, givin' him another migraine, Megan. Or you'll have me to answer to." She slammed the door shut behind her.

Meg drew a deep breath. Showtime. "So, I take it Sue Ann doesn't know?"

Dad leaned back in his chair, crossing his arms over his chest. "That was long before Sue Ann came into the picture. Didn't see any need to talk about it ever again."

"Obviously."

He pointed a finger at her. "Lose the attitude, young lady, or you can get your butt right out of my office."

"That's just what you want, isn't it? To find yet another excuse not to talk to me about my mother. What if I'd started dating a cousin without knowing it? Or that Haley might one day? It could happen in a town this small."

"I'm well aware of that possibility. We finally got through it with you, and now because you went catting around, I have to worry about it all over again."

"I loved Josh. Getting pregnant was an accident. I'm not a cheater who got herself impregnated by her lover like my mother did. You need to separate the two."

"Nice way to talk about your own mother." Dad huffed out a breath. "My biggest fear was that you'd end up like her. Hell, you look just like her, and have a chip on your shoulder as big as hers was."

"I'm just stating facts. Something you seem to have a problem with. But now I want the truth. Why did you fight Grandma and Grandpa for me once you figured out I wasn't your child?"

He closed his eyes and ran his hand through his hair. "Being an Anderson brings along a certain amount of responsibility. Something you've never been able to embrace. It would have been an embarrassment to my parents, my siblings, and to your brothers and sister too, if everyone knew the truth. It was just a happy coincidence you were born looking like your mother rather than your father. It helped people question the rumor that had been going around long before she died."

"So you kept me to save yourself the embarrassment. But you never forgave me for being the product of my mother's affair. At least now I can finally understand why you've always hated me."

"I don't hate you, Megan." He slowly shook his head. "But you've been the biggest challenge of my life. You acted out so often as a kid it was a relief when you went away to college and then to Denver. One less thing for me to worry about."

Just what a girl likes to hear. "Maybe if you had treated me more like the others, I wouldn't have tried so hard to get your attention. Granted, I went about it the wrong way, but all I ever wanted was just once to hear you say you were proud of me."

"Maybe I would've, if you'd ever done anything to make me proud."

Knife to the heart. "Why can't you see how I've changed? I'm not that mischievous kid trying to get your attention anymore."

"It is what it is, Megan. I did the best I could. And now you'll thank me by digging it up and getting Amber and her family riled up again too."

"Amber's known for years. And I do thank you for putting a roof over my head and paying for my college. But I did the math yesterday. All the rent you collected from my house would add up to well over two hundred thousand dollars by now. So, I'd say we're even."

She stood to leave before she said something even uglier about his lack of compassion. Just as she reached the door, he said, "All that money is in a separate account. Because I'm damned good at investing, there's almost three hundred thousand now. If you'd show me rather than just tell me how you've finally become a responsible adult, maybe I'll let you have it."

Three hundred grand?

She slowly turned and faced him again.

His lips curled into a smug smirk. "Well, now. That got your attention, didn't it? Everyone in this town has secrets. Some bigger than others. Your mother had more than just this one, things no one should have to know about their mother. Showing up with a smile on your face on Founder's Day and keeping this to yourself would help me believe you're one step closer to earning that money."

"Really? You're going to use that to buy my silence? As much as I'd love to use that money to fix up my house, it wouldn't be worth having you hold it over my head the rest of my life. I'm done caring what you think of me!"

She slammed his office door behind her. Blood pounded so loudly in her ears she couldn't hear a word Mrs. Duncan said to her.

No way was she going to give him any more power by touching a dime of that stinking money. She'd take the risk, gather more pre-booking money, and then pray she'd be able to get her lodge open on schedule. She wouldn't fail this time. She'd show him he was wrong about her and do just as Grandma said, steal away some of his clients and make a good living despite him.

Why should she care what he thought of her anyway? She didn't need his approval anymore. She'd just focus on making the people who actually cared for her and who were in her corner proud.

She ignored everyone who called out a greeting and kept her head down as she made her way to the hotel. She'd pick up Haley from Casey and then go hammer or strip the crap out of something at the lodge.

Just as she started across the grassy park, Haley called out a happy, "Hi, Momma!"

Her anger dimmed by half at the sight of Haley's sweet, smiling face. "I didn't expect to see you here." Meg lifted her up and spotted Grandma sitting on the wooden bandstand steps nearby.

Meg plopped Haley onto the step and then sat between her and Grandma. She'd been trying to think of what to say to Grams all morning. "So, I guess Casey told you what I was doing, huh?"

Grandma nodded. "Figured you'd run outta there with your panties all in a twist. We've all seen what an idiot you can be when you get like that. Thought we'd stop by to be sure you didn't do anything stupid."

"I wasn't going to . . . well, anyway, I want to say thank you. For being there for me when you didn't have—"

Grandma thumped her cane. "What nonsense is this now, Meggy? Do you love me any less since you found those files?"

"No. I think I love you even more." She drew her grandmother into a hug. "Even if you are the crankiest person I've ever met."

"Well, there you go. And for the record, there's never a dull moment when you're around, and I like that about you . . . most of the time. You've done some pretty idiotic things, but I got no time for boring people."

Meg laughed. "Thanks. I think?"

Grandma struggled with her cane as she slowly attempted to stand. "I'm off to the grocery store. I don't want to hear about those files ever again. Got it?"

"Got it. Why don't you give me your list, and Haley and I will go for you?"

"What list? It's all up here in the steel trap." She tapped a finger to her forehead. "I'm not so old I can't do my own damned shopping. Besides, looks like you got bigger trouble on your hands." Grandma pointed her cane. "Amber's heading this way. Casey said you're gonna talk to her about it too. Not sure yet if that's going to be one of your more idiotic moves or not. Guess we'll see." Grandma stuck out her hand. "Haley, why don't you come along with me? You can pick out the ice cream you like best."

"Okay. Bye, Momma." Haley tilted her chin and pursed her lips.

"Bye, baby." Meg gave Haley a kiss, then flagged Amber down.

Amber walked slowly toward her, suspicion dancing in her eyes. "What's up? Wondering if I got my invite to the silly little girls' thing you guys are having on Friday?"

"It's Pam's party. I have no idea who she's inviting. Do you have a minute? I'd like to talk to you about something."

Amber glanced at her watch. "Make it quick."

"Okay, uh, you want to sit?" Meg waved a hand toward the bandstand's steps.

"I'm not sitting on those dirty steps. Jeez, what the hell, Meg? Just spit it out."

Meg sat, but then realized that left Amber in the power position, lurking above her head, so she stood again. Being short sucked when trying to give attitude. She still only came up to Amber's store-bought cleavage. After hopping up on a step, she finally stood eye to eye with Amber. "I just found out something I was told you already knew. About our father?"

Amber's jaw clenched. "Did the person who told you about this also tell you what a whore your mother was? And how she ruined my mother's life?"

A strange urge to defend a woman she had no memories of rose up in Meg. "It takes two cheaters to have an affair. One's not any better than the other."

"Men cheat, Meg. Society gives them a free pass. You've always been so naïve that way. But what's your point?"

"I just wanted to . . . I don't know. For God's sake, Amber, we're sisters. Our kids are cousins. I just want this polite war between us to end."

"Easy for you to say. My mother's life was destroyed, and I had to grow up with practically nothing, while you and the rest of the Andersons and Grants lived in mansions. Worse, you got a freakin' free pass every time you screwed up because you were the mayor's so-called daughter. My mother told me your mother was just a slut who enjoyed tempting weak men away, not caring who she hurt in the process. I have no desire to have anything to do with that woman's spawn."

"At least you had a mother who loved you. And we're both the spawn of the same weak father. But if you really feel that way, then why were you coming on to Josh? You'd think after what happened to your mother you'd never cheat."

Hurt flashed in Amber's eyes for a nanosecond before she shut it down. "Randy and I have an open marriage. No man will ever destroy me like my mother. I'm late. I have to go."

An open marriage? That couldn't have been Amber's idea. When they were kids, Amber wanted that prince in shining armor who'd only ever have eyes for her as much as any other starry-eyed little girl who'd seen every Disney movie ever made.

Meg couldn't help it—she had to know. "So, do you even love Randy? Or did you steal him away just to hurt me for what my mother did?"

Amber whirled around. "Everyone knew Randy was guaranteed a great job from his father after college. Set for the rest of his life. No way was I going to let you continue to live the life I deserved. But look at you now, Meg. Little Miss Rich Girl who hasn't got two dimes to rub together and is living in her grandmother's guesthouse.

Karma's a real bitch, right?" Amber poked Meg in the chest. "I'm already taking steps to run your sorry ass out of town. Nobody wants you here, Megan." She spun on her ice pick heels and left.

Meg sank down on the steps and watched Amber walk away. Was it true? Did people want to see her gone?

Where was that great comeback, Muck? Why was it easier to stand up to her father, the most powerful man in town, than to Amber?

So much for being tough.

Hard to believe she'd once idolized Amber and loved being her friend. All those sleepovers every weekend and staying up all night talking about boys. She hadn't seen the dark side until it was aimed at her. Casey had mentioned Amber had found out about their father in their junior year of high school. That had been right when Amber had changed.

After Amber had turned into the queen bitch, she'd reduced many girls to tears by betraying trusts and revealing everyone's most sacred secrets. Amber was probably serious about trying to run Meg out of town.

According to her dad, everyone in Anderson Butte had secrets—but she didn't. So what could Amber do that'd be so bad? The even bigger mystery was, why did her confrontation with Amber make her more sad than angry?

"Megan?"

She looked up to find Walt, one of her potential contractors, standing in front of her with a fat envelope in his hand.

She sent him a smile and said, "Hey. So how'd we do? Somewhere in the ballpark we discussed?"

"Well, no, actually." Walt cleared his throat. "There's been a shortage of manpower, so everything's more than . . . well, here. Let me know what you think after you've had a chance to look things over." The sheepish look on his face as he handed the bid over didn't bode well.

She tore open the envelope and searched for the bottom line. It was twice what she'd estimated and her heart sank.

The numbers made no sense. She'd gone over some of the costs with the lumber store herself.

But then, Walt had always been in love with Amber. He'd still do anything for her. So maybe this was step one in the "run Meg out of town" plan?

When she looked up at Walt again, he couldn't meet her direct gaze and looked away.

That hurt. They'd been friends since elementary school. Did Walt want her gone too? "Tell Amber good try. But I won't let this stop me. See you around."

As Meg forced herself to calmly walk away, Walt's sputtering apology confirmed she was right. Meg tossed the bogus bid into a trash can on the corner.

Well, Amber, game on. She would not allow her half sister or her so-called father the power to defeat her. They were dealing with the new Meg now.

CHAPTER Sixteen

Meg headed across the square toward the hotel. She needed to talk to Casey. Amber's little power play was a good one, so Meg had to act fast.

Contractors from Denver would charge a surplus for working out of town. And the other smaller contractors in nearby towns didn't have any openings for such a big job. She could only hope Amber hadn't gotten to Beau Bailey yet.

Meg stuck her head inside her sister's office, but Casey wasn't there. She hated that she was going to have to ask for help. She'd built up her courage to ask all the way there.

Meg checked the kitchen next. Dax was pulling something sinfully chocolate-smelling from the oven. He was built like a Navy SEAL, but made delicate soufflés. He gently laid it on the granite counter. "Hey, Meg."

"Hi. Dibs on any leftovers. Do you know where Casey is?"

A slow smile tilted his lips. "She's in the throes of a cute little snit. We're shorthanded today, so she's down at the dock packing the boat with picnic supplies."

"Thanks." Meg turned to leave, but stopped. "So, do you have a thing for my sister, Dax?"

He shrugged one of his big shoulders. "She's the boss, so she's off limits, right?"

Yep. He did. "Casey's a bit of a rule follower that way. See you."

Meg hoped her sister would be willing to break a rule or two for her, just this once. She headed out the back door and down to the dock. Casey was hauling boxes onto the pontoon boat with a deep scowl etched on her face. Maybe it wasn't the best time for favor asking.

Casey spotted her. "Here. Make yourself useful. Load this onboard." Casey shoved a cooler into Meg's hands.

"What's going on?"

"Chris is out sick, Billy is on vacation, and Toby is nowhere to be found. I've called and sent him numerous texts, but he's ignoring me. He's supposed to take some guests out to Sunset Cove for a picnic lunch. If he doesn't show, I'll need you to take them."

Meg was tempted to point out she wasn't allowed to work for the hotel anymore. If Dad found out he'd be furious, but she'd risk it for Casey.

Besides, she used to enjoy taking guests out for picnics at Sunset Cove. It was a beautiful, secluded spot. Good for fishing, cliff diving, swimming—and the best place on the lake for skinny-dipping.

Maybe she'd take Josh out there later on the Jet Ski and finish up what they'd started in the shower earlier. The thought made her smile.

When Casey's back was turned, Meg grabbed her phone. Toby always returned her texts immediately. Something that would probably irritate both her sister and Josh.

Where are you? Casey's about to blow a gasket. You have a charter in ten minutes!!!!

After about thirty seconds, her screen lit up with Jeez I forgot. On my way, babe.

Meg put her phone back and helped finish up the last of the boat prep while Casey muttered under her breath all the ways she'd like to kill Toby.

He finally showed up with a wrinkled T-shirt, tousled hair, and a smug "just got laid" grin. He lost it as soon as he spotted Casey's scowl.

Meg took the opportunity to slip off the boat while the dressing down took place. Casey would be quick and to the point. She'd never let the guests see her in a temper, and they were already on the end of the dock, excitement lighting their faces in anticipation of their picnic.

Meg greeted them and helped fit them into their life jackets. When Toby joined them, he thanked her and took over.

She caught up with Casey as she marched back to the hotel. "So it all worked out, right?"

Her sister sighed. "Sorry. I was mad at Toby, not you. Thanks for the help."

"You're welcome." Probably as good a time as any to ask. "But now I need *your* help with something."

"Excuse me?" Casey pulled up short. "Is the apocalypse happening and I missed the memo?"

It had taken all her might to ask, and her sister was making light of it? Meg was tempted to tell her sister to forget it. She'd figure it out on her own. But she really needed Casey's help. Ignoring her sarcasm, Meg sucked in a deep breath and told Casey about her conversations with Amber and then Walt.

Casey's smirk quickly vanished. "Let's go to my office. Too many ears out here." Casey led the way down the hall. She closed the door behind them and then sat behind her desk. "Beau told me he wasn't sure he'd be able to fit a job as big as yours into his schedule."

Settling into a guest chair, Meg said, "He told me that too, but he said he'd think about it. Can you help me convince him to take on my job? At a reasonable rate? Amber is determined to see me fail. But I can do this if I can get Beau to help."

Casey's lips tilted as she nodded. "Beau has been after me to go away with him for a long weekend before the boys get back from France. I've been putting him off because I thought people would put two and two together if we did that. But I just told him I'd go before I went to pack the boat, so he should still be in a good mood. Let's see." She picked up her cell and tapped out a text.

Relief whooshed through Meg as her sister finished her text to Beau asking for his help. "Thanks, Casey. I owe you one."

"You owe the bank for your loan, you don't owe your sister for a favor. And see? Trusting me enough to tell me your problem and then asking for help wasn't so bad, was it?"

"I guess." Meg owed her sister the truth about Josh too. "You'll probably be mad at me for this, but I told Josh I'd give our relationship another try." Meg braced for her sister's fury. Casey had warned her about handing her heart to Josh. But she hadn't given it to him all the way. Just enough to test out the waters.

Casey nodded. "I figured as much—" Her ringing cell cut her off. "It's Beau." She picked up the phone. "Hello?"

Meg scooted to the edge of her seat.

Please let him say yes.

Casey's face turned all soft and mushy. Doodling little curlicues on her paper as she listened, she finally said, "Yes, I think we could include some of that as well." She was quiet for a minute before she said, "Mmmmm, yeah. That too."

Meg stood to give them some privacy, but Casey lifted a finger and shook her head.

"'Kay. See you later, then." When Casey hung up, her expression quickly slipped back to normal, but Meg was pretty certain her cheeks were still fifty shades of pink.

"So? Was that a yes?"

"Yep. He said the numbers you talked about were close enough, he'd send a formal bid and a crew to start tomorrow, and that I was going to owe him big-time." Casey sent her a quick eyebrow hitch. "I'm looking forward to paying him back. But you'll be interested to know, Amber offered to sleep with Beau if he refused to do the work for you."

"Well, it's lucky for me you're such a wild woman in the sack then, right? He might've caved if you weren't keeping him so . . . *satisfied*."

A magazine flew at Meg's head, but she dodged it. She headed for the door before objects more solid began to fly. "Thank you, Casey. You're still my favorite half sister."

"And you're still a brat!"

———

Finished with rigging up the trigger device on Meg's old car, Josh decided to take a break. "Zeke, I need to run a little errand. Be back in a bit, okay?"

The old man nodded and went back to the carburetor he was rebuilding.

After Josh had called Meg and confirmed she was at the lodge and that Haley was napping with Meg's grandmother, he jumped into his truck.

Their time in the shower earlier still tortured him. Nothing helped. Reciting box scores, the periodic table, and even the alphabet backward couldn't redirect his thoughts.

He pulled up to the lodge and then circled around back. Meg wore big safety glasses as she swung a sledgehammer that had to weigh half as much as she did against one of the deck's main support posts. Apparently the whole thing was coming down.

Later.

And he'd do it for her. It could be dangerous.

He moved into her line of sight. She stopped mid-swing and smiled. "Hi. What are you doing here?"

"I haven't been able to stop thinking about you since this morning." He took the sledgehammer from her hands, slid her safety glasses off, then picked her up and kissed her.

When they came up for air, she stared into his eyes. "Me too. I planned to take you somewhere nice later—"

He cut her off with another kiss.

When she moaned and wrapped her legs around his waist, snuggling her soft chest against his, he wasn't sure they'd make it all the way to the bedroom.

He started for the back door, reluctant to break their kiss, but he needed to see where he was going. "Let's go finish what we started this morning."

"I'm all hot and sweaty." She leaned back and smiled. "But okay. If you insist."

"I do."

As he carried her inside she nibbled on his ear, then whispered, "You're bossier than you used to be."

He kicked the master bedroom door open all the way before he dumped her on the bed and covered her curvy little body with his. "I've been taking lessons from you."

He laid his lips softly on hers, surprised at how much he suddenly wanted to please her. Show her how much he'd missed her. How much he loved her. As urgent as his desire had been before, he wanted to go slow. To savor their first time together again.

But Meg wasn't having any of that. As usual.

She writhed beneath him as she stripped down to her underwear. "You next." She grabbed the hem of his shirt and yanked it off. Then she went for the zipper on his jeans.

After she'd tossed all his clothes aside, he grabbed her busy hands and lifted them above her head, trapping them against the sheets. "We're doing it my way this time."

Meg grunted. "See? Bossy."

"We're always in such a hurry. Let's slow down and enjoy it. And each other. Or are you afraid you'll be in so deep you'll let your defenses down, forget to hide that secret gooey center you guard so fiercely with your sarcasm?"

Her eyes narrowed. "Maybe I just like sex the way I like it. Using *both* of my hands."

He shifted her wrists into one hand, freeing up his other. "You're afraid to give up control. Be totally vulnerable. Admit it."

Meg never backed down from a direct challenge. She'd do it.

"Fine." She rolled her eyes. "I'll just lie here like a limp noodle, the blood draining from my hands while you do whatever you'd like. Wake me up when you're done." She yawned for effect.

He nibbled on her cute little earlobe and got a shiver out of her. "Liked that, huh?"

"Been three long years, Dr. Freud. Not gonna take much."

He loved how a woman who just barely passed the height restrictions to board most roller coasters could put up such a big front. He'd have her begging in no time.

Starting from her shapely calf, he ran his hand up her smooth leg, slowly trailing his fingers up her side, raising goose bumps in his fingers' wake. When he finally reached her breasts, he gently kneaded and squeezed, taking the time to please both of them before he unlatched the front clasp of her lacy bra and parted it.

He took a moment to just look. To appreciate her beautiful body.

Meg huffed out an impatient breath.

He ran slow kisses across her jaw, her soft neck, and after he laid a light kiss just in front of her ear, whispered, "Am I annoying you?"

"Yes! You're driving me nuts!"

He laughed, then kissed her pouting lips again. He'd missed her smart mouth as much as her sweet kisses. He'd kiss her for the next five minutes straight, just to drive her really crazy. Meg used to love that.

It wasn't long until her body finally softened under his, and she let out a quiet sigh.

Progress.

Still kissing her, he slowly slid his hand lower, his fingers caressing her smooth belly. Only her skimpy panties remained.

When he slipped his hand under the soft material, he found her wet and ready for him. He stroked and teased her until she moaned against his mouth. "Now?"

"Not yet."

He moved to her chest, exploring her breasts with his mouth. Sucking, teasing, until Meg moaned. "Josh . . . for the love of . . ."

He trailed lazy soft kisses lower, past her belly, to her shapely thighs. Using his teeth and a thumb, he slipped her panties off, then lapped up her moisture. Her hips jerked before she threw her head back.

Meg's breathy gasps hardened him like steel.

He wasn't sure how much more he could take. He wanted to go slow, but maybe he'd have to save that for the next time.

When her hips rocked in time with her need, he almost lost it. But he wanted her blind with passion for him first, so he slid two fingers inside her.

Her back arched as she called out his name.

Meg just wanted to touch him. To run her hands all over his sexy, hard body . . . but he still held her wrists prisoner over her head.

He was killing her . . . in such a good way. Who knew how incredible letting him have his way could be?

She was about to go over the top without him, when suddenly her hands were free. He'd leaned over to grab a condom. Thank God.

She loved how Josh stared hungrily into her eyes as he slowly slipped inside of her. Filling her with long, slow thrusts that felt so familiar.

So good.

Her hands wandered over his hard back muscles, then ended up tangled in his soft hair, pulling him closer as he groaned with pleasure.

She'd missed the way he looked at her, his eyes filled with fierce desire as he strained to hold back.

For her.

She closed her eyes, opened her heart, and let his intensity wash over her, through her. The pure, raw desire for him stole her breath. It was heaven to just savor, enjoy, and let go completely. To lose all control.

For him.

The years without his touch, the pent-up desires and needs, slammed into her all at the same time. She gasped as overwhelming pleasure swept her up and threw her to the top, like riding the perfect wave. Her body convulsed around his in hard, pounding contractions. She opened her eyes and stared into Josh's intense ones again as he matched the frenzied pace of her hips. Then she gave in to it, and to Josh, and let go.

He smiled before he closed his eyes and joined her.

Josh's heavy weight suddenly pinned her to the bed, and he sighed. "That was incredible."

"Ummm hummm." She slowly ran her fingers through his hair while they both caught their breath. She hated to admit it, but his way was pretty great. She felt so relaxed, sated, and . . . happy, even if it was only for a few more minutes before she'd draw her defenses back up.

When Josh rolled halfway off her, she could finally take a full breath again. He snuggled his face on the pillow beside her.

Instead of whispering, "I told you so," like she'd expected, his lips brushed her ear as he said, "I saw it in your eyes. You love me too."

Her heart used to be filled with such naïve joy and love for him. Not unlike what she'd just allowed herself to experience a few moments ago. But was she ready to take that leap of faith?

She stared into his eyes, struggling with what to say.

"I . . . can't yet."

"Okay." Josh nodded and closed his eyes.

She wished she could tell him she loved him, but it was just too soon for her.

Snuggling against his side, she laid her palm on his cheek and whispered, "I don't mean to hurt you, by not saying it."

When he opened his eyes and met her gaze, she worked up a smile. "I will admit this, though. Your way *was* a lot more fun."

She expected a smug grin, but he just stared into her eyes in that unnerving way of his. Waiting for her to address the situation instead of avoiding it.

"Oh, all right." Propping her head up on her hand, she returned his steady stare. "You were right when you said earlier that I'm afraid to be totally vulnerable. To allow myself the possibility of being hurt again. So if I say I love you, that's when you'll know I'm ready."

"Fair enough." He slipped an arm around her waist and pulled her closer. "I shouldn't have put you on the spot like that. Won't happen again, okay?"

She nodded while swallowing back the emotion clogging her throat. "'Kay."

His lips stretched into a grin and the fun Josh returned. "Told you so about slowing it all down though, right?"

And they were back to normal.

She poked his shoulder before she rolled out of bed. "I already admitted you were right, so go away. I have a deck to demolish."

"How about I pick up a pizza for dinner, then after we eat, *I'll* tear down the deck?"

Meg tugged her clothes back on. "Pizza sounds great, but I can do the deck on my own."

"I know you're capable, but what if you get hurt while you're all alone out here? Promise you'll let me do it, Meg."

"Whatever." *That* she could give him.

He quirked a brow. "So was that a yes?"

"Yes!" She leaned down and laid a hard kiss on his lips. "And for bringing me pizza, I may just let you have your way with me again after Haley goes to sleep tonight."

Then she'd see if it was as mind-blowing the second time. Because really, after so long, any sex would have probably been great. Maybe it was just what she needed so her heart would finally know what to do.

"Sex for a pizza delivery. Works every time." Josh rolled out of bed and scooped up his jeans.

"Yep. A total win-win. I've trained you well."

She laughed at the befuddled look on his face as he tried to work out who had just achieved the upper hand on that one.

CHAPTER SEVENTEEN

Almost the whole town stood behind Zeke's garage to watch Meg's car get blown to bits. Josh smiled at the turnout, hoping it'd give people a chance to see he wasn't the villain he'd been made out to be.

The volunteer fire department moved into position, ready for the drill, while the whole police force helped corral the people behind the barriers Josh had set up. Because most of the police were also volunteer firefighters, that made a total of six guys.

He'd give the people a good show, but he'd made sure the explosion would be controlled and burn out quickly. He'd just finished removing the last tire when he glanced up and caught Meg's brother Ryan watching closely, with a suspicious gleam in his eyes. Ryan would get proof his sharp instincts were right soon enough.

Meg strolled up with Haley on her hip. "Hey."

"Hey, back. How are my two favorite girls?"

"Good." Meg shot him a smile that smoldered with heat. They'd been enjoying making up for lost time in bed the last couple of days. "But I guess this is goodbye to my poor old car. May she rest in peace." She gave him a quick hug.

In front of the townspeople. More progress.

And it spoke volumes that Meg would allow him to take Haley to the ranch later, albeit reluctantly. When they got back, she was even going to let him babysit while Meg went to her girls' thing.

He'd made a point of giving Meg a break every day and taking Haley on little outings, getting ice cream at the diner, going to the toy store, or just playing in the park, but he hadn't had her alone more than a few hours at a time.

He loved spending time with Haley and listening to the funny things that came out of her mouth. Especially stories about Meg that he'd teased her about later. Apparently no family secrets were safe with a two-and-a-half-year-old around.

He'd told Meg he could handle the longer day, but he hoped to God he'd know what to do with a little girl for that many hours straight.

"Hi, Daddy." Haley reached her arms out for him to take her.

As Meg handed Haley over, she asked, "So what's with the little slips of paper in the sack going around?"

"Ever heard of Zozobra?"

Meg nodded. "The fifty-foot-tall ugly puppet guy they burn to the ground every year in Santa Fe. You calling my car ugly?"

"Absolutely. But Zozobra embodies gloom. So anyone with worries can write them down and we'll put them all inside the car, like they do the puppet. By destroying their worries in the flames, people can feel free to move on. Might even help someone forget the past and give a guy another chance. Wanna try it?" He handed her the piece of paper and pen in his pocket he'd put there just for her.

"Thank you, Mr. Subtle." She sent him a smirk. "But I suppose it couldn't hurt. Turn around, I need your back to write on."

When he turned, he spotted Meg's grandma making her way toward them. She carried a rifle over one shoulder and a cane in her other hand, looking like a fierce Annie Oakley with a limp.

Haley waved. "Hi, Grandma!"

The woman actually smiled. And she still had all her teeth. He'd never seen anything but a scowl before.

"Hello, sweet girl."

She could be nice? He'd always assumed mean was just her nature. She must really hate him. "Hi, Mrs. Anderson. How are you today?"

She cocked a brow. "Old. Tired. But still one of the best shots in these parts. I come to prove it to you, so you'd know I'm serious about shooting you again if you mess up, boy." Before he could respond she asked, "So what've we got here? How's it all going to work?"

Meg popped her head from around his back. "Hi, Grandma. We should probably save you for last, or this show's going to be over before it starts."

Ryan joined them too. "Yeah. At that distance, not many are going to be able to make that shot, Granger. I'm not even sure my men could hit that small target you got marked there."

Josh nodded. "Didn't want to take the chance on anyone getting hurt by being too close. I'll go last if I have to. I can make the shot, and I guarantee it'll be worth the show."

Grandma grunted. "Cocky, aren't ya?"

"Nope. Just a really good shot."

Ryan asked, "Yeah, about safety. How much gas is in that tank, Granger?"

"None. It's all under control." Josh had rigged it so a bunch of small explosions would go off, making a lot of noise for effect, but controlling what and how high things went up.

Crossing his arms, Ryan said, "How does a software guy know how to blow up cars?"

"YouTube. Are we all set?"

Abe, the fire chief, placed the bag with the worries on the front seat and then gave him the thumbs-up. Josh handed Haley back to Meg. "There's going to be a really big bang, Haley, and then some fire, but nothing to be scared of. Okay?"

"Momma said it's gonna go BOOM!" She flung both hands up in the air to demonstrate.

"That's right." Satisfied he wouldn't scare the crap out of his kid, he accepted the rifle Zeke held out.

Josh turned to the crowd, put two fingers in his mouth, and whistled for everyone's attention. "Ready to blow this rig?" After the cheers settled down, he said, "So, we'll all use this rifle. You'll get three shots. Hit the target dead on, and then she'll blow."

Brewster called out, "What's the prize if we hit the target?"

"Bragging rights and a damn good show."

The men smiled and nodded. The women rolled their eyes.

Meg's grandma spoke up. "That's a tough shot. We should use my Remington to give people a better chance. Got a problem with that, Granger?"

He'd calibrated Zeke's scope. It was as close to perfect as it could be. But maybe he'd score some points with Meg's grandma and let her have her way. "Sure. Why not? But do you mind if I take a practice shot to test it out?"

"Go ahead." She handed over her gun. "Let's see you take off the side mirror first."

Josh moved up to the bales of hay that surrounded the car and assumed a position slightly behind the vehicle to give him an angle. Taking aim, he held his breath, then slowly squeezed the trigger. The mirror dropped straight to the ground. He'd taken out the small support that held it to the car. "Looks true."

Grandma let out an unimpressed grunt.

Josh handed the gun to Toby first. "You any better at this than darts?"

"Yep." He turned to Meg. "So if I make this—"

Josh laid a hand on his shoulder and squeezed. "Not happening. Got it?"

Toby smiled. "Loud and clear." He made a show of rolling his shoulders and moving his feet into position, finally taking a shot. He came close, but missed all three times.

After the next few shooters were unsuccessful, Meg's grandma jumped the line and declared it was her turn. When no one argued, she hobbled over and accepted the gun from Josh. "Because I'm interested in knowing just how good you think you are, Granger, let's have us some fun before we blow the car up. What do you say?"

The gleam in the woman's eyes and the soft chuckles from everyone should probably have warned him off. "I'm game. What did you have in mind?"

"Let's see how you do with something that's not standing still. See those two big pinecones hanging side by side on the tallest tree at the top of the ridge there? I'll go first. The one on the left." She leaned her cane against the hay in front of her and aimed the rifle. After taking a moment to gauge the sway in the light wind, she popped off a shot. The pinecone burst into pieces, then drifted to the ground.

"Nice shot, Mrs. Anderson."

He accepted the gun and calculated the range of movement, then took out his pinecone.

She slowly nodded. "Not bad. Okay, how about we add a little pressure. There's an old, run-down shed a ways over there. Through the trees. There's one window left with four panes. See it?"

He searched the stand of trees, finally glimpsing sunlight reflecting off the glass. It wasn't far away. But getting a straight line of sight would be the challenge. "I see it." Although he wasn't sure how she was seeing it through her wire-rimmed glasses.

In a raised voice, she said, "I told Meggy earlier I didn't like the idea of you taking Haley away in that truck of yours. I'm not convinced you'd bring her back."

That wasn't going to help his credibility, dammit.

Grandma continued, "Shoot out a pane and you can take Haley to the ranch. Miss, or don't take the challenge, and she stays here with me. All safe and sound."

All eyes turned to him.

The chances of making that shot were less than 50 percent, even for him. The interest brewing in the people's eyes was evident as they all stared at him. Waiting.

Meg called out, "Grandma, stop!"

Meg moved by his side. Then, loud enough for everyone to hear, she said, "You don't have to do this, Josh. I know you'll bring her back."

A little trust from Meg. At last.

He shot her a smile, but if he didn't at least try, the rest of the town wouldn't fall in line. His negotiation training told him upping the stakes on the other side would be the next move. Remembering something Zeke had told him the other day, he said, "I'll take the shot, but only if you take the shot too. If I hit and you miss, you'll have to break down and finally accept Zeke's offer for dinner and a movie."

Chuckles sounded all around.

Zeke called out, "Never known you to back down from a direct challenge, Ruthie. What's it gonna be?"

Meg's grandmother sent Zeke a scowl.

Josh added, "But if we both miss, the whole deal is off, except you'll have to quit pointing guns at me when I come to visit Meg and Haley." He held his hand out for her to shake.

Everyone waited silently as Meg's grandmother stared at Josh's hand while she considered. "You think you're pretty clever, don't you, Granger?"

Meg laughed. "Welcome to my world."

Meg's grandmother turned and checked out the target again. "You figuring what I am? Maybe thirty-five, forty percent chance we can hit that?"

She might be old, but she was still sharp. "Yep."

"And you're still willing to take the challenge?"

He nodded.

"Okay then, we got ourselves a deal. A body's gotta eat dinner anyway and a movie won't kill me." She returned the shake. "You want to go first or second?"

"Ladies first."

As Meg's grandmother moved into position, Josh grabbed a handful of straw and tossed it up so they could both see how the wind took it. "A little to the left if it holds steady."

Her eyes shifted toward his. "But it's gusting a bit. What we're both going to need is luck." She lifted the rifle, stared down the sight, then whispered, "You bringing her back, Granger?"

"Yep."

"I'm so old I'll just plead Alzheimer's or something and take you out if you're lying to me."

"Understood."

He moved aside as she set up for her shot. After she pulled the trigger, the flapping of startled birds filled the air, but no glass breaking.

"Darnation!" She handed the gun to Josh.

He glanced at Meg, silently asking what he should do. If he missed, it'd save her grandmother's pride, she wouldn't have to go on the date, he'd be safe when he visited the guesthouse in the future, and he'd still get to take Haley to the ranch.

He should probably throw it.

After Meg shrugged, her grandmother called out, "What's this going on between you and Meggy there, Granger? I'll have to accidentally shoot you in the ass too, if you don't get up there, be a man, and give it your best shot!"

Clearly, this was where Meg got her attitude from. Related by DNA or not.

After Meg smiled and nodded, he stepped up to the bale of hay and lifted the rifle to his shoulder. Slowing his breathing and his heart rate, he blocked out all the sounds around him, lining up the pane of glass glistening in the sunlight. He set his body, closed his eyes, then moved only his trigger finger, waiting for the outcome.

The sound of glass breaking sent a cheer up from everyone except for Meg's grandmother. "Guess we got ourselves a date, Zeke. But that doesn't include any monkey business. Just making that clear right now."

Zeke chuckled. "We'll see. Might be, you'll finally see what a charming guy I can be when I put some effort into it. You'd be worth the effort, I reckon."

Grandma rolled her eyes.

Still smiling at his victory, Josh handed Meg's grandma the gun. "I respect a woman who drives a hard bargain. I think you should have the honors of blowing up the car."

"Don't mind if I do. Nice shootin', Granger."

She took aim, pulled the trigger, and then winced as the big boom filled the air. The car's body blew five feet straight up off the axle, just as he'd planned. By the time it landed, fire engulfed the inside, flames flaring out all the window openings to add drama.

It'd worked perfectly.

"Now that was fun." Meg's grandmother smiled. "If you have any trouble with Haley this evening, you know where to find me."

"Thanks."

Ryan appeared beside him. "YouTube, huh?"

Josh tilted his head as he watched the fire crew trip over themselves as they tried to put out a fire that'd go out on its own if they didn't hurry. "The Internet is an amazing thing." He clapped his hand on Ryan's shoulder, then went to talk to Meg.

He'd risked exposing his skills because it wouldn't be much longer before he could tell the truth anyway. Hopefully the Zozobra legend worked on cars as well as tall puppets. Having Meg firmly in his corner before the truth came out would be good.

Meg checked Haley's backpack one more time to be sure she had everything she'd need if her asthma acted up. Then she added another juice box, more crackers, and a banana in case Haley got hungry.

Josh took the backpack from her hands and tossed it in the backseat of his truck, next to Haley's car seat. "We're not going to Siberia, Meg. We'll stop and get something if she gets hungry."

"Okay. Haley likes chicken nuggets, grilled cheese—"

"Kid food. Got it." He leaned down and kissed her. "We'll be fine. Have fun at your girls' thing."

Meg leaned inside and gave Haley a kiss. "Be a good girl, okay, Bug?"

Haley nodded. "'Kay."

"And if you have trouble breathing, tell Daddy right away."

"Okay. Bye, Momma."

Meg's stomach hurt. Josh didn't have much experience alone with Haley. Even worse, he had to babysit until her girls' night was over. She turned to him. "You know what? Maybe I'll go along with you guys and just be late to Pam's thing."

"You don't trust me to bring her back?"

Seeing the flash of pain in his eyes, she laid a hand on his arm and gave it a quick squeeze. "No. It's not that. What if Haley has trouble breathing with all that dust in the barn?"

Josh moved Meg aside and closed Haley's door. "Then I'll know exactly what to do. Stop worrying."

Meg huffed out a breath and crossed her arms. "When she has to go to the bathroom—"

Josh laid his fingers over her lips. "I can handle this. But how about we stay at the guesthouse tonight so your grandmother will be close by? Would that make you feel better?"

She nodded, but he didn't move his fingers.

"Great. Now smile and wave goodbye, so Haley sees how you aren't worried."

His new bossiness was getting on her nerves.

When she narrowed her eyes, he quickly removed his fingers and whispered, "I know how you get after these girls' things. All that talk about men, too much to drink. You'll be all hot and bothered. Begging me to put you out of your misery." He got in, rolled down his window, and sent her a sexy grin. "I'll wait up."

"How considerate of you." As Josh and Haley backed out of the drive she plastered on a fake smile and waved. "Text me when you get there. And when you're back!"

Josh sent her a salute, then headed down the highway.

Lord, this could be a disaster.

CHAPTER EIGHTEEN

*J*osh smiled as he headed south toward the ranch. Meg letting him take Haley had been a leap of faith for her. The ultimate show of trust. Big step.

He'd get her to tell him she loved him yet.

Josh glanced in the rearview mirror at Haley again. She'd just awoken from her forty-five-minute nap and was squirming around in her car seat. He reached for the end-of-the-world survival kit of a backpack Meg had sent along. His hand landed on some chunky cardboard books, so he tugged them out. "Want to look at these?"

Haley nodded and took the books. "I have to go potty."

"Oh. Okay." They'd just passed through a small town. It only had a busy convenience store that sold gas. The next town was bigger, but twenty minutes away. Better not risk it. Josh slowed the truck and then turned it around.

"Hurry, Daddy!"

Hopefully Meg had sent along a change of clothes just in case. "Almost there."

After they pulled into the last empty space in front of the store, he jumped out and opened the back door. After tackling the crazy harness system, he finally freed her from the car seat and then jogged toward the glass doors. He yanked one open and headed for the rear. There was a line outside the women's restroom, but thankfully not one outside the men's. Just as he was about to push the door open, he stopped and looked at Haley. Her face was scrunched as she strained to hang on.

He couldn't take her in there with guys at urinals showing their junk. Unless maybe he covered her eyes and made a dash for the stall? Probably a bad idea.

He checked out the women standing in line. Maybe he could ask one of them to take her. The next one in line was tatted up, and had purple hair and fingernails shaped into deadly points.

Nope.

Haley couldn't wait for the third woman in line who had a kid of her own.

He turned and raced back to his truck, grabbed the backpack, and then headed behind the store and into the woods. "We're going to have to go out here, okay?"

Haley's eyes widened. "Outside?"

"Boys do it all the time. It's fun." He moved in front of a tree, suddenly realizing it didn't work the same with girls. He'd have to get creative if they were going to keep everything dry. Josh shifted her in front of him and placed her tennis shoes against the bark. Then he widened his stance to keep his boots out of the way. "I'll close my eyes, and then you pull everything way down to your shoes and let it rip."

Haley giggled. "Okay."

She wiggled around, and then the telltale splatter hitting the dirt at his feet signaled success.

She said, "Now we have to wipe and wash our hands."

Dammit. Being a guy was so much easier. He held Haley tight with one arm while his free hand groped around in the back-pack. Please let Meg have included something to clean up with. He finally found a pack of baby wipes and handed one to Haley, hoping she could do that part on her own.

"All done."

Thank God. He put her down and dealt with extracting more wipes from the container. When Haley appeared beside him again all dressed, she reached for a juice box. He caught her hands and used a wipe to clean them. Then he reluctantly handed her the juice. Inevitably she was going to have to use the bathroom again. He hoped they could make it all the way to the ranch so they wouldn't have to find another tree.

He handed her a bag filled with the orange fish-shaped crackers she'd asked for, and then carried her to the truck with a newfound respect for the well-equipped backpack. He'd had missions less complicated than taking a little girl to the bathroom. He should have let Meg finish whatever she was going to tell him about that.

Back on the road again, he glanced at Haley looking at her books and stuffing crackers into her mouth. An unfamiliar warmth surged through him as he watched her.

He'd feared he wouldn't know how to be a good parent because of his background, but he hadn't been prepared for how quickly a kid could take complete control over his heart. Seeing her joy at the simplest things and watching her learn was amazing. He didn't know he could love anyone other than Meg so much.

He still had a lot to learn about how to care for her, but luckily Haley often told him if he was doing something wrong. So far, so good. Meg had nothing to worry about. He could do this.

After he pulled up beside the barn at the ranch, Josh grabbed his cell and turned to Haley in the backseat. "Wave hello to Mommy."

He snapped a picture of a smiling Haley, her hands, face, and shirt smeared with orange crumbs and her shorts twisted funny from their pit stop.

Josh sent the picture to Meg with the caption We're here. She gets her table manners from you. Hopefully Haley wouldn't mention their outdoor bathroom adventure to Meg.

Not a minute passed before Meg replied. Wipes in the back-pack, funny guy. Use them!

Will do. Stop worrying.

Can't.

Try harder. Love you.

There was a long pause before she typed back. I'm still working on that. Thx for remembering to text me. Have fun.

He shook his head and then put his phone away. Did the "still working on that" part refer to the worry for Haley, or about saying she loved him back? Probably both. He hoped.

After a quick wipe down, he grabbed Haley from the backseat and plopped her onto the ground. "Let's go see Charlie."

They circled around the barn because he worried about the dust and Haley's asthma too, and walked to the back pasture. Eric and Mr. J were inside the fence working on Charlie's hoof. Other horses were milling about. Mr. J lifted a hand in greeting, but Eric didn't seem to notice they were there. Probably had his earbuds in again.

When Haley saw the puppies and their mother, she let out a yelp. With their stubby little tails wagging, they all ran full tilt toward her.

Giggling and trying to pet all four dogs at once, Haley sat down and let them crawl all over her. Pure joy lit her face as she rolled around with them.

Yeah, she needed a puppy. The trick might be getting her to pick just one.

With Haley content, he hopped the fence to see about Charlie.

"Hey, guys." When he got closer, Eric finally turned around. The kid had a shiner under his left eye, a busted lip, and cuts and bruises all along his arms.

Eric nodded, then quickly looked away.

Hot anger, mixed with memories of his own humiliation at the hands of bullies, made Josh tilt his head, silently asking to speak with Mr. J alone.

His former mentor said, "Eric, why don't you finish up here while I talk to Josh for a minute?"

Eric nodded and got back to work.

Once inside the barn, Josh asked, "When did that happen?"

Mr. J's jaw twitched in annoyance. "Last night. And the night before last. He's miserable here and not making friends. I've looked into other options, but no one can take him until August. I called his grandmother this morning to see how she's doing. She's in the hospital again so she can't take his guardianship back."

Josh was supposed to be staying detached, dammit. Maybe helping at the ranch, with all the memories, hadn't been the best idea. He might have to rethink that and find another venue to help.

But Eric was a good kid who needed a break. And for the first time in his life, Josh was in a position to help. "So Eric just needs a place for a couple of months?" Meg could probably use some cheap manual labor at her lodge. Or maybe Eric could help out in Zeke's shop.

When Eric screamed, "No, stop!" Josh whirled around.

Haley had followed a puppy under the fence and into the horse corral. His heart lurched as he took off at a full run.

Josh laid a hand on the fence and swung his feet over. As his boots hit the dirt, Eric scooped up a crying Haley and then the pup, hauling them both out of harm's way. Eric handed Haley to Josh. "I'm sorry I scared her. I didn't want her to get hurt."

Josh took Haley and held her close, not sure who was more scared—her or him. "Thanks, Eric."

The kid smiled. "My little sister always did dumb stuff like that too. You gotta watch them all the time." When Eric's smile

TAMRA BAUMANN

slowly faded and sadness flashed in his eyes—missing his little sister, no doubt—Josh was a goner.

He was going to take the kid and the damn dogs Eric loved too. It was just for a few months. There'd be plenty of room at the lodge for all of them. And they'd find homes for the other dogs.

Meg was going to kill him.

Meg sat next to Casey on the couch at Pam's house. With girls' night in full swing, Meg reached for her phone again, but still no word from Josh. They should have been back an hour ago.

Casey whispered, "They probably just stopped for dinner. Here." Casey stuck a glass of wine into Meg's hand. "Drink up. I'm gonna get some more nachos."

"Bring me some too, please." Pam always threw a fun party, but Meg just wasn't feeling it. Especially after Sarah had told her that Amber had tried to convince Sarah's husband, an electrician, not to work at the lodge.

Hopefully Beau would be able to convince the subs to ignore Amber too, or Meg might be in trouble. She had more pre-booking money now and couldn't afford to open late. Her stomach ached thinking about what would happen if she couldn't finish in time and had to return money already spent.

Pam sat down beside her on the couch. "So what's up with you and Amber? She said if you were coming to the party tonight she wasn't. When I told her that was stupid, she said she was too busy anyway. Some PowerPoint thing she had to get done for Founder's Day tomorrow."

Meg usually told Pam everything, but had decided not to tell anyone about her and Amber being sisters—yet. Not because her father asked her not to, but because she didn't need any more complications at the moment. "I'm sure she's just being her usual drama-queen self."

"Yeah, probably. So how's it going with you and Josh?"

Casey returned with three bowls of nachos. After she handed them out, she said, "Yeah, Meg. Spill."

"Wait. We want to hear too." Meg smiled as Sarah, the married love of Ryan's life; the new dentist, Tara; and Aunt Gloria gathered around.

"The sex is fantastic. But that wasn't ever our problem. When we first met, Josh was super attentive and sweet. But as time went on he changed. He became such a workaholic it was hard to get him to put away his phone or laptop long enough to watch a half-hour television show with me. But now he's back to the way he was before. He asks about my day and we talk about his, we take turns making dinner, he takes Haley for little outings every day, never checks e-mail while we eat, and actually pays attention when I tell him something. I used to have to send him e-mails if I wanted him to remember things we had planned. It's pretty much great between us now."

Casey took a deep drink from her glass. "There's an unspoken 'but' in there. What is it?"

Her sister knew her too well. "Besides being concerned he might slip back into workaholic mode, I'm worried that after having that high-powered job he's going to get bored with small-town life and leave us again. I mean, seriously? No matter how much he tells me he's happy getting his hands dirty for a change, how can a guy who used to work practically nonstop and made a gazillion dollars doing it be happy working on copters and engines with Zeke?"

Meg took a quick nacho break. They were just too good to ignore. "I'm pretty much committed to staying here now, no matter how badly Amber wants to run me out of town. So I'm afraid to take that final leap and dive in all the way. It hurt too much when he left the last time."

Pam nodded as she popped another nacho in her mouth. "Yeah, and didn't you say he wants to work with troubled kids? Not enough of those around here to keep him busy with that. You may have a point."

Aunt Gloria shook her head. "I see the way that man looks at you. And the way you look at him when you think no one is watching. You're already in, whether you want to admit it or not."

Was she? While she pondered that, Meg's phone vibrated in her back pocket. "Maybe this is Josh."

Meg tapped the text icon. Got delayed with some paperwork, but we're back now. Have a few surprises for you. Maybe you can ask the ladies if anyone wants a puppy?

Josh had already mentioned the little boy at the ranch needing to find homes for the dogs. But paperwork? Something was up. What kind of surprises? Don't tell me you brought a puppy home!

Okay, I won't tell you. Gotta go. Haley's hungry.

Dammit.

She looked up at all the women, who were waiting patiently to see what was up. "He brought a puppy home. I'm going to kill him."

Tara, a tall, thin, beautiful blonde, laughed. "That's the sign of a committed man, if you ask me. I saw the picture he posted at the diner. Those are some pretty cute pups. I've been thinking of taking one now that I'm all settled in my house."

Sarah, always so quiet and sweet, smiled. "They really are adorable. I asked, but Ed won't let me have one. It just melted my heart when Haley told me at the fund-raiser how badly she wants a dog, Meg. You have all that room now."

Aunt Gloria nodded and took another slug of wine. "Dogs are good for kids. Teaches them responsibility."

Pam stood and grabbed another bottle of wine, then went around topping off everyone's glasses. "You always had a dog growing up, Meg, so why shouldn't Haley?"

Casey nodded and opened her mouth to add her opinion, but Meg held up a hand to cut her off. "Okay. Fine. She can keep the dog. But Josh is going to have to do the housebreaking." Relieved that Josh and Haley, and a new puppy, were back and safely tucked into the guesthouse, Meg drained her wineglass, ready to have some fun.

⎯⎯

Just before midnight, Meg reached for the handle on the guest-house door. Josh hadn't locked it like she'd expected. Which was a good thing because she didn't have her keys with her. Hopefully he'd waited up. He'd been right earlier—a hot roll in the hay would be the perfect ending to a pretty great day.

As she quietly swung the door open, three little balls of fur slipped past her feet. A bigger version walked out slowly behind.

What the . . . ? She'd wrapped her head around one dog, but not four! Josh was so not getting lucky now.

She waited while they all did their business, then shooed them back inside. There was an overturned box by the door that must've been where the pups were supposed to be sleeping. She righted the box and then wrestled the dogs back inside while the momma dog laid down to watch over the whole affair. One pup who looked like a little pirate with a patch over one eye tried to make a run for it, but Meg snagged him. When she lifted him to eye level to scold him, a rough little pink tongue slipped out and licked her cheek. Instead of chastising him, she kissed him on the top of the head, then plopped him into the box with the others.

She reinforced the box with extra weight at the bottom, then turned and pulled up short. A boy with a bruised face was sound asleep on the love seat and Josh and Haley were both asleep on the couch. An open book lay facedown next to Haley's head on Josh's chest. They must've fallen asleep reading.

It melted her heart.

But not for long, because the house was a disaster. There were books, toys, and torn-up stuffed animals all over the floor. The puppies must've gotten ahold of them after they'd busted themselves out.

Josh was usually a light sleeper, but it looked like he'd slept right through the stuffed-animal murders. Two kids and four dogs must have worn him out. Served him right.

Josh had some serious 'splaining to do in the morning.

After getting ready for bed, Meg switched off the light and crawled under the sheets. Just as she was about to drift off, soft whining accompanied by scratching on her door made her throw the covers back. At this rate, she was never going to get any sleep.

Whipping the door open, ready to scold the momma dog, she looked down. A lone escaped pup looked up at her and wagged his stub tail. It was pirate face.

Resigned, she huffed out a breath and lifted the pooch up. After creating a makeshift bed out of towels and a laundry basket, she settled the pup in and laid the basket next to her bed. "I'm right up here, see? Now go to sleep."

Just as she closed her eyes, the puppy whined again. Meg reached down and petted the dog until it quieted. But no sooner than Meg had fallen asleep, the whining started again. It was like having a newborn.

This dog was lucky it was her favorite of the three puppies or she'd make Josh deal with it. She reached down and petted the dog until it settled again. Brother. Look at her, getting all attached after only a half hour.

Closing her eyes, she gave up and just left her hand on the puppy's back, willing herself to sleep.

Meg awoke to a warm tongue licking her tingling, numb fingers. It was morning, but just barely. The pooch probably needed to go outside again.

With her stiff arm, she lifted pirate pup from the basket and stared into his adorable, furry little face. "I hereby dub you Captain Jack Sparrow. No. What the heck, maybe I'll just call you Johnny Depp. You're both pretty darned cute. And you'll probably have the chance to meet him. He's a big tipper and one of my favorite guests."

And, she was talking to a dog.

Sheesh.

When she opened the bedroom door, the boy was up. His hands were full of stuffed-animal guts and the room was almost tidy again. Josh and Haley were still asleep on the couch.

She whispered, "Hi. Thanks for cleaning up. I'm Meg."

Relief flashed across the kid's face. "There's the missing one." He dumped the stuffing into a garbage bag and then held his hands out for the pup. "I'm Eric. I'll take him outside with the others. I made a pen for them."

"Thanks, Eric." Meg handed the dog over and started for the kitchen. A kid who cleaned up and figured out how to make a pen all before six a.m. didn't seem like the kind to get into fights. There must be some big story behind Eric and the dogs. Best to load up on caffeine before she and Josh got into it.

As she flipped the switch for the coffeemaker, a big set of hands slipped around her waist.

"Morning." Josh pulled her against him and wrapped her up tight, trapping her arms at her sides. Then he nibbled on her neck. A move that would have normally driven her wild.

"Not gonna work, pal. But you're smart to restrain my fists. I'm tempted to belt you."

He kissed her cheek. "I deserve it, but will you hear me out first, please?" He let his arms fall to his sides, releasing her.

It was hard to fight with someone who admitted his guilt right up front and sounded so sincere, but she was willing to try. Spinning around, she said, "You knew I didn't want a dog right now."

He crossed his arms. "That's why my plan was to get a puppy for myself, so you wouldn't have to deal with it. But then things got complicated."

Struggling to keep her voice low so as not to wake Haley, she said, "It doesn't work that way with kids."

Josh's brows crumpled in confusion. "What do you mean?"

"She's going to fall in love with it and think of it as hers, no matter if it's mine or yours."

"I didn't think of that. But why does that matter?"

Temper flaring, she blurted out, "I don't appreciate you making this big a decision about our daughter without me. I understand this is all new to you, but if things don't work out . . . well, it just adds a complication we don't need right now!"

Josh's jaw tightened. "If things don't work out? I thought—" Eric came back inside, so Josh took her arm and guided her to the bedroom. He shut the door behind them. "I thought we were on the same page here. Clearly we're not."

He was angry too. But holding it together better.

Haley's puppy was going to be one more thing they'd have to share for years to come. Bonding them even tighter. Half of her liked the idea, but her other half was terrified.

Meg sank to the edge of the bed. As she opened her mouth to try to explain, he said, "I'm in this for the long haul, Meg. I thought you were too."

She stared into his eyes; they were swimming with pain and frustration.

The girls had all ganged up on her the night before, telling her she needed to deal with her trust issues. Those junior shrinks concluded it had started with her dad, and then Amber made it worse when she'd suddenly turned on her. That's why Meg had kept most people at arm's length and picked emotionally remote men whom she expected to dump her.

Until she'd met Josh. He was the first guy she'd allowed herself to trust. Then he'd left her too. But, unlike the others, he'd come back. That had to count for something. People make mistakes; she'd certainly made her share.

Casey had admitted she actually liked Josh, thought he was good for Meg.

If Casey liked him, then maybe he wasn't the usual type Meg always picked. Casey's approval made the decision easier. Maybe it was time to break the cycle and get over it. He'd changed, so maybe she could too.

"I'm sorry. What I should've said was that when it comes to Haley, we need to start making decisions together—especially something as big as getting a dog, Josh."

He cringed. "Well, then maybe I'd better tell you the rest. About Eric. But first, I'd like to tell you what it was like for me growing up at the ranch."

Josh opened up for the first time about his past. It was a subject he'd never wanted to talk about, so she'd never pressed. It had made it that much easier not to tell him about her past either.

She couldn't imagine Josh as a skinny kid, getting beat up regularly. There were few who'd take him on now. No wonder he was so good about going to the gym and keeping fit. It must have given him a sense of control he never had as a kid.

By the time he'd finished his story she felt so sorry for Eric, there was no way she could be angry at Josh for taking the kid away from the pain and the bullying.

But keeping a kid and four dogs at the lodge while it was being renovated was no small thing and he should've at least called her. "Fine. Eric can stay for the summer. And one pup. I vote for the little pirate. But no more decisions like this without talking to me. Got it?"

"Yep." He smiled so sweetly it weakened her defenses, as usual. "How about I lock the door and we finish making up?"

"Or, how about you go out there and make breakfast for that crowd while I take a shower and try to figure out how to find homes for those other three dogs before Haley gets too attached?"

"Or I can do that." He stood and opened the door. "Thank you, Meg. I knew you'd understand. You have a big heart under all that bluster. It's what I love most about you."

She opened her mouth to deny it, but when he quirked a challenging brow, she stopped. He'd always seen right through her. That's what had made her fall so hard for him when they first met. How he seemed to know her and understand her so quickly. Like no other man ever had. It's why she'd let her defenses down for the first time and allowed herself to love him.

She rose from the bed and gave him a hug. Laying her forehead against his hard chest, she whispered, "That I didn't kill you over this probably means I love you too." She gave him a squeeze. "I might know for sure if you make me French toast."

Chuckling, he gave her butt a light smack. "I'll get a straight-up confession of love out of you yet. But I'll take this one for now, even if it is French toast blackmail."

She rolled her eyes at his bad joke, then crossed to the bathroom and turned on the shower.

She was all in now. Hopefully she hadn't made a big mistake. Again.

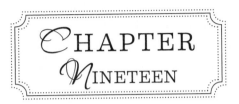

CHAPTER NINETEEN

Because it was Saturday morning and sleeping in might be involved for those lucky enough to be able to, Meg waited until ten o'clock to set out on her mission to find the puppies a good home. She knocked on Tara's front door, juggling the basket on her hip with two wiggling pups inside. Hopefully it hadn't been the wine talking when Tara said she wanted a puppy last night.

When the door swung open, Tara stood before her in cute jogging attire and a little white towel slung around her moist neck. Her lips slowly tilted. "Josh brought *all* the puppies home? Is he still alive, or are you here for an alibi? Your brother Ben is more my type, but I guess I could be persuaded to say you and I spent the whole night together." She reached inside the basket to pet the dogs.

Meg laughed. "You'd totally be my type if I were into women. Especially if you look this good after a run. That's just not right."

Tara smirked. "Lie to me. Butter me up so I'll take a pup. I'm on to you, Megan."

No lie. Tara was the prettiest woman Meg had ever met. It was just a bonus she was nice too. "Which one would you like? Or if you just can't decide, why not take both?"

Tara grabbed the basket and then stepped aside, inviting Meg in. After leading the way to a living room right out of an interior decorating magazine, Tara took the dogs out and played with them on the shiny wood floor.

"I'd like to take both and then give one to Sarah as a gift. She wants one so badly, but I got the impression her husband holds all the power in their relationship."

That was the understatement of the year. Ed was a downright bastard sometimes. "Yeah. Nice thought, but when Ed's unhappy, Sarah pays for it."

Tara frowned as she stroked the pup curled up in her lap. "I hate to hear that. Sarah deserves better."

Sarah deserved Ryan, but too late for that.

The other pup made a run for it, but Tara stretched out and grabbed it. Her shirt rode up, exposing some nasty, jagged scars on her stomach and back. Not wanting to stare, Meg quickly looked away.

But Tara noticed.

"Those are a story for a future girls' night. Suffice to say, I totally understand your reluctance to trust Josh again after being hurt." She brought the sleepy pup from her lap up to eye level and smiled. "I'll take this little cutie."

"Thanks, I owe you one, Tara." Meg wanted to ask who or what had done that to her. But it didn't seem Tara wanted to talk about it. Might be one of the reasons a young dentist would move to such a small town where she didn't know a soul, when she could probably make a whole lot more money in Denver. "Are you coming to the Founder's Day dinner later?"

Tara shook her head. "Nope. Looks like I have a date tonight with my little man here."

"We'll miss you, but staying home means you won't have to endure my dad and his windy speeches about the history of Anderson Butte. I'd skip too, if I could."

As Meg rounded up the other wiggly puppy into the basket, Tara said, "So, I'm dying to know. Did our pep talk work last night? Did you finally commit, and are you and Josh on speaking terms today?"

"Yes, but I really should have made him work a little harder for it. Not only did he bring all the dogs home, but he also brought home a ten-year-old boy who's going to stay with us for a few months. Speaking of that, Eric got into a fight the other day and finally admitted to Josh this morning his front teeth are still hurting. Do you have time to see him on Monday?"

Tara's brows spiked. "If he's in pain, I'll see him right away. Let me get cleaned up and I'll meet him at my office. Forty-five minutes?"

One of the benefits of living in a small town and not Denver anymore. People did favors because it was the right thing to do. Tara was going to fit right in. "Do you take puppy chow in payment? Josh has a truck bed full."

Tara laughed. "I think we can work something out."

Meg walked to the front door. "Thanks, Tara. Now I owe you twice."

Tara snuggled with her new puppy and sighed. "This little guy makes us even."

She'd have to remember to tell Ben that Tara thought he was cute. He needed to quit dating bimbos and get serious for a change. Tara would be perfect for her brother.

Just as Tara was about to close her front door, she said, "Wait. Mrs. Jenkins was in to see me last week. Her dog died recently and she'd seemed pretty upset. Maybe she'd like another?"

"I'll stop by there next. Thanks."

Meg texted Josh about Eric's dental appointment and asked him to bring along dog food, then reluctantly headed up the hill to a quaint little cabin with a blue metal roof, nestled among the trees.

Mrs. Jenkins, a widow, the leader of the Three Amigos, and Meg's former principal, was not Meg's number one fan. Hopefully the pup would soften her up a bit.

Meg spotted her struggling with a wheelbarrow full of weeds. "Need a hand?"

The old woman stopped and wiped her brow. Then her eyes narrowed. "What have you got there, Megan?"

"A puppy who needs a good home." Meg laid the basket at Mrs. Jenkins's feet and then lifted the wheelbarrow. "Where did you want this?" She'd let the puppy sell itself.

Mrs. Jenkins stood with her hands on her hips, lips pursed as she peered down into the basket. "Around the back. I'm making a pile to burn later."

Meg found the pile and dumped out the contents, then hurried back. Mrs. Jenkins was still staring at the dog. "You think giving me a puppy will make up for all the grief you've caused me over the years?"

Always back to that with her. "No, I don't, but Tara mentioned you're missing your dog, so I thought this little girl would cheer you up for a few minutes, even if you don't want to take her in."

Mrs. Jenkins picked up the pup, then brought it to the porch steps and sat down. Tears welled in her eyes. "I do miss my Bella. This sweet little girl is cute, but I'm not sure I'm up for another dog quite yet."

"I understand. I'll go fill this up again while you take a break."

Meg went to the garden to pull weeds. It was the least she could do after all the crap she'd dealt the poor woman years ago.

Luckily, there weren't many weeds left, so she picked up a pair of dusty gloves that lay on the fence post and set in. Pulling weeds in her grandmother's garden was one of Meg's usual punishments as a kid, so she was well trained. And darned fast because it was boring.

Must be lonely living all alone like Mrs. Jenkins. No one to talk to before she went to sleep at night or when she woke in the morning. Meg had missed that after Josh left. It'd been nice to have that back. The great sex made it even better.

After the wheelbarrow was full, she dumped it along with the other weeds in back and then went to find Mrs. Jenkins. She had the puppy all set up with a bowl of water and a chew toy on her front porch.

"All done. You have a nice garden going, Mrs. Jenkins." Meg put the wheelbarrow in the shed, then made her way back to the house. "We'll get out of your way now."

"Thank you for finishing up my weeding, Megan. I appreciate it, but you know, a simple apology goes a long way."

"That would make a difference to you after all this time?"

"If you really meant it."

Meg sat on the porch and let out a breath. "Looking back, I realize now why I acted out so much. It was meant for my dad. I never set out to cause everyone else so much misery, it just always seemed to turn out that way." She stared into the woman's rheumy eyes. "So I hope you'll accept my apology for all the trouble my bad behavior caused you and the school, Mrs. Jenkins."

"Wait until I tell Edna and Mable." She slapped her knee and laughed. "They're never going to believe those words came from your smart mouth. Apology accepted, Megan." She picked up the pup. "And thank you for bringing me my new little Bella. I'm keeping her."

That she might finally be forgiven by one of the Three Amigos sent an unexpected wave of relief through Meg. "Awesome. Going to the dinner?"

"Yep. I've got a crate to keep this little one out of trouble while I'm gone. But it looks like rain. We'll probably end up eating supper in the gym again. Coach Wilson is going to hate that."

Meg glanced at the gathering dark clouds above her head. "I'm sure Coach is already there, laying down that thick paper to protect his precious wood floor."

"I imagine. Say, Amber asked me for some old photos and such the other day. She's been asking everyone, so maybe she has something nice to entertain us with this year."

Nice? Fat chance of that.

"Maybe." Meg gathered up the basket and gave the pup one last pat. "See you later. And thanks, Mrs. Jenkins. For everything."

Josh pushed Haley in the swing at the park as he waited for Eric to finish up at the dentist's office. He stared into people's faces as they strolled past the town square, looking for the person Watts promised to send during the celebration. The agent would be dressed as a tourist, casually window-shopping, scoping things out before they made their move.

Then he spotted her. Watts had done that on purpose, the bastard. Of all the agents in their department, he sent a woman Josh used to hook up with occasionally between missions before he'd met Meg.

Evans met his gaze and lifted her chin slightly in greeting before turning to stare at the display in the T-shirt shop's window.

It was go time. Time to find out what was going to happen if Megan's father was sent to jail, and how Meg would react when she learned of his role.

And there was Meg now, strolling toward them with a big smile on her face. She surprised him when she threw herself at him, wrapped her legs around his waist, and planted a noisy kiss on his mouth. "I found homes for both the pups and you'll never believe what just happened!"

Josh glanced over Meg's shoulder in time to spot Evans and the sneer on her face before she moved on to the next shop.

Meg grabbed his face with both hands, forcing his attention back to her. "Hey. You've got the 'old Josh' look on your face. What's the matter?"

He forced a smile. "The 'old Josh' look? What's that?" He needed to pull it together. Get his head in the game. He couldn't afford to be responsible for blowing the one mission that would finally set him free.

"The look where you get all serious and distracted. Something wrong?"

Haley called out, "Push, Daddy!"

He sent Haley flying so high she giggled as Meg slid down his body. "I was just thinking it was taking Eric an awful long time. Maybe I'd better go check on him now that you're here to watch Haley?"

"Okay." Meg frowned like she didn't believe him. But after giving Haley another push, a smile slowly lit Meg's face. "Mrs. Jenkins took the other puppy. Tara will be glad to know. Tell her, will you?"

"Yep." He gave her a quick kiss. "Be right back."

Relief filled him as he turned to go check on Eric. Seemed Meg believed him after all. He was so damned tired of lying to her. Hopefully in a few days it'd all be done with and he could finally start his life over.

His phoned buzzed with a text from Watts. Hey, didn't catch the time the movie starts. Hope it's not three hours long.

He wanted Josh to let him know when the mayor was giving his speech and how long Evans had to get the task completed. Josh was trying to steer clear of the whole thing, but it made sense to help this one last time. Need to check showtimes.

After he put his phone away and crossed the street, he felt her presence. They weren't out of Meg's sight yet, so Evans stayed just behind him.

She said softly, "I've missed you, Sam. Let's get together after."

Megan and Watts were the only ones who knew his real name before. Even among his fellow agents. He'd wanted to leave his old life completely behind. But the wariness and the deeply buried vulnerability in Megan's gaze when they'd first met made him need to tell her the truth. At least about his name. Even if he'd had to lie to her about everything else.

He increased his pace. "Negative."

After tugging Tara's office door open, he walked inside and then took a second to compose himself.

Evans could be trouble. She might not know he'd quit and think he was undercover playing a part. Hopefully she'd take his curt response for what it was meant to be and leave when she was done planting the tracking software.

Tara had told him to go on back when he returned, so he ventured past the empty receptionist's desk and the torture chairs. He found Eric and Tara laughing and playing with her puppy on the floor in her office.

Eric's cheeks had turned red when Tara smiled at him when they'd first met. He obviously wasn't too young to appreciate a pretty woman.

But Tara had fear in her eyes when she'd greeted him. Someone had hurt her. Probably someone Josh's size. So now he pasted on a friendly smile. "How'd it go, guys?"

Tara turned and looked at his chin as her smile faded. "We fixed his cracked tooth, so he should start feeling better soon. But his x-rays showed a few other problem areas we should see to right away."

Eric's face turned panicked. "I don't know if I have enough money to pay you. Maybe I can ask my grandmother?"

Before Josh could tell Eric not to worry about it, he'd cover it, Tara said, "Well, how about a payment plan? I'm going to need someone to walk my puppy now and then while I'm busy seeing patients. We'll work something out." Tara stuck her hand out for a shake. "Deal?"

Eric smiled and returned her shake. "Deal." Holding her hand pinked up Eric's cheeks again, so he quickly hopped up and stood beside Josh.

Josh gave Eric's shoulder a sympathetic squeeze. It was tough to be ten and crushing on an older woman.

When the boy didn't flinch at his touch, Josh left his hand on Eric's shoulder. "Meg said to tell you Mrs. Jenkins took the other pup."

Tara stood and finally looked him straight in the eyes. "That's great. You guys have fun at the dinner this evening." She quickly turned and picked up her dog.

He had an overwhelming urge to look into her situation, to be sure she wasn't still in danger, but he quickly shut it down.

He was almost done with that part of his life.

Forever.

CHAPTER TWENTY

With Haley on her hip, Meg led the way through the pouring rain toward the high school's steps for the Founder's Day celebration. Josh and Eric jogged closely behind. Her father expected the family to be in place first, so the parking lot was empty and they found a spot right up front. She hadn't taken the extra time to get all fixed up just so the rain could ruin her makeup, so she powered forward.

As they approached the big set of doors, she expected Josh to move ahead and open it for her like he usually did, but he was busy with his phone. Again.

He'd been engrossed with his phone ever since the park. Had she spoken too soon when she'd told the girls Josh had changed?

Meg switched Haley to her other hip, then yanked the heavy door, and they all entered the quiet building. With Eric's wet sneakers squeaking against the highly polished floors and Josh bringing up the rear, they trooped past long rows of lockers. Eric walked beside her, his head swiveling back and forth, checking things out. He was a curious kid. Always asking questions. Just like her nephews.

But it was kind of embarrassing the lanky ten-year-old was almost as tall as she was. Even in her heels. "I hope you're hungry,

Eric. There's going to be a ton of food and tables loaded with yummy desserts. And you can go back as many times as you like. It's all on my dad, so eat up." Josh had told her earlier how Eric was worried about money, so she wanted to be sure he knew the food was free. The kid needed to put some meat on his skinny frame.

Eric grinned. "Thanks. This is a big school for a small town, isn't it?"

"Yeah. We're one of the few towns around with a high school. Kids from all the surrounding areas get bussed in. My dad fought hard to have it built here."

It hadn't been an easy battle. Her father had donated the land on the edge of town and spent many hours lobbying the state school board on behalf of Anderson Butte. Her dad wasn't *all* bad.

"I was in the first class to ever go through all four years." She detoured them down a wide side hallway to the front of a big glass case that held various awards. Pointing to some in the back, she said, "I still hold two school records no one has been able to break. In track and field, and swimming." She pointed out her picture, smiling and sopping wet, holding up a medal. "See, Haley? That's Mommy when I was younger."

Haley nodded but couldn't have cared less.

Eric's face scrunched as he studied the engraved plaques. "Wow. After *all* these years, no one has ever broken your records? That's awesome!"

"Hey. It's only been ten. I'm not that old!"

Eric surprised her when he smiled shyly and said, "Just teasing. It's really cool."

Her sports records were the only thing she could be proud of from her high school days. She wouldn't tell Eric, but she probably still held the record for most hours in detention too.

Josh stood behind them, his fingers still flying over his phone, just like he used to. Was the phone-obsessed Josh surfacing again? She'd had enough.

"Who've you been texting all day?"

His head whipped up and he sent her a weak smile. "People from my old work. There's a problem with something I used to be in charge of. Just helping out." He quickly slid his phone in his back pocket again. "So, how's this whole deal work? Will it last long?"

Was he on some sort of time schedule all of the sudden? "Normally, it's outside on the football field. Everyone eats and plays games while my dad carries on over the stadium's PA system. Afterward, we watch a fireworks show my brothers take great pride in putting on.

"But since it's dumping rain it'll all be inside. We'll get our food from the cafeteria and then everyone goes to the gym to sit on the bleachers and eat while my dad bores everyone to tears. Haley and I will have to sit up front on the raised dais with the rest of my family."

Josh nodded. "So . . . what? A couple of hours, then?"

"Got big plans after or something? There's no set time, we just eat and visit until we're done. Small town, remember?"

"Sure." He turned and punched Eric lightly on the shoulder. "Want to try and set a new school record of our own for the most plates of food consumed?"

So Josh *had* been listening earlier. And he'd put his phone away and was interested in the plans. Maybe she was just being paranoid about the whole thing.

Eric sent an elbow to Josh's ribs. "Bet I can beat a lightweight like you."

"You're on." He held his knuckles out for a bump.

When Eric tapped his fist against Josh's, Meg smiled. That was probably Josh's sneaky way of getting some meat on Eric's bones.

The kid was going to fit in with them just fine for the summer. Hopefully the paperwork would get settled so Eric wouldn't have to go back to that ranch.

———————

Keeping an eye on the mayor to be sure he stayed put while Evans planted the tracking software, Josh held back a wince when Eric suggested just one more brownie. He was going to hurl if he had another bite of anything. Where did the kid put it all?

"No can do." He held up his palm for a high five. "You win."

"Yes!" Eric slapped Josh's hand and grinned from ear to ear. "Be right back."

As soon as Eric left, Zeke took the vacated seat next to Josh on the wooden bleachers.

"Granger. How's it going?"

"Great. The food was fantastic." He'd have to run five extra miles to make up for all he'd eaten.

Zeke slowly nodded. "I've been thinking about something I'd like to talk to you about."

"Sure. What's up?"

Zeke cleared his throat and sat up straighter. "I don't have any children to pass my business on to, and I've worked too hard to let one of my numbskull nephews run it into the ground, so I've been putting off my retirement. But, now that you're here, and have taken to the work like a duck to water, I was wondering if you'd consider letting me help you get certified to work on helicopters so I can finally retire? Then after that, I'd like to hand over my business to you. You'd keep all you earn."

Josh started to speak, but nothing but air passed his lips. Shock that anyone would be so kind to him, offer him something so huge, rendered him . . . amazed. "What would your family think of that, Zeke? Me running your shop and keeping all the profits?"

He shrugged. "None of their business. And you might be surprised how much my shop brings in. All the equipment is paid for, so you'd make plenty for your new family, and maybe even some extra so you can help a few more kids like Eric."

He'd love to run the shop as long as he could find a way to help kids like Eric too. It'd be the best of both worlds, but things were going to get complicated very soon. "Zeke, I don't—"

He plowed on, cutting Josh off. "I'm not giving you the equipment, just letting you use it for as long as you like. I'd appreciate it if you didn't share this next part because Meggy doesn't know, but I've left everything to her when I die. Those lazy relatives of mine weren't going to get anything anyway. But knowing Meg, she'll give them something because she'll feel bad for them. She talks a big talk, but deep down she's just a big marshmallow who'd bop me over the head for telling you that."

He knew that, but what Zeke didn't know was Josh's secret. The old guy might not be so quick to hand over his business once he found out Josh had been lying to Meg for years. Especially if Meg didn't take the news well.

"Thank you, Zeke. I appreciate the generous offer. But how about we see what the next few weeks bring, then after that, we'll talk about it again?" Josh held out his hand for a shake.

Zeke frowned. "What's the next few weeks got to do with the price of eggs?"

"Time to get used to the idea. To think it through."

"Okay." Zeke smiled and shook Josh's hand. "Enjoy the rest of the evening. I'm gonna sneak out before the mayor gets going. Heard all he has to say a time too many as it is."

The rain continued to pound on the skylights above as the mayor went on and on about Anderson Butte and its long history.

Eric was slumped over Josh's phone, playing a game with the sound muted, when the speech finally ended.

The thunderous clapping probably wasn't for the content, but because it was finally over. But one thing was for sure. Megan's father had a true passion for his town. Be a shame if he had to spend the rest of his days behind bars.

Evans would have had plenty of time to get in and out, but he still needed to let her know the mayor had left after his speech. Just in case.

Josh nudged Eric's shoulder with his. "I need to send a quick text."

Eric frowned, but paused the game and handed the phone over. Josh had just finished tapping out the text to Evans when a text came in from Meg. Could you come get Haley, please? She needs to run around a bit.

He looked up at Meg where she sat on the stage, and nodded. "Eric, I'm going to take Haley out in the hall for a minute. Stay here, please."

"Okay." Eric reached out for Josh's phone to continue his game.

After Abe, the fire chief, gave his usual speech detailing the need for more volunteer firefighters, Meg sat alone on the raised dais. Over the last half hour, after their father left, the rest of her siblings had found reasons to leave. She didn't care to stay for Amber's mystery presentation coming next. She'd done her duty and Haley was at her limit.

Meg gathered her things and stood as the lights went out and Amber's voice came over the PA system, asking for everyone's attention for a special presentation.

Perfect time to slip out.

A huge image of a smiling baby was projected on the wall. It took Meg a second to realize it was her up there.

What was Amber up to? Meg sank into her chair again.

Sending Meg a sneer, Amber stepped to the podium and grabbed the mic. "In honor of our town daughter's recent return, I thought you'd all enjoy this little stroll through memory lane. It'll answer some of your lingering questions, like who really egged Mrs. Beckett's car that summer when she'd been away for three weeks so it sat in the hot sun baking away. If you'll recall, it ruined her paint job."

The image changed to a picture of Megan with pigtails and braces. Not her finest look. Not her finest moment either.

Amber laughed. "And here's your culprit."

All eyes cut to Meg.

Amber had been standing right next to Meg that day, encouraging the whole thing. Seemed Amber wasn't confessing her role, though.

Before Meg could figure out what to do to make it stop, Amber said, "But let's start way back at the beginning. Be sure to note in all of Megan's family photos who she's never standing by. That's right. Our beloved mayor. Why do you suppose that is?"

A series of photos appeared in rapid succession of various groupings of her family, starting with her when she was just a baby, up until the beginning of the evening when they'd all lined up for a group shot.

Meg's stomach dropped. This wasn't going to end well.

"As some of you may have suspected, the truth is that Megan isn't an Anderson at all. That story about how my father was killed trying to help Meg's mother after her car went over the edge of the road was all made up by the mayor's brother, who many of you know was the sheriff at the time. The truth is, Megan's mother and my father were leaving town with their illegitimate offspring, Megan, when the accident occurred and they were both killed."

A collective gasp filled the air. Followed by low murmuring.

"Megan just recently found out her family has lied to her about it her whole life. And to all of us as well. But hang tight, people, it gets better. It'll be my pleasure to show you all who my half sister truly is."

Meg's heart beat triple time as she fought back the anger and tears rising in her throat. She wanted to crawl under the table but wouldn't give Amber the satisfaction. Worse, Eric still sat in the stands seeing all of Meg's dirty laundry revealed on the wall, twenty feet high.

Amber added, "And remember when the mayor's office window got busted out? Yep. You guessed it. Megan again."

Yeah, but it was a snowball, for God's sake. Meg hadn't known Amber had filled them with rocks before she'd encouraged Meg to launch one at her dad's window.

As Amber told them about Meg's secret crush on Jake the— obvious to everyone but Meg and Pam—gay mailman, laughter rose from the crowd.

Now she felt bad for Jake too. Hopefully he'd already left so he wouldn't have to endure the laughs because of her. Would he ever talk to her again after this?

Each new image on the wall made Meg look worse and worse, reminding her of things she deeply regretted.

The old, familiar urge to run crept slowly up her spine. It was dark; she might be able to slip out a side door. But that wouldn't solve anything. No. She'd stay and take her medicine.

Closing her eyes, she forced her reeling mind to focus. There had to be a way to end her public lynching short of forcibly taking Amber out.

But was Amber right? After all Meg had done—and it was playing out right before everyone's eyes reminding them—maybe she didn't deserve to be welcomed back to town. She couldn't even claim a family connection earned her the right because she wasn't an Anderson and now everyone knew it.

When she opened her eyes, an image appeared on the screen of Mrs. Jenkins with whipped cream dripping down her face.

The crowd roared with laughter as Meg's stomach clenched with deep remorse.

It was the time she'd tricked Mrs. Jenkins into manning a booth at a swim team fund-raiser called "Stump the Principal."

She hadn't told Mrs. Jenkins what would happen if she couldn't answer a question correctly.

Meg had found obscure facts on the Internet that no one could possibly know. Mrs. Jenkins had four whipped cream pies to the face that day but had been a good sport about it—until afterward. Meg spent a month in after-school detention for that one.

She turned to find her former principal in the crowd. Mrs. Jenkins had forgiven Meg just hours before, but probably wanted to take it back after being made the butt of that cruel joke all over again.

When she locked gazes with the older woman, Mrs. Jenkins mouthed, "Apologize."

A wave of hope rose through Meg as she remembered Mrs. Jenkins's earlier words—that it *would* make a difference, even after so much time had passed. She'd said only if Meg really meant it. She did. She was truly sorry for her bad behavior.

Unable to stomach any more, Meg stood and walked toward the podium. Amber was so engrossed in the next picture on the wall, she didn't notice when Meg slipped beside her and punched the power button on the laptop. When the wall went dark, Amber turned around and Meg yanked the mic from her half sister's clutches.

"Could someone hit the lights please? I have something to say."

When the lights came back up, Amber stood with her arms crossed. "Ready to leave town now, Meg? I think after seeing this, everyone agrees you're not welcome here."

Amber stood close enough so the mic picked up her words. When a few called out their agreement, it warred with Meg's newfound courage. Maybe she should just leave before it got any worse?

As quiet murmuring came from the bleachers, she looked for the answer in Mrs. Jenkins's eyes. She nodded, urging Meg to do what she got up there to do.

Courage renewed, Meg said, "It's true. Amber and I are sisters. Who would've seen that one coming, right? But I want to thank my sister for this opportunity."

The crowd slowly stilled.

"We hadn't gotten to the part in Amber's thorough presentation, but I'm sure it was there, about how we'd sneak out at night and let your cows out, Mr. Bower. And Mrs. Wilson, I owe you a few lawn gnomes. I see you can still get them on eBay, so I'll get right on that. And Mrs. Beckett? I'm sorry about the paint job on your car. I didn't know the eggs would do that in the hot sun, but I'll find a way to pay you back after I get my lodge up and going."

She held up her right hand. "But I swear, it's been over ten years since I've stolen apples from anyone's trees, thrown snowballs at windows, or even plucked daisies from your lovely garden, Mrs. Mitchell. I used to do that and then give them to Casey because they're her favorite. I just liked to see my hardworking sister smile."

Meg swallowed the tears welling in her throat. "I plan to stay this time, but I also plan to apologize to each and every one of you, individually, for the things I did when I was a kid. I know it's not enough for me to stand up here and tell you I've changed. I'm going to have to prove it. And I will. If you can find it in your hearts to give me the chance. If not . . . I understand."

Amber leaned close to the mic. "Nice try, Meg. But we all know you're a liar and just trying to save face."

A liar was the one thing she was not. She'd just been about to leave, but couldn't let Amber get away with that. It was tempting to tell them all how Amber had been there encouraging many of those stunts, but that was all in the past. Time to move forward.

Recalling the interesting things she'd learned about Amber at girls' night, all confirmed by Casey, Meg faced her half sister. She was just about to air Amber's dirty laundry, but Meg paused. Stooping to Amber's level wasn't the answer. She needed to be the bigger person. "I guess time will tell if I'm not being truthful, won't it? But I wish *you* nothing but the best."

After Meg turned off the mic, she whispered to Amber, "Leave Randy. No one deserves to be treated that way. And I'm honestly sorry about your mom."

Amber's eyes grew wide as she whisper-yelled back, "Who told . . . those are just more lies, Megan."

It was too small a town. Everyone knew the truth. The "story" was, Amber's mother had moved to California, but she was in a mental institution. And Randy was too much a jerk not to brag about all his women to the guys when he'd had a few drinks.

After Amber's head swiveled, probably checking to see if anyone else had heard, she said, "Whatever, Megan. I'm outta here." Red-faced, Amber marched down the stairs and out the side door, slamming it behind her.

Silence hung heavy in the air as two hundred sets of curious eyes bore down on her, wondering what Meg had said to set

Amber off, no doubt. She gently slid the mic into its stand, then turned and stepped off the stage, struggling to hold it together.

Throwing her shoulders back, she aimed for the rear set of doors, where Eric stood waiting for her. While taking her walk of shame, thoughts of crawling into bed and pulling the covers over her head until next month sounded pretty good.

Once outside, she let her pent-up tears fall.

Josh stood beside Haley in the hallway, waiting for her. "I heard the tail end of that. You did good, Meg."

When he spread his arms, she melted into his warm embrace and whispered, "I'm sorry you had to hear any of that."

He held her tight. "What I heard were the words of a brave woman with a big heart who cares enough to apologize to anyone she hurt. We all have a past, Meg. Let's go home."

Later that night, still lying wide awake long after everyone else had fallen asleep, Meg tried to slip out of bed without waking Josh, but his long arms reached out and pulled her back against his chest.

She whispered, "I thought you were asleep."

He grunted. "You were thinking too loud."

"Sorry." She chuckled and turned in his arms. His eyes were closed but a cute grin tilted his full, irresistibly sexy lips, so she gave them a quick peck. "I'll go make some tea and try to think quieter out in the living room so you can sleep."

Josh rolled over and trapped her under his big, heavy body. "Instead, why don't I give you something better to think about?"

The gleam in his eyes challenged her to put her troubles aside for a few minutes and play with him.

Why not? Her worries would be right where she left them in the morning. "What did you have in mind?"

"This." He trailed soft kisses up her neck. "And then maybe some more of this."

When he nipped lightly at her earlobe, she closed her eyes and sighed. She loved the way he always took his time, pleasing her before himself.

Maybe it was time to turn the tables a bit. Show him how much she loved that he'd stood outside the gym, waiting for her, even though he'd just seen some of her ugliest parts she'd wanted to keep hidden from him.

She whispered, "I'll play. But let's do it my way. Roll over."

Josh said, "Bossy woman," but complied with a smirk.

"I want it to be all about you this time, Josh." She tugged off her tank and panties, then stretched out beside him, staring deeply into his amused eyes until they grew dark with desire for her. She loved when he looked at her that way. Like she was the last hot fudge sundae with a cherry on top left on earth. "Hold your hands above your head and just pretend your wrists are bound together, because I don't want to get that kinky. And no cheating. Got it?"

He smiled. "Tying my wrists isn't all that kinky, Meg. There's a lot more kink in the world than that."

"Shhh. No talking. Just close your eyes and enjoy."

When his eyes were closed again, she straddled him and then slowly lifted his T-shirt over his head. He separated his hands, but put them right back after, so she didn't call foul. Tossing his shirt aside, she sighed as the reflected moonlight from the lake danced across his hard, chiseled body. He had the sexiest chest and abs she'd ever had the pleasure to pleasure. And the rest wasn't bad either.

Up to the task, she slowly ran her hands over his hard shoulders and neck, kneading and rubbing until the muscles relaxed and became putty in her hands. After whispering soft kisses across the stubble on his jaw and then his cheek, she moved to his neck, breathing in his unique, intoxicating scent. Soap from his shower mixed with shaving cream and then something unidentifiable, but potently male, made her want to lick him. Instead, she nibbled on his earlobe because he really liked when she did that.

It made him groan.

Pleased with her results, she worked her way lower, running her hands over his hard pecs, loving the definition and strength. As her lips toyed with his hardened nipples, his hands ran slowly up and down her back. When he gave her bottom a gentle squeeze, the sexy haze lifted from her brain long enough to scold him. "Hey. Hands above your head, buddy."

He quickly lifted them back up. "You're killing me, Meg."

"Sweet torture is the plan. But now I'm going to have to punish you, bad boy."

He laughed. "Please. You can't even tie my hands together. Or kill a bug. This I gotta see."

"Shush. No talking, remember?" She ensured his silence by laying her mouth on his and kissing him the way they both liked it. Slow, sweet, and deep. The kind that always made her heart turn to mush and her blood boil. She hoped it did the same for him.

Her tongue danced and tangled with his as her hands slid lower, tracing the bumps across his hard abs before diving under the waistband of his boxers. When she took him in her hand, he made a low noise in the back of his throat.

Josh was hard and ready for his punishment, so she slid slowly down, making sure her breasts rubbed along his body the entire way. While she inched his boxers off, she ran her tongue around his length, spending extra time at the tip.

His hips jerked. "God, babe."

Smiling, she took him inside her mouth, sucking, stroking,

squeezing, and driving him so wild, the muscles in his neck strained until he cried out, "Meg—"

Taking the hint, she slid slowly up his slick body and slipped her hands into his. Entwining her fingers with his much larger ones, she smiled and stared deeply into his eyes as she straddled him and slowly let him enter her, sliding up and down his length. With his hands still trapped in hers, he leaned forward and kissed her, hard and sexy, as his hips begged for a faster pace.

When he ended his urgent kiss and opened his eyes, he'd apparently had enough of her game because he quickly flipped their positions, keeping their joined hands above their heads as he buried himself inside her to the hilt.

His eyes stayed locked onto hers, staring intensely with desire as he made love to her. It made her heart burn with even more love for him. The sensation grew stronger as each thrust grew harder and deeper, faster, more intense. Her whole body ached for him to put her out of her misery, hovering at the edge of the cliff, when he finally drew her over the brink along with him.

After a few moments, Josh rolled onto his back so that she lay sprawled on top of him, her hair fanned over his chest, the strong beat of his pounding heart under her ear. He kissed her temple. "That was . . ."

"Yep." She could lie like this in his arms all night long. Tucking her face into the crook of his neck, she smiled. "It's never been this good for me with anyone else, Josh. Only you." She laid a soft kiss on his neck. "But you cheated and didn't let me have my way all the way with you."

He slowly ran his big, rough hand up and down her back. "I think we fulfilled the 'all the way' part just fine, no matter who had their way with who first."

"Because that nonsense actually made sense to me, I must be more tired than I know." She closed her eyes and whispered,

"Thank you for still loving me, Josh. Even after what you saw today. That means more to me than anything in the world."

He brushed another kiss along her temple. "I love you even more for it. And I guess that's another of your roundabout ways of saying you love me too, so shut off your busy mind and get some rest."

"'Kay. Night." Tomorrow was probably going to be one rough day. She'd have to face the whole town at church. And whatever Amber had in mind for retaliation.

She snuggled closer to Josh and smiled. No matter what happened in the morning, it'd be okay. She had Josh in her corner, and that was all she'd need.

CHAPTER
TWENTY-ONE

Haley's laughter outside the bedroom window woke Meg. She stretched her arms above her head as sweet memories of the way Josh had made love to her the night before filled her tired mind. But then, the other memories of the Amber debacle at the gym came rushing back, quickly replacing her nice ones.

Humiliation slowly crept into her gut.

Worse, it was Sunday. They had to go to church and face the town all over again. As much as she'd like to lay low at the lodge for a few days, she'd promised the Three Amigos she'd be there. She didn't need to give them any more reasons to hound her.

Should she cut her losses, sell the house, and move back to Denver? It'd be easier for Josh to go to school there. It wouldn't matter as long as they were together, right? But she needed to show everyone in Anderson Butte how much she'd changed, that she could stick, and that she could run a lodge and do it well. And then there was that big fat loan she'd need to repay.

There really wasn't any choice to make. She had to stay. Things would get better eventually. They couldn't get much worse.

Meg threw the covers back, then got up and tugged on a pair of shorts and a tank top. She needed coffee. And a big dose of antidepressants, aka her chocolate stash, which was in for a serious pillage.

Thankfully Josh had started the coffee for her, so she grabbed a mug and poured it out. Then she found her bag of Dove milk chocolate treats and dug in.

Hearing more happy shrieks outside, Meg moved to the kitchen window as she popped candy into her mouth. It wasn't the breakfast of champions, but it was hard to be totally depressed with chocolate melting on your tongue.

Josh ran around the yard, Haley on his back, with Captain Jack barking and chasing Josh's heels.

It almost made her smile.

But the weight of Amber's verbal beating the night before kept her lips locked in a tight line, only to be interrupted long enough to shove more chocolate inside her mouth.

Eric sat at the end of the dock with his feet dangling over the Jet Ski, his arm around the momma dog, staring out over the lake.

They were going to have to keep that dog too, dammit. She followed Eric everywhere, and the kid obviously loved her. Probably they should give the pooch a name.

Thinking of Eric's problems quickly slammed Meg's into perspective. The poor kid had lost his whole family, and his grandmother wasn't doing well. He'd probably lose her soon too, leaving him with no one in the world who loved him. Just as Josh had been at that age. Even if her dad and half the town didn't love her, she'd at least always had Casey and her brothers. And Zeke and Grandma, Uncle Brewster, Aunt Gloria, and Pam . . . she needed to get over herself.

Meg slipped out the back door and down to the dock. She sat next to Eric and handed him some chocolate. Giving the dog a pat, she said, "Morning."

"Hi." Eric unwrapped his treat. "Thanks."

"You probably don't think much of me after last night, huh?"

Eric shrugged and mumbled around his candy. "Some of those pranks sounded pretty awesome."

Meg grunted while she drained her coffee mug. "I wouldn't recommend repeating them. I spent most of my high school afternoons in detention."

Eric slowly ran his hand up and down the dog's back. "I didn't know adults still got bullied like that. I figured I'd just have to stick it out a few more years and then it would finally end when I got bigger."

Damn, Amber.

"There are always going to be bullies in the world, Eric. But it's easier to deal with them when you have people in your corner. Anyone who tries to bully you here will have to answer to me." She laid her arm around Eric's bony shoulders and gave him a hug. "What Amber did to me was mean, but I needed to make things right with the people I hurt anyway, and I will. Then Amber can't hurt *me* anymore. What those boys did to you was ten times worse and so very wrong. I'm sorry for it."

"What Amber did to you was wrong too. Especially because she's your sister. I was mean to my brother and sister sometimes. Now I wish I could tell them I'm sorry."

What a sweet kid.

"They know, Eric. My brothers still tease me, and as much as it can annoy me, I know they love me." She handed him some more chocolate. "I can only imagine how rough it is not having your parents and brother and sister anymore. But I just wanted you to know we're here for you."

Blinking back tears, he nodded. "Josh said he'd pay me to do work around here. But I'd do it for free if I could stay longer. I really love it here."

Now Meg struggled with tears. No kid should have to negotiate for a safe place to live. She hugged him a little tighter. "I'm pretty sure my brother would arrest me for violating child labor laws if we did that. Take the money and save it for college if you want, but you're welcome here, for free, as long as the paperwork gets settled with your grandmother and we can keep you. Okay?"

His answer was a silent head bob against her shoulder.

Meg held on for a few more minutes, then reluctantly released him. "So, I think we're going to have to keep this hound too. What should we name her?"

The dog's tail wagged, as if she knew they were talking about her.

"Really?" Eric beamed a gigantic smile. "We can keep her?"

"Yeah." Teasing, Meg said, "I think she looks like an Edna."

"Edna?" Eric rolled his eyes. "That's totally lame. I call her Oreo, 'cuz she's black and white. And because that's my favorite cookie."

Eric sometimes seemed thirty instead of ten years old, but that he'd name a dog after his favorite cookie proved he was still a kid. She'd have to be sure Oreos went on the shopping list. "Oreo, mother to Captain Jack Sparrow. Doesn't get better than that." Eric's big smile made her want to keep it there. "Ever been on a Jet Ski?"

"Nope."

"Well then, let's go!"

"Right now?"

"Sure. We've got a few hours before church starts. Let me grab some life jackets."

She turned to get the jackets, but stopped when he laid a hand on her arm. "Thanks for letting me stay with you guys, Meg."

The sincere gratitude in his eyes melted her heart. "You're welcome. We love having you here, Eric. Be right back."

Spending the morning watching Eric's grin as he drove a Jet Ski for the first time had lifted Meg's spirits. But happiness quickly turned to dread as they pulled up to the church in Josh's truck. The large group of people gathered out front all turned to stare as Josh parked. Toby waved and parted from the group, making his way toward them. At least she had one ally.

While Josh hopped out to deal with Haley's car seat, Toby opened Meg's door. She ignored Josh's quiet grunt and smiled at Toby. "Thanks."

"No. Thank *you*." He beamed one of his classic "surfer dude" smiles. "We were all taking bets on if you'd show up this morning. The few of us who said you would just made a killing."

The few who said she would? Great. "Glad I could be of assistance." She patted his shoulder. "Thanks for betting on me."

"Yeah, well, you'll never guess who I'll have to split the pot with. Your dad, and all Three Amigos. Bye." Toby strolled away.

Even Dad had bet on her showing up?

Maybe things would go better than expected today.

She turned to see what Josh thought of her dad betting on her and caught him checking his phone again. Then his head popped up and he leaned around his truck, as if searching for someone.

He had that look on his face again.

She leaned around the truck too and saw a few tourists milling around the square, but then she spotted Zeke walking toward them. That must be who Josh was looking for.

Josh handed Haley over to her. "Why don't you guys go on in? I'll catch up."

Before she could ask what was going on, Josh turned to leave. She called out, "We'll be way up front, second row on the right."

Josh just lifted a hand in acknowledgment as he crossed the parking lot.

He'd been acting so weird since the picnic.

Shaking her head, she said to Eric, "Pastor Brian is really loud, so I wish we could sit in the back and save our eardrums, but everyone has their usual spots and we can't mess up the system. Unfortunately all the Andersons sit right up front."

Eric nodded. "Because your dad's the mayor. Makes sense."

Not to her. She'd always wished she could sit in the back row with Pam. Maybe one of these days she'd do it, just to buck the system. But not today. Today was all about showing everyone she belonged.

Luckily Amber was always late, so Meg nodded and forced smiles at the folks who sent curious glances her way as she walked up the long aisle toward her usual pew in the second row.

Sue Ann, sitting in her spot at the end of the first row, was powdering her nose in the reflection of her little hand mirror. When she turned and greeted them with a smile, Meg wasn't sure what to do.

"Uh. Morning, Sue Ann. I'd like you to meet Eric. He's staying with us for the summer." She turned to Eric. "This is my dad's wife, Sue Ann."

Eric stuck out his hand. "Nice to meet you."

"We're glad you're here, Eric." Sue Ann shook his outstretched hand.

Holy crap, Batman. Had the whole world gone mad? First her dad bet on her and now Sue Ann was being nice?

After they were settled in, her father slipped beside her and whispered, "I heard about what happened last night after I left."

Meg's stomach seized. "Yeah. It wasn't pretty. You're lucky you didn't have to see that. And I'm sorry about that snowball through your office window. I didn't know about the rock inside."

"Always figured that was you." Dad crossed his arms. "Well, at least you didn't screw up last night. You finally apologized and acted like an Anderson for a change."

Her jaw was still in her lap as he stood to go take his seat next to Sue Ann. The world *had* gone mad.

Josh followed a few feet behind Watts and Evans as they slipped around the back of Town Hall. When Josh caught up to them, Watts lifted his chin in greeting. "Thanks for coming."

The text Josh had just received said they were planning a takedown during the church service.

Josh said, "Why not wait until tomorrow? Arrest them in the office. Doing it here, in front of everyone, is . . ." He wanted to say as cruel as what Meg had to endure the night before, but didn't. "It could be dangerous. What if one of them has a concealed weapon?"

Evans shook her head. "The warrant will be here any minute. We need to strike now, while we have them contained. One of them could have a friend in the right place who could tip them off. I say we do it and be done with it."

Watts glanced at Josh. "We just wanted to let you know the plan. They've probably started the service by now. You'd better get going."

Watts's way of blowing Josh off. "It'd be easier on Meg, and her family, if you didn't do this in front of the whole town."

"She has you whipped." Evans shook her head. "What's happened to you, Sam? You used to be the biggest hard-ass I knew. It's like you lost your balls and grew a heart or something."

He met her gaze and raised a brow. The pain in her eyes betrayed the sharp words. She'd been in love with him, but he'd been honest with her. He didn't love her back. He used to fear he wasn't capable of love. Until he'd met Meg. Was Evans trying to hurt Meg to get back at him?

Done with their staring match, she huffed out a breath and looked away. "I just want this over with so I can move on."

He wasn't getting anywhere. If that warrant came through, they were going to do it. Best to be with Meg and the kids in case things got rough. "I better go."

Josh slipped quietly into the back of the church. The pastor was bellowing about the power of forgiveness. That couldn't be a coincidence. He'd been at the dinner last night too.

Josh quickly moved up the side aisle and then slid into the pew next to Meg. She lifted her hands from her lap in a "where the heck have you been" gesture, so he laid his arm around her shoulders and pulled her close. He whispered in her ear, "Sorry."

Drawing a deep breath for calm, he considered saying a prayer for that warrant to stay tied up. Doing a takedown during the church service was excessive. But then, Watts always liked to play up the busts big, thinking it made him look better to the brass above. The ass.

As the pastor droned on, Josh checked the location of all the exits. Two on the sides, one in front, off to the side of the pulpit, and the large bank of doors at the rear. They'd probably come in one from the rear, another from the side.

After what seemed an eternity, the pastor appeared to be wrapping things up. Josh reached for his phone to check the time. Meg snatched it from his hand and slipped it into her purse before sending him a quick elbow jab to the ribs.

Right. Probably not polite to check phones during church. But he was just checking the time. He tapped a finger on top of his wrist. Meg tilted her chin, indicating a big clock that hung on the wall high above them. It had been just over an hour. Maybe they'd make it out before the warrant came, yet.

The final hymn had just ended when Evans entered through the back doors and Watts through the side exit behind Josh.

Evans called out, "FBI. Everyone please take a seat."

Josh glanced at the mayor to gauge his reaction. Genuine confusion, not fear of arrest, knit his brow as Anderson remained standing and said, "What's going on here?"

Ryan, the only other one still standing too, said, "Dad, sit down." Then he called out, "Sheriff Anderson. How can I help you?"

Evans said, "Sheriff, we appreciate your cooperation. If everyone will just please remain quiet and in their seats." Heads swiveled from the front of the church to the back again, as if watching a tennis match. Waiting for Ryan's response.

Instead Watts spoke and everyone turned to the side. "We're here to take two people in for questioning. We need the mayor and Mrs.—"

Gasps rang out as Ryan held up his hand and cut him off. "No one is going anywhere without a warrant."

"It's all here." When Evans held up the papers, Ryan walked down the aisle to inspect them. People quietly mumbled among themselves, speculating. Many commented that the last two days had been the most interesting in years when a loud commotion broke out on the other side of the church.

Mrs. Duncan, the mayor's secretary, bolted from her seat and ran toward the pulpit. Watts was too far back to catch her, so Evans yelled from the rear, "Sam! Go!"

Options flashed through Josh's head. Meg would find out the truth before he had a chance to explain if he went after Mrs. Duncan. But his sense of justice was too ingrained to let the woman get away. He took off after her.

Blowing his cover.

CHAPTER
Twenty-Two

*C*haos broke out in the church around Meg. What the hell was going on? Why had that woman called Josh "Sam"?

Meg turned in time to see the male agent follow Josh out the door, both chasing Dragon Breath. Why would she be running from the FBI? When Meg turned around again, the female agent was reading Dad his rights and handcuffing him, all while Ryan stood by, rubbing the back of his neck and studying the warrant she'd handed him.

Meg passed Haley off to Grandma and said to Eric, "Stay with my grandmother, please." Then she hopped up to see why her dad was being arrested.

"Ryan, what's going on?"

The crowd noise had become deafening, so she had to lean close to hear him say, "They found evidence on computers in Dad's office of an illegal gaming scam, money laundering, and wire fraud, among other things."

"What? Dad doesn't even know how to use a spreadsheet. That makes no sense."

Josh and the agent returned with Mrs. Duncan in handcuffs. She was spitting mad and yelling about her rights being violated.

Ryan said, "Nope. But what makes perfect sense to me now is that Josh is obviously an undercover agent. And his name is Sam."

The air whooshed from Meg's lungs as it all began to sink in.

Meg made her way through the people milling around and squeezed next to Josh. "What's going on? And why did she call you Sam?"

The female agent holding her dad's arm said, "Because that's his name."

Josh shook his head. "No, Josh Granger is my name. Sam Coulter is an alias. Watts will confirm."

The woman's eyes narrowed. "After all those years together, you never even told me your real name?"

Meg turned to Josh. "Who is this?"

The agent tugged on Dad's arm and said, "I'm the one before you, honey. Good luck."

Meg's head spun with confusion as the agents dragged her father and Mrs. Duncan through the back doors. Josh took her arm and led her outside. When the metal door slapped closed behind them, she ripped her arm from his grasp and threw her hands on her hips. "Explain. Now!"

"Meg, please—"

Josh tried to touch her, but she evaded.

He held up his hands, palms out in a gesture of peace, but Meg was far from feeling serene. Blood pounded in her ears. That son of a bitch had been lying to her. The one thing she asked him never to do.

"I was an FBI agent. Three years ago, your father was a suspect. I was asked to talk to you and find out if you knew anything. When we met, I was undercover, posing as a software developer for a firm that was a front for the mob. Right after we broke up, I exposed the operation and then had to go into hiding along with other witnesses from the company, until the trial was over. There were some nasty mob players involved. I broke up with you because I needed you guys to be safe. Not because I didn't love you. After the trial was over a few weeks ago I quit the FBI so I could be with you and Haley."

She blinked at him, trying to absorb it all. How the hell could someone be that good at lying? She'd lived with him twenty-four seven. "So that first night, at the talk I was giving, your 'assignment' was to chat me up? Flirt with me, and get information out of me?"

He slowly nodded. "Yes. But as soon as we started talking I knew there was something special about you and I wanted to know—"

"Wait." Meg held up a hand to cut him off. "So you had a file on me? Knew what I liked to do, what I did for a living, that kind of thing? So all that instant connection I was feeling with you was because you already knew everything about me? You were using that knowledge to trick me into giving you information about my father? I should've known you were too good to be true." Tears burned the back of her eyes. She'd fallen for him the first night because of a fake connection. It'd all been a ploy.

She was an idiot. Josh was no different from every other guy who'd hurt her.

"Meg, listen—"

She poked him in the chest. "So how many other women have you charmed into bed with that trick? Did you get any of them pregnant and then leave them too?" A thought sent a hard punch to Meg's gut. "For God's sake, please don't tell me you're married!"

"No. I'm not married." Josh closed his eyes and ran his hand down his face. "And I don't have any other children. After I joined the agency, I never slept with anyone who wasn't a fellow agent. Until you."

"Yeah, about that! Why did that woman think your name was Sam? You obviously slept with her too. Who are you lying to, Josh? Her or me?"

"The only person at the agency who knew my real name was

my boss, Watts, the man you saw inside. Everyone else knew me as Sam Coulter. Call the FBI's main number and ask for Watts. He'll answer any questions you have."

Meg crossed her arms, swallowing back her angry tears. "Why bother? He'll probably just lie to me too. So was any of what you told me about your past even real?"

"Most of it."

"So you went to college, but didn't work as a programmer? You joined the FBI when you graduated?"

"Yeah. My specialty was extracting the truth from all levels of scumbags. I'm good at knowing when people are lying. I was so immersed in that filth I had no outside life and was losing it. I needed a break. That's why they assigned me to this case."

"So did you . . . torture people to get the truth?" She wasn't sure she really wanted to know, but needed to ask.

"Not physically. But psychologically . . . yeah." He looked away.

She didn't know him at all. "I don't understand why you couldn't have just said something like 'I work for the government and can't discuss it, but I need to leave for your safety.' I believed all your other lies. I certainly would have believed that statement too!"

He shook his head. "Undercover doesn't work that way, Meg. An innocent slipup on your part could endanger others' lives. It's a strict no-tell policy we all live by."

"So, when you asked me to move in with you, it was just for the case? To make it easier to check up on me, or to see if I talk in my sleep?"

"No. I asked you to move in because I fell in love with you."

She stared into his eyes, searching for the truth—but that was pointless. The man lied so well it'd do no good. "How could you sleep with me again, knowing you'd be sending my father to jail soon, Josh? He and I have our differences, but he's still the man who raised me. As someone who grew up with no family, maybe you can't understand, but that's a deeper betrayal than even all the lies you've told me. Pack your things and leave."

When she turned to walk away, he said softly, "That's not entirely true, Meg."

She stopped walking, but wouldn't look him in the eye. She couldn't. It hurt too much. "Then what is?"

"I'm not the one sending your dad to jail. I told Watts I couldn't investigate your father the night I met you. I have no idea what they have on him. I haven't wanted to know. If you'd like me to find out, I'll do anything I can to help."

He laid his big hands on her shoulders, gently turning her around to face him. "I'm sorry, Meg. For every single lie I've told you. I'll never lie to you again. But we have a deal. I get to stay until the end of summer."

"The only thing I've ever asked of you was not to lie to me. So our deal is null and void. We're done. I want you out of my house and out of Anderson Butte."

"If I could have told you the truth I would have." He slowly slid his hands from her shoulders and took a step back. "I love you, Meg. But I'll move my and Eric's things out of the lodge. And I'll take the dogs." He turned to leave.

She called out to his retreating back. "Eric and the dogs can stay. I'll sign whatever papers I have to for his guardianship."

He stopped walking and faced her. "What about Haley? I need to be part of her life."

Meg bit her lip, struggling to hold it together. How was Haley going to react to all of this? She loved Josh. "I don't know yet. I have to think about that. But not right now. With my dad being arrested and now you being . . . it's just too much at once. Just leave!"

Fighting back a sob, Meg went back inside the church to get the kids. Everyone was gone except for Zeke. "Where'd everyone go?"

"Your grandma took the kids to her house and said to take your time."

Meg slumped down into the front pew and held her head in her hands. Zeke slipped beside her and sat quietly.

Every new so-called fact buzzed around inside her head, clashing with each of the lies Josh had told her. If she believed in signs, they'd all be pointing to the highway and back to Denver, away from Amber, the people in this town who judged her, her father, and away from Josh and his maze of lies.

"I can't take much more, Zeke. It's tempting to pack up and go."

"I'd sure hate to see you leave. Especially now that the cat's out of the bag about you being my favorite niece. You belong here, Meggy. And you deserve to be happy. I've never seen you happier than you've been with Josh these past few weeks."

"You were my favorite uncle even before I knew you were my real one. But how can I live with a man like that? He's a trained agent who can look me in the eye and sell me a pack of lies. How do I even know he's telling me the truth now?"

"You don't. And I guess you never will. If you want him, you'll have to learn to let go of all your mistrust and give him the benefit of the doubt." He gave her hand a quick squeeze and then stood. "I've got a carburetor calling my name. Take some time to cool off. Nothing has to be decided today. But if it matters to you, I still trust him."

Zeke walked slowly down the long aisle and through the back doors. After they closed with a loud thud behind him, Meg sat alone in the silent church, afraid to ask what else could possibly go wrong in her life.

Josh drove around the lake to gather his things from the lodge. His knuckles whitened on the steering wheel. Fury, not only at the situation, but also at himself for failing, burned in his gut. She loved him, he'd seen it in her eyes. But maybe love wasn't enough? Meg's distrust of people already ran deep, and he hadn't helped. Had he betrayed her trust one too many times?

He needed a new plan. But what could he say or do to fix what he'd done?

It might just take some time to win back Meg's love, and he'd do whatever it took to keep Haley and Eric in his life. He'd not fail there.

When he pulled into the drive, Ryan waited on the front steps of Meg's house.

Great. That's all he needed.

"Watts filled me in." Ryan stood and crossed his arms. "But I still have some questions, Granger."

Josh nodded. "You can ask while I pack. Meg wants me out right away."

"Can you blame her?"

"Nope." He led the way to the master bedroom.

He grabbed his duffel from the closet and threw it on the bed. The letter he'd written to Meg the day he'd broken up with her was still taped to the bottom of the bag. Wouldn't much matter after what happened earlier. Meg knew the truth now.

He ripped the envelope out and tossed it into the trash can by the door.

Ryan leaned against the wall, silently watching as Josh packed his things. He expected Ryan to lash out, but his voice was steady when he said, "Meg has a thing about people keeping the truth from her. She'd always wondered about our mother when she was a kid and hated when no one in town would talk about her. She didn't understand they were keeping the promise they all made to my dad. No one wanted to risk retaliation."

Josh stopped packing. "Retaliation?" Ryan hadn't said that many words since Josh had met him. He hoped he wouldn't stop now.

Ryan shrugged. "My dad convinced everyone years ago the only way for our small town to thrive was to provide a place for celebrities to come where they could have complete privacy. The town was on the verge of bankruptcy, so Dad made everyone promise we'd never go to the rags or alert the paparazzi. In order to have a retirement fund and net profits, we had to sign the 'pact.' It's a profit-sharing corporation. But my dad has all the power. He controls the land, the buildings, and all the money. So far, everyone has stuck to it because while so many small towns are failing, ours is thriving. Anderson Butte wouldn't still be here if not for Dad's business smarts. Everyone knows it. So when he *asks* for a favor, they don't go against him. Never have."

Josh grunted. "I *knew* that was Jim Carrey."

Ignoring that, Ryan said, "Didn't help that Dad was always extra hard on Meg. She never understood why."

"Because he's not her father?" Josh stuffed the rest of his shirts into the bag.

"Partly. But mostly because she's a lot like our mother was. But we've all noticed a real change in Meg since she's been back this time. Maybe even since she's had Haley."

"Meg's the same person I've always known. She's a great mother." Josh only hoped he'd be as good a father to Haley.

"Speaking of Haley, what are your intentions there?"

The challenge dug at Josh. He met Ryan's gaze, unflinching. "To be her father. Meg asked me to leave, but I'm not going far."

Josh crossed to the bathroom and grabbed his dopp kit. When he returned, he found Ryan settled on the edge of the bed, looking like he'd gone ten rounds. "That's what she'd expect you to do. Leave her while she pretends it doesn't matter to her—like the others have."

"Others?" Meg kept her past as close to her chest as he did.

"Meg's track record with men isn't great. It started with Randy, who ran off with Amber, and it just got worse from there. I wanted to beat the crap outta each and every one of them."

"Me included?"

"You most of all. You got her pregnant and *then* ran off on her." Ryan's hand balled into a fist before he shook his head and relaxed his fingers again. "My dad convinced Meg she's not worth loving or something. No one's ever fought for her."

"I'd like to *beat the crap* out of your father for that." Josh tugged the zipper closed on his duffel and looked around one last time for anything he might have missed. "So I should stay, even though she asked me to go?"

"Yeah. But you didn't hear that from me."

"Would I be wasting my time asking Casey for a room?"

One side of Ryan's mouth quirked up. "Casey will take Meg's side. But you could beg and come clean. Then, maybe . . ." Ryan stood. "Can you help me decipher some of these federal charges against my father? My dad can be a real SOB, but he's not tech savvy enough to pull something like that off. I'd like your help to prove it."

Josh hadn't gotten a guilty vibe from the mayor during the arrest. And he trusted his instincts . . . with most everything but Meg. The Duncan lady was going to jail for a long time. Watts would give Josh's opinion weight. "Let me see about a place to stay, then I'll make a few phone calls. Catch up with you at your office?"

"Yeah." Ryan stood and held out his hand. "Appreciate it."

"No problem." Josh returned the shake.

As they walked out together, Ryan pointed at Josh's bag. "Besides your truck, is that really all you own?"

"Nope." Josh cranked his truck's door open. "I have a registered gun, and those two dogs in the pen over there. See you later."

Josh drove to the other side of the lake and pulled up to the hotel. He left his bag in the truck. It'd be a tough sell to get Casey to agree to let him have a room. He might have to stay at the hotel fifteen miles down the road, but he wasn't going any farther away than that. Hopefully Zeke would still let him keep his job.

He wouldn't be like the other guys who left Meg, but if she couldn't love him back, he'd stay for Haley and Eric's sake. Even if it'd kill him to see Meg every day, knowing he could never have her.

When the lobby doors swished open, someone he hadn't met stood behind the front desk. She smiled and said, "Hi. May I help you?"

"Looking for Casey?"

"She's in her office."

"Thanks." Josh made his way down the long hall, then tapped a knuckle on her doorjamb.

She had her eyes closed and was rubbing at her temples. When Casey looked up, she sighed. "Go away, Granger. Haven't you done enough damage for one day?"

"You all lied to Meg for her own good. I did the same." He held his hand out toward the chair in front of her desk, silently asking permission to sit.

When Casey rolled her eyes, he took that as a yes and settled in. "I love Meg and Haley, Casey. I was just doing my job. And I'm going to help your brother prove your dad's innocence. Will you let me explain? Please?"

She leaned back in her chair and crossed her arms. "You get five minutes. Go!"

Angry, confused, and hurting even worse than when Josh had left her three years ago, Meg gave Josh time to get his things out of her house by taking the kids to the diner for a treat.

She licked the last remnants of chocolate mousse pie from her fork, looking for her usual comfort in good old reliable chocolate.

Her stomach protested as she stared at her empty plate. "Awesome, as always, Aunt Gloria." Meg faked a smile, suddenly realizing all she'd consumed for the day was coffee and chocolate. No wonder her gut ached.

Eric nodded enthusiastically. "Really awesome!"

When Haley added a "Yay!" Gloria smiled as she wiped down the long counter. "I'm glad you guys liked it. Eric, what grade will you be in come fall?"

Eric chugged his milk. After using the back of his hand to wipe his mouth he said, "Fifth."

"That means you'll have Mrs. Grant. She's a fun teacher. You'll like her."

Eric shook his head. "I'm just here for a few months. Until they can place me somewhere else."

"That so, Meg?" Gloria lifted a scolding brow. "Seems a shame Eric would have to move and start all over again."

A dose of guilt from her aunt was the last thing she needed. Josh had just ripped her soul out. It was all she could do to fight back her tears. "Josh is in charge of that. I don't have any say in the matter."

"Speaking of Josh, any news yet? Are they pressing charges?" Gloria's forehead crumpled.

Meg didn't want the kids to hear about that, so she said, "Eric, why don't you and Haley go pick a pie from the cooler to take home?"

"Awesome!" Eric jumped off his stool and took Haley's hand.

When they were out of earshot, Gloria said, "If your dad ends up in jail, Sue Ann certainly can't keep this town running. And he's too stubborn to hand over the power to you kids until he draws his last shaky breath. I can't keep my diner afloat without the celebrities the hotel brings in. We're all worried, Meg."

Gloria was right. Her dad was the reason everyone in town had 401(k) plans and health insurance. He'd probably try to run the town from jail. But he couldn't have pulled off anything like the FBI was accusing him of. He didn't do it. "I haven't heard. Maybe I should text Ryan?"

"Why don't you text Josh? Seems he'd be able to find out. Being he's one of them."

Because she didn't wanted to talk to Josh. Ever again. She'd just text Ryan.

"While you're at it, consider making up with him." Gloria shook her head. "Who'd a thought he was an FBI agent?"

"Former. He says he quit recently. If you can believe a word that comes out of his mouth." And the making up wasn't happening. Only an idiot would go back for more heartache.

Meg reached into her purse for her phone and came up with Josh's. She'd forgotten she still had it after confiscating it from him in church. She shouldn't do it, but hey, he'd lied to her since they'd met. He deserved any snooping she could pull off.

She swiped the "slide to unlock" icon. The next screen asked for a password. Pondering for a moment, she typed in the name of the horse he loved, Charlie, but the letters on the screen shook back and forth, telling her no dice.

Next she typed "Haley," but that didn't work either, so she tried "Meg," pretty certain her snooping would be shut down posthaste.

When his phone came alive, she grunted. He'd probably chosen her name because she was part of the case he'd been assigned. Not because he really cared for her or anything.

His conversation list popped up on the screen. A quick scan proved he'd been talking to people from his old job, just like he'd told her. He hadn't lied about that. But how to separate the lies from the truth? It was as if he'd become a complete stranger to her in between heartbeats. Who was the real Josh Granger?

Overwhelming guilt for snooping poked at her conscience, so she quickly shut the phone down and put it back in her purse.

When her phone beeped with a text, she reached for it. Ryan, finally. Maybe she'd get some news about her dad. Josh is going to help. I'll let you know.

She tapped back. Thanks.

She started to put her phone back when it beeped again. He was just doing his job, Meg.

Yeah, and part of that job was to play intense mind games with people. *When necessary.* And to lie so well that his girlfriend, who lived under the same roof, had never known he had a whole other life. How could she have been so freakin' blind?

But worse, that instant mutual attraction she thought they'd both felt had been one-sided. The one thing that had made her let her guard down for the first time with a man. One who understood her and yet accepted her for who she was.

He probably had a complete file on her. How could she *not* have fallen for a guy who seemed to like all the things she liked, loved to do the same things she loved to do? Who understood her so thoroughly? He'd played with her mind just like he did with the criminals he dealt with.

What did she really know about him? Was he the intense guy like in Denver or the laid-back one of the last few weeks? Anyone could be mellow for a few weeks. But not everyone had the ability to lie like that.

The kids returned with the boxed pie. Haley said, "Can we go home, Mommy?" She rubbed her eyes.

Nap time.

They'd ridden over in Josh's truck, so they didn't have a car. She glanced at her phone to check the time. He was probably done clearing out his stuff by now.

"Let's go see if Aunt Casey can give us a ride."

Aunt Gloria appeared and held out a paper to-go bag. "For later. No one should have to cook dinner after a day like you've had."

Grateful tears threatened to spill over, but Meg blinked them back. She accepted the bag and the hug her aunt offered.

While she wrapped Meg in her arms, Gloria whispered, "Don't judge him by the other scumbags you've dated. He's different. You know you're still my favorite niece, Anderson blood or not, and that I love you, right?"

Not Aunt Gloria too. It was nice her aunt still loved her, but couldn't anyone be on Meg's side and understand how deeply Josh had betrayed her trust in him?

She could only nod, for fear she'd fall apart. She mouthed a "thank you" before she took Haley's hand and headed for the door with Eric trailing behind.

As they crossed the park, a soccer ball zipped across their path. Eric trapped it with his foot, added a little hop and a flip, and then launched the ball like a rocket back to the kids on Toby's soccer team who were practicing their drills. A wistful smile lit Eric's face as he watched the ball sail through the air.

"Wow. That was fantastic, Eric." Meg smiled despite her black mood. "Did you play on a team back home?"

He nodded. "I used to. Until . . ."

Until his whole life had been turned upside down.

As hers had in the last few days. They had that in common.

Toby had obviously seen Eric's fantastic pass, because he was jogging in their direction, his whistle bouncing off his chest. "That was impressive, dude."

Toby nodded at Meg, then turned to Eric. "We could really use a guy like you on the team, bro."

Eric's face lit up as he turned to Meg for permission. "Can I stay and play?"

"Absolutely." She turned toward Toby. "Can you give him a ride home when you're done?"

"Yep." Toby grinned and threw an arm around Eric's shoulder. "Come meet everyone, buddy."

That was the life Eric deserved. Soccer practice with great coaches like Toby encouraging him. Aunt Gloria was right. Meg needed to find a way to keep Eric longer than just the summer. Unfortunately, that would involve more dealings with Josh.

Tears burned her throat again as she picked Haley up and started for the hotel. She needed to hold it together. At least until she got home. When she was alone and Haley was asleep, then she could fall apart.

CHAPTER
TWENTY-THREE

*J*osh hung up Ryan's office phone after speaking to Watts. In the middle of Josh explaining the charges to Ryan, the sounds of a hysterical woman echoed outside of Ryan's office. Sue Ann burst through the door with black mascara streaks running down her face. "You"—she pointed to Josh—"are the reason my husband is in jail. Figures Meg would bring trouble with her." She planted her hands on her hips. "She's going to have to deal with me this time."

Ryan sighed. "Sit down, Sue Ann."

Her fury switched to Ryan. "How can you ask me to sit in the same room as . . . him? He and Megan need to get their sorry asses out of town before I grab my gun and chase them both out myself!"

"You do that, and you're going to jail too. And for the record, Meg had nothing to do with this." Ryan stared at her until she huffed out a breath and dropped into a chair.

Ryan turned to Josh. "You were saying, Granger?"

"They can hold him longer than the standard forty-eight hours while deciding to charge him or not because of the fraud across state lines. When I told Watts I don't think your father had anything to do with it, he said he'd take that into consideration."

"Thanks. So what about Mrs. Duncan?"

"They've searched her home but came up empty. I guess she and her husband have been estranged for quite some time? He's taken a job overseas, right?"

"Yeah. We haven't seen Hal for three or four years. When he left, he told everyone they were taking a break."

"Phone records show they don't communicate, and banking records show Duncan has been living way over her means. She's trying to pin everything on the mayor, saying because he lacked computer skills, he instructed her to do it. She's using the 'pact' the town has made as her reason. Says she feared retaliation."

Ryan winced. "Not a bad argument."

Sue Ann jumped out of her chair. "Not a bad argument? Everyone in this town would be on welfare if it wasn't for your father!" Sue Ann spun toward Josh. "What are you going to do about it?"

Ryan glanced at Josh too.

Apparently the ball was in his court. "Meg told me Duncan runs the town webpage and lives for gossip. Someone like that would need recognition for what she'd gotten away with. From someone she trusts. Does she have a best friend?"

Ryan and Sue Ann said in unison, "Barb Haney."

Josh stood. "Then there's your next move. Probably couldn't hurt to use the power of the 'pact' on her when you question her. Miranda her up, then scare the crap out of her by telling her you already know Duncan has told her what she's done. Get a full confession. But do everything by the book so it can be used in court."

"Will do. Want to sit in on the interview, Granger?"

Josh shook his head. "Nope, I'm done with lying scumbags. You have good instincts, Ryan. You'll do just fine." He glanced at Sue Ann. "I hope everything works out, Mrs. Anderson."

Her shoulders slumped as fresh tears filled her eyes. Seemed her anger had faded to worry for her husband again. She whispered, "It had better, or you'll pay."

What a piece of work.

Josh headed out the front door and down the stone steps. He needed to get his phone back from Meg so he could keep in touch with Watts about the case. But he dreaded looking into Meg's big blue eyes again as they swam with the pain he'd put there. Maybe he'd give her a little more time. He refused to admit to himself that he was terrified he wouldn't be able to convince her to forgive him.

He'd go talk to Zeke first. Make sure he still had a job.

He hadn't realized just how much he wanted to take over Zeke's business until now, when he might not get the chance. Looking back to when he was a kid, he was happiest when he'd gotten to leave the ranch to work at the garage in town. He'd been good with his hands, and no one gave him a hard time when he'd worked there. He'd gotten nothing but praise for a job well done.

Now he liked the challenge of puzzling out the problem and fixing it. Maybe he could find a way to work at the shop and help kids at the same time.

He walked slowly toward Zeke's place, trying to figure out what he'd do without Meg if he couldn't convince her to give him another chance. The thought of being with Meg again had gotten him through the last three years. His chest ached at the possibility he might never get her back.

He passed through the big double doors and found Zeke sitting at the long workbench, bent over a carburetor. It was the first time he'd ever known Zeke to work without music blaring in the background. That couldn't be a good sign.

He'd come to care for Zeke too. He'd made more friends since he'd been in Anderson Butte than he'd had in the last twenty years. Zeke's offer to hand over his business had been the nicest thing anyone had ever done for him.

Not sure what to say, Josh picked up a wrench and started where he'd left off on the engine he'd been working on before the disastrous weekend.

After a few minutes, Zeke stood and stretched out his back. "So, that was what you meant last night about seeing what the next few weeks bring before you accepted my offer, huh?"

"Yeah." Josh laid his wrench down and wiped his hands. Here came the part where Zeke would probably tell him to hit the road too. "I couldn't possibly accept your offer without you knowing the whole truth."

"And you couldn't tell me the truth." Zeke scratched the stubble on his cheek. "That was the right thing to do. I'll give you that. Wish you hadn't hurt Meg in the process, that's all."

"Me too." Josh joined Zeke at the workbench, leaning against it. "I understand if you've changed your mind."

"Now, don't be putting words into my mouth that aren't there. I was only stating facts. And if you'll recall, I gave you the job in the first place because I didn't trust you and wanted to keep an eye on you. But, after what happened today, it does make a man wonder if you really have feelings for Meg. Because if you don't, then I'll have to ask you to leave town and let her and Haley be. Meg's had some rough patches. She don't need any more caused by you."

"I love Meg. And I'm not going anywhere. I have Haley and Eric to consider. I may have failed with Meg, and I'm still hoping she'll come around, but I won't fail the kids."

"That's what I figured." Zeke shrugged and sat down to work on his carburetor again. "The offer still stands, Granger. And just a piece of advice from an old man. Meggy is as stubborn as they come, but anything worth having is worth fighting for."

The sharp click of a rifle cocking snapped Josh's head around. Meg's grandmother lifted her gun and pointed it straight at his heart. "You're coming with me, boy. Now!"

With a sound-asleep Haley on her shoulder—and since when did Haley weigh so dang much?—Meg made her way down the long hall that connected the hotel with Casey's living quarters. She'd checked Casey's office first, and then the lobby, but she was nowhere to be found. It was her sister's day off, so maybe she was at home for a change.

Meg held the pie box and to-go bags in one hand and Haley in the other. Just as Meg lifted her foot to kick in lieu of knocking, the door swung open. Casey frowned as she listened to someone on her cell phone. When she spotted Meg, her shoulders jerked in surprise. "She's right here. I'll take care of it."

Meg said. "Take care of what? Who's looking for me?"

Her sister crooked her finger and held the door open wider. "Why don't you lay Haley on my bed?"

Meg followed Casey to her bedroom. After Casey lifted the covers back, Meg slipped Haley under them, then kissed her forehead.

When they were in the living room again, Casey asked, "So where's Eric?"

"At the park playing soccer. Toby said he'd bring him by later. What's going on, Casey?"

Her sister gave such an innocent shrug it had to be fake. "I just wanted to keep the kids so you could have the evening to yourself. I'll let Toby know to bring Eric back here. Now let's get you and your dinner on your way home."

Meg let herself be dragged for a few feet until it hit her. "How did you know this was my dinner? Who were you talking to when I showed up?"

"Aunt Gloria." Casey stopped pulling and huffed out a breath. "She was worried about you, that's all. Now get going, would you?"

Something was up.

"Is it Dad? Have you heard something?"

Casey crossed her arms. "No. But before you hear it from someone else, I should probably tell you that after I heard Josh's side of the story I let him have a room."

Hot fury ripped through Meg's veins. That's why Casey was trying to get rid of her? "How the hell could you do that to me, Casey?"

Utterly betrayed for the second time that day, she turned to leave.

But Casey was quicker and wrapped her long arms around Meg's shoulders to stop her. "I didn't do it to you, I did it *for* you. I didn't want you to push him away like you've done to every man who's cared for you."

Meg turned to face her sister. "What's that supposed to mean?"

Casey sighed. "You'd never fully commit to the men you dated, so of course they treated you the same. Or you'd pick a guy so wrong for you, it was for the best when he'd leave. You push men away so they can't hurt you first. You're not the hard-ass you like people to think, Meg."

"I committed to Josh and look what that got me."

"Then you must love him enough to give him a second chance. He was just doing his job and you got caught up in that. Josh loves you, and I don't want to see you throw it all away because you're afraid to be hurt."

"How can you say that after your nasty divorce? I hated how badly Tomas hurt you."

Casey nodded. "I hated how much he hurt me too, the cheating bastard. But I don't regret marrying him. I have my boys I wouldn't trade for the world. And we were really happy for a while. The best thing I took away from my divorce was it made me realize I'm strong enough to deal with whatever life throws at me. I'm responsible for my own happiness. If you push Josh away, will that make you happy?"

"But I'm not strong like you, Casey." Meg fought to stop them, but warm tears rolled down her cheeks. "He broke my heart again and I'm just barely hanging on here. I'm trying to stay brave in front of the kids, but what if I'm *not* strong enough to deal with whatever life throws at me and I screw everything up again? And now I have Haley to worry about too, so then what?"

Casey pulled Meg toward her and squeezed tight. "Then we'll be here to pick you up and dust you off just like before. But you *are* strong enough, Meg." Casey kissed the top of Meg's head. "I've always believed in you. I just wish you'd believe in yourself for a change."

"Easier said than done." Meg let Casey hold her for a few minutes while she pulled herself together. She wanted to go home, hide under the covers, and hope the pain would ease by the morning.

Wiping her tears, she leaned back. "Can I borrow a Jet Ski to get home?"

"I had Trent leave you one at the end of the dock. I love you. Call me later, okay?"

"'Kay. Love you too." Her mind whirling with what her sister had said, Meg slowly made her way down to the dock. She slipped into her life jacket, stowed her food, then turned the key that was dangling in the ignition. Cranking the gas, she tore away from the dock.

What was she going to do? Just because everyone told her she should consider forgiving Josh didn't mean she could. His betrayal made it hard to even think about him, much less look at him. How could she let someone with the power to hurt her so deeply back into her life again?

She wasn't Casey. She wasn't the girl who had all the answers and did everything right. She was the screwup her dad worried would ruin his fine reputation. And now Amber had made sure the whole town remembered that was exactly what Meg was.

Pulling up to her new dock, she spotted Grandma's car in the drive.

Great. That's all she needed. Someone else telling her how to feel.

She tossed the life jacket and her dinner onto the dock, then hauled herself up and made her way to the back door. She crossed through the laundry room and into the kitchen to put the food in the fridge. She unloaded the bag and found a meatball sub, a bag of chips, a turkey sandwich, and a fruit cup.

Her grandmother called out, "Megan? What in tarnation took you so long? Get in here right now, young lady."

Steeling herself for one more conversation she didn't want to have, she grabbed her bag of Dove chocolates off the counter, went to the living room, and pulled up short.

Grandma sat in a rocking chair pointing a rifle at Josh, who was sitting on the couch with his arms crossed.

Meg tossed the bag of candy on the coffee table. "What's going on, Grandma?"

Grandma slowly rose from her chair, threw her gun over her shoulder, and picked up her cane before heading for the front door. "You two are going to stay in here until you work everything out. I'll be right outside on the front porch, so don't try anything funny."

The front door closed firmly behind her.

Crap!

So everyone had been in on it. Aunt Gloria, Casey keeping the kids, and Grandma kidnapping Josh at gunpoint. Never a dull day in Anderson Butte. But just for once, couldn't everyone mind their own business?

When she finally met Josh's gaze, the pain in his eyes matched hers, and her stomach sank. What was she going to do?

What she really wanted was to curl up in a ball in her bed. Was that so much to ask? She said, "You can go out the back if you want. There's a Jet Ski that needs to be returned to the hotel anyway."

Josh's right brow popped up. "And risk getting shot by your grandmother again? I don't think so."

"She won't really shoot you."

"Says the woman with cute little buckshot scars on her ass to the man still recovering from the last time your crazy grandma shot me." He rubbed his left arm where Grams had tagged him.

He stood and walked toward her.

She stepped backward with each of his forward steps until her knees hit the rocking chair Grandma had been sitting in. "I can't do this, Josh."

"I hated that I had to lie to you, Meg. I'm willing to do whatever it takes to fix this."

She shook her head. "There's nothing that will fix what you've done to us. I'll . . . just . . . go."

He reached out and took her hand, but she pulled it out of his grasp. On a sigh he said, "Your grandmother can't force you to forgive me. And neither can I. Only you can decide if you will or can." He tilted her chin with his finger and stared into her eyes. "Tell me you don't love me, Meg, and I'll take my chances and be the one to go."

He'd always seen right through her. It was his so-called superpower in the FBI. If she told him she didn't love him he'd know it was a lie. Because she did. Maybe too much. It was the trusting he wouldn't hurt her again that she struggled with.

She couldn't think straight when he touched her. "I'll be right back."

Meg slipped around him and practically ran to the master bedroom. She smacked the door closed behind her and crossed to the bathroom sink. After washing her face and blowing her nose, she sank onto the bed and held her head in her hands. Why wouldn't everyone leave her alone so she could work everything out by herself?

Easy for all of them to say that he was just doing his job. They weren't the ones who'd have to live with a man who'd lied to her since the day they'd met.

Her girlfriends were right. Trust didn't come easy to Meg. But could she trust her heart, which was screaming that it wanted Josh's love even if he'd probably hurt her again?

Even if she could forgive him the lying, her old worry that Josh would get bored in Anderson Butte and leave raised its ugly head again. And now she was committed to staying. But would she wake up one morning with a note on her pillow telling her he had to go?

If he up and left them, Haley would be heartbroken too.

She flopped onto her back and closed her eyes as tears leaked past her ears. What was she going to do?

After a few minutes, she got her emotions back in check enough to go tell her grandmother to leave. Meg needed some time to figure things out. On her own, without anyone's help. Just like her father had said.

As she walked toward the bedroom door, she tossed the tissue still wadded up in her hand into the trash can. It landed on an envelope with her name on it.

Curious, she pulled the envelope out and went back to sit on the bed. It was Josh's handwriting on the outside. The letter was addressed to her, care of Anderson Butte, Colorado.

Why would he have written her a letter?

She ripped it open and unfolded the slightly faded, handwritten note. It was written on lined yellow paper. The date on top was the day they'd broken up, three years earlier.

Meg,
If you're receiving this, the worst has happened, but I couldn't leave this world with you thinking I didn't love you and our unborn child. I couldn't tell you before, but I'm an undercover FBI agent. I had to leave to keep you and our baby safe.

My will leaves all I have to you, so you should soon receive a large sum of money to help raise our child. If not, please contact Agent Watts at the FBI and he'll be sure you do.

I wish we could have watched our child grow together, but I take comfort in knowing you'll be his or her fantastic mother. You're the strongest, kindest person I know even though you'd be the first to deny it. My greatest hope is that our child will have your incredible spirit. I'll miss that about you. You brought light to my dark when I needed it the most.

Maybe after reading this, you'll be able to forgive me for falling in love with you at the worst possible time. But the short time we had together was the best of my life.

Love, Josh

He'd written the letter in case he got killed? The words swam with her tears as she read the letter again.

He thought she was a strong person? And a good mother before Haley had even been born? But was she strong enough to handle whatever might happen if she took Josh back and it didn't work out again?

Josh evidently believed it.

He'd been doing his job and she'd gotten caught up in it. Just like Casey had said. He really did love her. He'd had no choice but to leave her.

And he had more faith in her than she did. She couldn't argue with the hard proof she held in her hands.

He'd just sworn to her he'd never leave her and Haley again.

She folded the letter and tucked it into her pocket to keep.

Forever.

To remind her the next time her stupid insecurities made her doubt his love for her again, because she tended to do that. Maybe one day she'd get past that tendency, but for now his letter had been just what she'd needed to give her the courage to try.

Meg jumped off the bed and ran for the kitchen. She pulled what she was after out of the fridge and then made her way to the living room.

When Meg walked into the living room with her hand behind her back, Josh's stomach clenched as he stood. "Did you decide what you want to do?"

"I think so. But I need to ask you a couple of questions first. Are you certain you can be happy living here, in such a small town and working for Zeke, long term?"

That she'd ask the question meant she was reconsidering. His knotted stomach muscles loosened a fraction. "I love it here. The way everyone knows everyone else. And I'd forgotten how much I enjoy mechanical work. Zeke has been wanting to retire, so he's giving me the business to run. He's also donating some land he owns just outside of town so I can start a summer camp for kids like Eric. I hoped you'd help me with that."

"You won't miss all the excitement and intrigue?" Her forehead scrunched. "Because I'm still not sure who the real Josh is. This guy who likes to work on engines and help kids, or the agent who lived an exciting life and can lie like no one I've ever met."

He took a step closer to get a better look into her eyes. Uncertainty shone brightly along with her unshed tears.

He wanted to hold her. To wrap her up and reassure her she'd always be enough for him. But she wasn't ready for that, so he stuck his hands in his front pockets. "I'm all those things, Meg. No doubt, I joined the FBI for the excitement, but more to be a part of something important. I was good at what I did, but I had no one to miss me if some of the guys I put behind bars decided to retaliate. Then you came into my life and showed me what I'd been missing. I liked to think someone would care if I was gone, that maybe you and Haley . . . needed me?"

"We did need you, Josh." A tear spilled over and down her cheek. "Still do. Dammit, I'm just going to do this." She whipped a hand out from behind her back. "Here."

He blinked for a moment, struggling to understand the meaning behind her gift. "You're giving me a fruit cup?"

"Yes. Don't you remember?"

When he shook his head, she sighed. "You told me nothing says love like a fruit cup. So I'm giving you one. Jeez. You aren't making this any easier on me, Josh!"

His heart nearly beat out of his chest as he laughed and pulled her close. "Say it. Or I'm not taking you back."

"I'm the one doing the taking back here!" She poked him in the ribs. "But all right."

She leaned back and smiled. "I love you, Josh. I don't know if things are going to work out, but I'm willing to try because I like my life better when you're in it."

"I've liked my life a whole lot better since the day I met you, Meg." He kissed her. "And I'm going to spend the rest of it showing you how much I love both you and Haley. Now let's go tell your grandmother the news. Maybe we'll be able to walk out of here alive."

CHAPTER
Twenty-Four

The next morning, Meg stood beside Josh and Haley as they watched Eric drive a soccer ball down the field. The score was tied, one to one.

Josh picked Haley up and then slid his arm around Meg's waist, pulling her close. She snuggled against his side, grateful for her family's meddling for a change. She would have pushed him away to save herself future pain, but now she'd made up her mind to live in the moment and take life as it came.

And for the moment, life was pretty darned good.

Pam walked up beside her and drank deeply from her to-go mug of coffee. "Morning. How are you guys?"

Josh smiled at her. "Great. How are you?"

Pam's eyes slid toward Toby. A sly grin tilted her lips. "Just fine, thank you."

Meg glanced at Toby in time to see a look pass between him and Pam. Grabbing Pam's arm, Meg dragged her away from everyone. "Are you sleeping with Toby?"

Pam chuckled. "We don't do much sleeping, but yeah."

Concerned for her best buddy, Meg said, "You know he's not the committing type. I couldn't bear it if he broke your heart, Pam."

Pam laughed. "I'm not giving my heart to anyone but Mr. Right. And he hasn't come along yet. Oh, I almost forgot, did you hear the news about Amber?"

Meg wasn't sure she wanted to know. "What? Has she cooked up a new scheme to make my life miserable?"

"No. Nothing like that. Randy's mother came in to see me for her perm yesterday. While she was under the dryer, Mrs. Jackson asked if it was true that Amber kicked Randy out!"

"Did she?"

Pam nodded. "Randy's evidently banned from their house until he breaks it off with that waitress he's seeing down south. He moved back home with Mommy yesterday."

Meg smiled. "Good for Amber." As much as Amber could be a pain, Meg really did want the best for her. She always had, even when Amber had turned on her when they were kids. Maybe there was hope for her and Amber to patch things up yet.

"Yeah. Well, gotta run. I have a cut and color in five minutes." Pam hugged Meg. "I'm so happy you and Josh worked it all out."

"Me too." Meg gave Pam a hard squeeze. "We're going to work on finding you Mr. Right next."

Pam sighed. "Well, I'm certainly well acquainted with Mr. Wrong, so that'd be a nice change. See you later."

"Bye." Pam wanted a husband and kids, but never complained. Meg would make it her mission to find a nice guy for her. Pam deserved the same newfound happiness Meg had.

She walked back and stood by Josh again. Turning her attention back to the game, she winced. She'd never played soccer and was a little surprised at how rough it could be. When a really big kid tripped Eric and stole the ball, she opened her mouth to protest, but Josh beat her to it.

He called out, "Where's the card, ref?"

She smiled as the referee tugged a yellow card from his back pocket and held it up. That set up some sort of penalty kick that had Eric lining up in front of the goal.

She wasn't sure she wanted to watch. What if he missed? It was just a game, but Eric seemed to love playing so much she hated to see him disappointed. He'd had way too much of that in his life recently.

She circled her arm around Josh's waist and squeezed as the ball flew toward the big goalie. It whooshed past the kid and into the net, and the crowd went wild. The ref blew time on his whistle and declared the Anderson Butte Rockies the winners.

Eric glanced their way and smiled as he jogged back to the sidelines to give his teammates and Toby high fives.

After Eric packed up his gear and joined them, he still beamed a giant smile.

Josh held up his fist for a bump. "Nice game, buddy."

Meg gave Eric a hug. "Glad you had fun today."

As she released Eric, Meg's phone vibrated in her back pocket. She tugged it out and opened the text from Casey.

Dad's back and called a family meeting. Grams'll keep the kids so you can come. Where r u?

Meg tapped back, Park. Be there in 5.

She turned to Josh. "Family meeting. Can you drop the kids off with my grandma?"

He gave her a quick kiss. "Yep. See you later."

"Thanks."

Meg hit the stone steps of Town Hall. Her emotions were mixed—relief her dad was back so everyone in town could relax warred with the familiar dread that surfaced every time she was summoned to her father's office. With Dragon Breath behind bars where she clearly belonged, Meg walked past the receptionist's desk and toward her dad's open door. Her brothers and sister were all deep in whispered conversation and had clearly started the meeting long before they'd invited her. Not sure what was up with that, she called out to her father, "Welcome back, jailbird."

Her siblings chuckled, but Sue Ann took her usual offense. "It's not funny, Megan. Can't you take anything seriously?"

Meg sat in the empty chair beside Casey. "You must see the irony here, Sue Ann. For once it's not me who's been in trouble. But we all knew Dad wasn't guilty."

Dad's brows shot up. "You never doubted my innocence? Not even for a moment?"

"Nope." Meg shook her head. "Besides your inept computer skills, you love this town too much to ever jeopardize it. That, and you'd never risk embarrassment to the Anderson name."

Dad leaned back and crossed his arms. "I'm glad you finally seem to get it, Megan. And since you're the computer whiz in the family, you need to help me clean up Mrs. Duncan's mess."

"Uh, sure. That'd be fine." Her dad had never asked her help for anything before. Although it was more of a demand, it put a little smile on her face.

"So." Dad cleared his throat. "The bottom line is, Mrs. Duncan had been running an illegal gaming operation, essentially stealing money from innocent people using the Internet, right here under my nose. She blamed me for it until Ryan got Barb's testimony, which led to Mrs. Duncan finally confessing that I had nothing to do with it. She's going to jail for a very long time. We're all going to forget it ever happened and move on."

Dad's gaze landed on her. "Agent Watts told me Josh believed I was innocent and that his opinion counts with them. He said Josh is a good man, Megan. Watts trusts Josh and is sorry he decided to leave the FBI. Seems your choice in men has finally improved."

Sue Ann added, "And he's pretty damn good-looking. I'm not sure you could do much better than him. Maybe he'll be the one who sticks for a change."

Not sure if that was a compliment or another slap, Meg said, "Well, I guess time will tell." She rose from her chair. "I'm glad it all worked out, Dad. After I get the work crews started at my house in the morning, I'll drop by and help with the computers."

As she started to leave, Dad said, "Wait, Megan. We need to talk about that. The Three Amigos came to visit me this morning. They said since seeing how you're sticking this time and are going to fix up your grandparents' place, how you've taken responsibility for your actions as a kid, and that you've taken in Eric, they wanted me to consider giving you another chance."

Meg flopped back into her chair in disbelief. "Really? They said that?"

"Yep. And since they can be a royal pain in my ass when they don't get their way, I've decided to give you that chance. You can have your shares back in the corporation. But this time, you'll be in charge of all the computer systems here, at the clinic, and the central reservations systems, with an appropriate salary. I don't want any repeats of what Mrs. Duncan got away with and I'm too damned busy to have to worry about that."

Before Meg could figure out what to say, Dad held out a white envelope. "When you came back a few weeks ago, jobless and hiding from Josh, I held little hope you'd ever change. But you've proved me wrong, and obviously some others in town too. This is all the rent money from your grandparents' home. There's a check for almost three hundred grand here. Fix up that lodge, but make it as nice as the hotel so you can book top celebrities. More rich clients will provide an extra shot of revenue for everyone in town. Don't screw this up, dammit!"

That must've been what they'd all been discussing before she got there. Better, her dad finally realized she'd changed. Didn't mean he loved her or anything, but at least he must not hate her if he was giving her the money.

She could live with that.

She glanced at her siblings to be sure they were okay with the new plan. When they all smiled and nodded, tears stung her eyes.

They hadn't lost faith in her after all.

She accepted the check, relieved she wouldn't have to worry about the possibility of returning the pre-booking money she'd taken the risk on. But it also gave her a little extra cash to do something she'd really wanted to do, but couldn't afford before. "Thank you. I'll do my best not to screw things up. Now, if you'll excuse me, I need to run a few quick errands."

<hr>

It was getting late and time to call it a day when Josh, elbow deep in an engine, sensed someone watching him. He lifted his head. Meg stood a few feet away with a tight smile on her face.

Warmth rushed through him at the sight of her. "Hey there."

"Hi. Do you have a minute?"

"Sure." She seemed nervous. Had her doubts about them crept back in again? He'd probably have that to deal with for a while yet.

He found a rag and wiped his hands, then gave her his full attention. "What's up?"

"First, thanks for helping my dad. We all appreciate it."

She came to the shop to tell him that? That made no sense. He'd see her at home in ten minutes. "I never wanted to see him in jail, Meg. But I can't be sorry I was assigned to his case. If not, we'd have never met."

Slowly nodding, she licked her lips. "I got my town shares back today and my dad hired me to be in charge of all the IT."

He crossed to her and pulled her into a hug. "That's awesome, Meg. Congratulations."

"Thanks." When he released her, she stepped back and cleared her throat. "Dad also gave me all the back rent money, so I'm kinda flush for a change, and I bought you a gift. I've been thinking about this whole commitment and trust thing between us. I know it's something I need to work on."

He held up a hand. "You didn't have to buy me a gift to prove that. I know you love me."

"I do. But this gift is a really big commitment so you'll have to agree to marry me first, or I'm taking it back."

His heart rolled over in his chest as he took her soft face in his hands and tilted it up. "If I had proposed to you like that, you would've kicked my ass. You don't even have a ring."

"True." With mischief gleaming in her eyes, she laid a quick kiss on his lips. "But what's outside is ten times better than a ring—if you're . . . you. And just because I'm asking you first, it doesn't let you off the hook. You still have to buy me a really big rock. So, what's it going to be?"

Meg waited for his answer, beaming that big, beautiful smile of hers at him.

He'd never been surer of an answer in his entire life. Clearing the emotion from his throat, he said, "Well, since you went to all the trouble to give me a fruit cup yesterday, and now some mystery gift . . . I guess marrying you is the least I can do. So, okay."

"The least you can do? And just okay? We may have to do this part over later so you can get it right." She took his hand and yanked. "Come outside. I'm dying for you to see what's out here."

He let her pull him outside into the dusky evening.

Charlie stood in the driveway, tied to a tree.

After Josh's mother had died and he'd had to harden his heart to survive being thrown into the cold world of foster care, Charlie was the only one he'd been able to love. Until he'd met Meg, and then Haley.

As he gave the horse a quick rub, he had to bite his bottom lip for fear he might embarrass the hell out of himself and cry. He turned to Meg. "You bought Charlie for me? He's ours now?"

She nodded. "Eric helped. He called and convinced Mr. J, who just dropped him off. He said you were always Charlie's favorite anyway. Mr. Bower has that big farm just outside of town and said we can board him there. This way you can see him whenever you like. See? Much better than a ring, right?"

"Thank you, Meg. I don't know how . . ." He couldn't finish. There weren't words to describe knowing that someone loved and truly understood him for the first time in his life.

Pulling it together, he said, "Yes, much better than a ring. But I want one of those too."

Meg slipped her arms around his waist. "I found the perfect rings online this afternoon. Mine is going to cost you, so brace yourself. And we're keeping Eric too, right? Forever?"

He lifted her up and held her close as he stared into her pretty blue eyes. "Yes. To any ring you want and to making Eric part of our family. Forever."

When she wrapped her legs around his waist, he kissed her, taking his time about it, wanting to always remember this particular moment in the best day of his life.

ACKNOWLEDGMENTS

I'm sure you've heard the one about a hard task taking a village to accomplish? Well, for me it was more like a smallish city. My road to publication has been filled with potholes and detours, but in that process I've met some pretty fantastic people who have graciously helped me along the way.

Probably best to start at the beginning and thank my parents, who always believed in me, including my most recent parent, who brought my dad happiness again after my mom died. To my sibs, Gary, Sue, and Lisa, for not telling on me when it mattered the most; to my aunts, uncles, in-laws, cousins, and many, many brothers-in-law, sisters-in-law, nieces, and nephews. (This might be a good opportunity to apologize to my neighbors for the noise level when we all get together.)

An extra special thanks to the three people I love the most. Mark, my husband, whose patience is appreciated when I'm too deep into a scene to make dinner, and our kids, Matt and Traci. Our children turned out to be two of the kindest, most hardworking, and dedicated young adults we know—despite their goofy parents.

I've had some pretty great critique partners along the way, starting with Shannon Bianco, Julie Pascal, Mindy Montgomery, and Darynda Jones. My current crit partners, fondly known as the Golden Meanies, consist of Louise Bergin, Shea Berkley, and

Robin Perini. Thanks, you guys. I love all of you even more than peanut M&M's.

Thanks for all the support my local RWA chapter, Land of Enchantment Romance Authors. The love and support this group provides is invaluable. LERA consists of some of my favorite people on this earth. They make the second Saturday of every month a guaranteed good time.

Also a big shout-out to my Golden Heart class, the Firebirds. A group of supportive, loving writers whose goal is to see all of our books in the hands of readers. You all hold a very special place in my heart. I will always be grateful to know each and every one of you.

Next I want to thank my agent, Jill Marsal, for taking that initial chance on me, for suggesting I write this story, and then for helping my book find its home. I *couldn't* have done it without you!

And a big thanks to my editors at Montlake, Maria Gomez and Charlotte Herscher. Thanks to Maria for envisioning what my book could be and to Charlotte for helping take it to that next level.

Thanks to everyone on the Montlake team, especially my patient copyeditor, Shari Miranda. (I talked to my neighbors way too much back in English class.)

I want to thank some of my other fun writer friends for just being awesome people. They live all across the country and around the world (one of the benefits of belonging to RWA): Tracy, Terri, Keely, Wendy, Lorenda, Babette, Kim, Pintip, Joanne, Susan, Heather, Sheri, Karen, Kathleen, Cathy, Kari, Jeffe, Shelly, Vanessa, Kat, the other Kim, Colette, Pam, Brenda, Barb, Jeannie, Gabi, Monique, Sarah, Jamie, Diane, and A.J. And last, but certainly not least, Gina Robinson and Laurie Sanchez, who have both become indispensable parts of my life too. Thank you, my friends, for being sounding boards when I need it most and for sharing all the knowledge along the way.

I think I'd be absolutely remiss if I didn't thank my co-workers at my day job, Stephanie, Debbie, Monique, and Corky, for putting up with my dual personalities.

And thanks to my hairdresser, for keeping up the illusion. Michael (and his partner, Gerald) brighten my days while lightening my grays the many times a year we visit. Thank you both for being such great cheerleaders.

Lastly, thank you, kind reader, for picking up my book in the first place, and then for enduring this long list and caring enough to be introduced to the people whom I value the most.

I have certainly forgotten someone, but not on purpose. If I have overlooked you, I promise you shall receive a bold and blatant double thanks in my next book.

ABOUT THE AUTHOR

Photo © 2012 Robyn Adams

Tamra Baumann is an award-winning author who writes light-hearted contemporary romance. Always a voracious reader, she picked her first romance novel off the bestseller table in her favorite bookstore and was forever hooked. (Thank you, Nora Roberts!)

She lives in the Southwest, where the sun shines most every day and the sunsets steal her breath away. She has two kids, both bilingual in English and sarcasm, and a dog who is addicted to Claritin because he's allergic to grass. Her husband, who gamely tolerates her many book boyfriends, has been her real-life boyfriend for almost thirty years.

Stop by and say hi at www.tamrabaumann.com.